P9-AOT-870

WEST GA REG LIB SYS
Neva Lomason
Memorial Library

GOOD COP, BAD COP

Other Forge Books by Barbara D'Amato

Killer.app

GOOD COP,
BAD COP

Barbara
D'Amato

A Tom Doherty Associates Book
New York

This is a work of fiction. All of the characters and events portrayed in this novel are either fictitious or are used fictitiously.

GOOD COP, BAD COP

Copyright © 1998 by PB Investment

All rights reserved, including the right to reproduce this book, or portions thereof, in any form.

This book is printed on acid-free paper.

A Forge Book
Published by Tom Doherty Associates, Inc.
175 Fifth Avenue
New York, NY 10010

Forge® is a registered trademark of Tom Doherty Associates, Inc.

Library of Congress Cataloging-in-Publication Data

D'Amato, Barbara.
    Good cop, bad cop / Barbara D'Amato.—1st ed.
        p.   cm.
    "A Tom Doherty Associates book."
    ISBN 0-312-86562-7
    I. Title.
PS3554.A4674G66   1998
813' .54—dc21   97-35922
                                                          CIP

First Edition: March 1998

Printed in the United States of America

0 9 8 7 6 5 4 3 2 1

To Deborah Schneider

ONE

THREE UNMARKED POLICE cars and one unmarked telephone truck sped west on Madison Street. Though the men didn't know it, every move they made in the next hour would be examined, cross-examined, deposed, praised, vilified, and chewed over in the press and in courts for decades to come.

It was December 4, 1969, a cold Chicago winter, still three hours to dawn, windy and dark. In the cars were fourteen men led by Chicago Police Sergeant Daniel Groth. Some were detailed from the Cook County State's Attorney's Office SPU, the Special Prosecutions Unit, and the GIU, or Gang Intelligence Unit, which was the local "Red Squad," and some were on loan from the Chicago Police Department. All wore black leather jackets and fur hats. None wore a uniform. Among them they carried one Thompson submachine gun, three 12-gauge riot guns from the Chicago Police Department armory, an M-1 carbine, and a sawed-off shotgun. They had their usual sidearms as well—twenty .38-caliber handguns and a .357 magnum. Their ammunition included both standard-issue and lethal nonstandard-issue rounds: dumdums and hollow-point bullets. They carried no nonlethal crowd control equipment, such as tear gas.

The cars rolled silently through the dark streets until they were within two blocks of their destination. Only then

did they inform the local Thirteenth District police dispatcher where they were going.

They glided to a stop 150 feet west of their target, 2337 West Monroe Street, climbed cautiously out of the cars and picked up their weapons.

The houses along the street were dark. Some of the buildings were actually dead, burned out the year before in the riots of 1968, their windows blank, interiors collapsed and decayed, the floors drifted with dirty snow that had blown in through the ruined windows. No one walked past on the cracked sidewalk.

The men had been briefed by Sergeant Groth. They had carefully studied the elaborate floor plan an FBI informant had drawn for them, showing a first-floor, four-room, two-bedroom apartment, detailed even down to the beds where the targets were likely to be sleeping. It pinpointed chairs, tables, the television set, a hassock. The front door of the apartment led into a hall with a closet dead ahead and a door into the living room on the left. The back door was up seven steps and had a window on its right. The entry led directly into the kitchen, with the stove on the right and the door into the rest of the apartment in the wall straight ahead.

Eight men moved toward the front door of the apartment. Six men moved around to the back door. Of the front door team, five were to go in, three to stand guard in front.

The youngest men detailed to take part in the raid had been told only that this was the lair of dangerous and vicious leaders of the Black Panther party. They were warned that there was a secret cache of Panther weapons in the apartment, which were intended for use in a revolution. The purpose of the raid, they had been told, was to seize that cache. They were told to expect violent, armed resistance, possibly a shootout.

The youngest of the officers was a slender white man

with black hair. Somebody said, "Come on, Nick," and he padded softly up to the front door with his team. His heart was beating fast and he was swallowing frequently, hoping his fear and tension didn't show. He kept his eye on the sergeant.

The sergeant rapped on the front door. There was a sound like "Who's there?" There was a shot. Another senior officer kicked down the door and went in first, low and shooting.

The young officer heard a shout, a crash, a shot that sounded like a carbine, then a shotgun blast, then a fusillade of submachine gun fire and screams as the night shattered around him in blasts of sound. He burst into the hall, from there leaped to the left into the living room, pitch black inside except for the flashes from gun muzzles. In spurts of this stroboscopic light, he saw a man lying on the floor bleeding, a woman on a mattress screaming, and officers firing through the back wall of the living room and through the darkened doorway into the bedrooms. There was a flashing sequence of bodies jumping, dodging. There were shots coming from the back of the house. He saw a movement beyond the door and fired. The leading officers leaped into the next room, a bedroom, while the young man and two others stood guard in the living room. There was a brief lull.

Another battery of shots, shouts, submachine gun rattle and the visceral impact of shotgun blasts. He thought, Wait! Are we firing at each other? Then he asked himself whether he was supposed to run in and help, but nobody had told him to, so he stayed, half crouched, weapon at the ready.

Suddenly, it was as silent as before, except for curses and sobs.

Chicago,
twenty-eight years later

TWO

IF ALDO BERTOLUCCI and Richard Dickenson had not drawn a late car, they would have been in the Furlough Bar by now. Instead, a half hour from the end of their tour, they were rolling west on Adams in the cold, dark winter night.

"*One eleven,*" the radio said.

Dick-dick was driving, and since the call wasn't for them, but for an early car on the next watch as the odd number told him, he just rolled quietly on.

"*One eleven,*" a voice acknowledged.

The dispatcher said, "*I've got a manager at the Sizzler Restaurant, 277 Wabash, says some people domesticatin'.*"

No answer.

"*Did you copy?*"

"*One eleven. We'll counsel them,*" the officer's voice said dryly. "*Ten four.*"

"Glad it's not us," Aldo growled.

If the truth were known, Dick-dick was afraid of Aldo. Aldo was large, fat, and to Dick-dick, old. Aldo was fifty-two. He was also of unpredictable temper, which was why he'd twice been dumped back to uniform, once from detective, once from Narcotics. Dick-dick was twenty-four.

But the truth would not be known if Dick-dick had any say on it. He maintained a cheerfully breezy exterior with

Aldo, as if the older man were a constant fount of amusing police lore. He was not as careful to cover the fact that he also admired Aldo. Aldo was tough. And he knew everything.

"What does he mean, 'domesticating'?"

"Well, he don't mean settin' up house. He means they're engaging in a domestic disturbance in a public place."

"Oh." The radio spat again. It sounded like *"Borgquat sheek—not display weap—zzzt."*

The dispatcher said, *"You got a bad signal, sir."*

"Skeeeek!"

"You're not making it with your radio, sir."

Adams Street around here was never dark, but parts of it were deserted at this hour. Aldo was leaning back with one leg crossed over the other and his seat belt unfastened when the dispatcher said, *"One twenty-eight."*

Aldo said, "Shit."

Dick-dick picked up and said, "Twenty-eight."

"Report of a woman screaming, corner of LaSalle and Polk. One twenty-eight, you respond?"

"One twenty-eight. We're on our way."

Dick-dick hung a left on DesPlaines and another left on Jackson, hit his lights and covered the nine blocks to LaSalle while the dispatcher came back on and said, *"I have a description from a citizen on that, twenty-eight. Probable ag batt. The woman is being hit by a male white wearing a black leather jacket and track shoes."*

Dick-dick, said, "Ten four."

Aldo mumbled, "That'll narrow it down to half the population. All we need now is he's young."

"One twenty-eight."

"One twenty-eight," Dick-dick said.

"Citizen says the white male is young, about twenty, twenty-two."

"We're there," Dick-dick said.

"Jeez, twenty-five minutes to the end of the tour," Aldo snarled. But he was out of the car like an explosion. Dick-dick stayed to shut it down and lock it. Turn your back on one unlocked in this neighborhood, he thought, and it's gone.

In a doorway shadowed from the street lights, two figures were struggling. If the woman had been screaming before, she wasn't now. Nor were there any witnesses around, including whatever citizen had called it in.

"Hey, *hairball!*" Aldo yelled.

The man turned, dropped the woman against a set of hanging wires once connected to doorbells, and drew back his hand to punch Aldo. Instead, Aldo punched him and the man fell, but his eyes were wild and he thrashed around trying to get up. Aldo dragged him up by his shirt, while Dick-dick cuffed his hands behind his back, palms outward.

"Grab her!" Aldo ordered. He dropped the man's shirt and lunged for the woman, who was running. Dick-dick had her first. She was making high-pitched keening noises that scared Dick-dick. They didn't sound human.

"Cuff her!" Aldo said.

"What? She's the victim."

"Shit, look at her!"

"Coke?" Dick-dick said.

"Ts and Bs, my guess. Talwins and blues. The two of 'em are havin' a drug beef. Get back to the car and get me an RD number. Wait a minute. You get their IDs. I'll call."

Aldo got to the radio. "No, tell 'em to take a slowdown. I got these two wrapped," he said. "But I got no cage. Can you send me somebody to bring 'em in?"

Dick-dick watched the two and listened to Aldo, knowing that he'd get out of the paperwork if he possibly could.

"No, they're kind of wild," Aldo said. "We need a cage car. Need a separate car for the woman, anyhow."

Dick-dick stared at the two prisoners, who were now both whimpering.

"Jeez, if we gotta," Aldo said. He came back to the prisoners and Dick-dick.

"You been popped before, hairball?" he said. The man shook his head. "You saw him throw a fist at me?" Aldo said to Dick-dick, drawing back his fist at the same time.

Instantly, the man said, "Yeah. I have."

"Nice felony-flyers you got there," Aldo said, looking at his shoes. "Buy 'em?"

The man, a skinny white guy with tan hair and a jiggling head, was now thoroughly terrified of Aldo. Dick-dick thought this showed good sense. "No, sir," the man said.

"Let's go," Aldo said. "With any luck they've got some connection to the hypes Coumadin's all bent out of shape about. Hey, get moving along here. I can practically taste the beer waitin' for me."

THREE

STANLEY MILESKI WAS laughing so hard he couldn't swallow his beer. A little sprayed onto the bar. He gulped and snorted. Officer Hiram Quail watched him expectantly, figuring either to hear a good story or to have to duck beer if Mileski really lost it.

"So the sarge is looking like he invented it himself, you know?" Mileski said. " 'This is AFIS,' he says, and he waves his arm at the room as if it's an Arab whorehouse and the recruits just have to take their pick. So they've had fingerprint

lectures in the academy, but here they are at the big copshop for the day, so they're kind of awed, right?"

Quail said, "Right." Mileski took another mouthful of his beer and started chuckling again. Quail swallowed, hoping the example would make Mileski swallow, which it did, much to Quail's relief.

"So the sarge goes, 'Until we had this system, every fingerprint had to be compared and categorized by hand. Every one by hand.' He's one of these people think it makes what he says more important if he repeats it. Right?"

"Right."

" 'Now with the automated fingerprint identification system, it's all done automatically,' he says. 'And practically instantly. You've studied whorls and loops and all'—he's pointing at this chart on the wall while he's talking, too. 'Well, now, this little box does it all.' So he pats the top of one of the terminals, and he tells them this here officer is going to show them how it's used.

"So Officer Cynthia Jones gets up from the terminal. And the sergeant—all the recruits are, you know, standing around in a sort of semicircle watching—he says, 'Let's take you, young man,' and they pick this kid, he's maybe twenty-one, skinny, got reddish hair. Matter of fact, he looks a lot like you, Hiram."

Hiram chuckled. He figured that was the best response to that sort of remark.

"Kid's grinning all proud and Officer Jones and the sarge do a ten-print, plus he's all agog because you don't use ink anymore and they just roll his fingers on the glass plate and the big print comes up on the monitor screen just like it was magic—and the tech scores two or three of the prints, however they do that, takes a little while, then they punch the data in the machine. Meanwhile Sarge is saying, 'This little

baby's matched unknown prints as far back as 1970. Every print we get off a felony scene goes in this here. Course, we still got some problems with it. There's a lot of different fingerprint systems around the country, and they can't all talk to each other yet. But it's just a matter of time. Now what the machine's gonna do is, it's gonna come up with the five closest matches to your prints, boy. And score them. How close they are. Like, twelve points of similarity in a print is considered lawyer-proof in court. Six or seven we can get to work on. Like, from a partial print? Now say your man is a convicted felon, Illinois, he's gonna be in here, name and all. Or say he's pulled some jobs but never been identified. The prints'll be in here. No name in that case, of course. And if there's nothing close enough, then your collar just isn't in here, like he's from Alaska, or maybe he's never been caught before.'

"So the machine's chugging and whoofing—"

"It doesn't chug," Hiram said. "Or whoof either—"

"Well, shit, Hiram! See if I try to lighten your day!"

"Go ahead, Stan."

"Machine's *humming*, goddammit, and out comes the matches. And all of a sudden we got Sergeant Asshole staring at this sheet and staring at the recruit, and staring at the sheet, and staring at the recruit, and finally he says, 'Holy shit! Thirteen points of similarity!'

"Then he gets real coy, and he says, 'Hey, kid. You ever been in Gary, Indiana?'

"Kid looks like the sarge just barfed on him. Backs up. Meanwhile the sarge is saying, 'This here finger has turned up at three felonies in Indiana. We got two payroll robberies and a jewelry store! Holy shit!'

"Then he turns to the recruits, like he's still got to do his bit for education, and he says, 'See, we got northern Indiana on the computer, and some Wisconsin.' Then he turns back

and says, 'Hell, kid, you gotta be wanted for at least three felonies! And here you are halfway to being a cop!'

"And the kid says, 'Wait a minute, boss. That was when I was a *teenager!*' "

Stan punched Hiram, who guffawed, slapped his glass on the bar, and elbowed Stan back. Both took a pull on their beer.

Stan stole a look at himself in the bar mirror. He tweaked some of his curly mud-brown hair with his left forefinger, getting rid of the groove left by the eight hours of pressure of his saucer cap. Between the dusty bottles of scotch behind the bar, he could see his face and he frowned at it, making the face look more ominous. At twenty-eight, Stanley had two ambitions in life: to make sergeant by age thirty and to be called "Iron Balls" Mileski.

Sergeant in two years wasn't likely, given Mileski's difficulties with spelling. But his heart yearned deeply for "Iron Balls."

Mileski's wife ran a china- and pottery-mending business out of their ground-floor apartment. YOU CAN'T TELL IT'S NOT BRAND NEW the sign said, and there was a little picture of a smiling teacup.

He helped when he was off, and he definitely had a way with china. Despite the fact that he was six feet four and had huge hands, the gold-rimmed pitchers and Dresden shepherdesses practically healed themselves under his magic touch. The business brought in a good piece of change; in fact, Stanley told his wife he'd have to be retarded, paraplegic, and with a dumdum bullet lodged in his frontal lobe before he could think of giving it up. But he lived in terror that some of his fellow officers would find out he did china mending—hell, even one of the other officers; whoever it was, would practically put it out citywide. That would shoot down his chances of being nicknamed "Iron Balls" for sure.

If the Furlough Bar had hung out a sign, NO YUPPIES WANTED, it couldn't have been more explicit. But it handled the problem nonverbally. The owners, two ex-cops, were careful never to wash the glass pane in the front door. A plastic sign, distributed by Pepsi-Cola in the late 1950s, was stuck not quite square in the door behind the antiburglar wire. It had the days of the week down the left side, and little slots where plastic numbers were inserted showing the hours the Furlough was open. The numbers hadn't been changed or updated since John Kennedy was shot. Several of them had fallen off and several more had fallen sideways. On Tuesdays, for instance, which this was, the bar was open from 0 to ∞. It was now 11:10 P.M.

If some granola-head in his Calvin Kleins happened to lose his way to trendy Chicago and wind up here by mistake, there was nothing in the Furlough to make him want to stay. There were no ferns, not a single green growing thing in the place, unless there was something living under the linoleum near the beer tap that nobody knew about. There was no stained glass. No designer water. There was no fresh squeezed orange juice.

If Norm or Hiram or Stanley or Suze had looked out of the window of the Furlough—which they wouldn't because it was too dirty to bother trying to see through—they would have seen the Chicago Police Department headquarters diagonally down the block. The CPD is on South State Street between Eleventh and Roosevelt Road, which would have been Twelfth if it hadn't been named for a president, and the Furlough squats stolidly at State and Thirteenth.

"Where's Aldo and Dick-dick?" Suze Figueroa asked Stanley. Suze was the only woman in the place and at twenty-six the youngest. She and her partner, Norm Bennis, sat at the bar just past Stanley, quietly drinking their beer.

"Not here," Stanley said. He had decided that somebody

named Iron Balls would give short answers to questions. The decision to become laconic warred mightily with his love of storytelling, so he confined it to times other people were doing the talking.

"Late car," Hiram Quail said. "Be here in a while."

Suze rubbed her hands together. She dearly loved a beer with the troops before going home. It was like being one of the guys.

Norman Bennis was a short, thirty-five-year-old black man, built almost exactly like an ax seen in profile. He was a wedge. Slender legs, narrow hips, wider chest, enormously broad shoulders.

"Well, hell," he said, "I guess we'll just have to kill time somehow."

He started to hold up four fingers for four beers, but the bartender was in no mood for cute and had slapped the glasses and bottles down on the bar before Norm got his hand up.

One beer later, Aldo and Dick-dick swaggered in. Dick-dick's swagger was a pale imitation of Aldo's, but he got better at it every day.

"Quick one," Aldo snapped at the bartender, who looked back at him with bland disdain. "Gotta get home." Nobody asked him why. It would trigger a spate of curses about his wife.

"Whyn't ya wash that window?" Dick-dick asked the bartender, trying to snarl like Aldo.

Aldo answered for the guy. "Keeps the yuppies out."

Suze said, "Hey, Aldo. How come you hate yuppies so much?"

"Ruinin' the country, that's what. Ferns. Jogging shoes."

"But Aldo, aren't yuppies exactly what we asked for?"

"What the hell you mean, Suzy?"

"Hey, it's not Suzy. It's Suze. Rhymes with booze."

"It's Suzy Q."

"Goddammit, Aldo—"

Norm said, "Chill, Suze my man."

"Call you what I want," Aldo said.

"About those yuppies," Norm said.

Suze said, "What I mean is, thinking of ourselves as professional law enforcers and therefore members of the larger society of professional advice givers, yuppies are doing exactly what we told them to."

Aldo said, "What're you talkin' about?"

"Well, look at it this way. We ask our young people not to run around mugging other people or lie down in alleys drinking rotgut. And sure enough, yuppies don't do that."

"Designer water! Hate 'em."

"And we ask people to eat sensibly. And to stay in school. Get degrees."

"College types. Hate 'em."

"And to dress nicely. Wear clean clothes. Tell our children to do their schoolwork, wear clean shirts, go to college—"

"Trendy clothes. Assholes!"

"—get a degree, get jobs, work hard, and you'll get your reward. They've done exactly what we've told them to do."

"Think they're better than everybody! Hate 'em!" Aldo said, finishing his second beer on a long, loud gulp, and he went out slamming the door. Dick-dick followed him. Mileski winced.

"You shouldn't bait him that way," Norm said.

"I'm not baiting him," Suze said. "I'm educating him."

"That's not a good move. Aldo's not a guy you want to make an enemy of. He's a grudge holder."

"And crabby."

"And crabby."

"Hey, Norm, what do you think—is Aldo getting worse?"

Aldo and Dick-dick crossed the street diagonally, angling toward the CPD parking lot, Dick-dick waving at a couple of cops coming out the front door of the CPD building. As he and Aldo reached the far sidewalk, a black limo drew up to the curb and a man in a tan camel hair topcoat was out of the car and approaching the doors to the building in seconds. His driver had tried to get around to open the door for him but wasn't fast enough.

One of the group at the curb had lifted his hand and said, "Evenin', boss," by way of greeting. Another had said "Superintendent," and Dick-dick actually saluted, but Superintendent Nick Bertolucci had gone past before they really got the words out.

Dick-dick looked at Aldo Bertolucci as his brother disappeared into the building. Aldo's face was red and congested. He was rolling his hands into fists.

"Well, hell," Dick-dick said. "I mean, there's a bunch of us here. He just didn't see you."

"Never mind," Aldo snarled. "Hell with it."

FOUR

SUPERINTENDENT NICK BERTOLUCCI charged through the lobby like a snowplow. He was a big man with a lot of upperbody muscle. Probably people would have made way for him

even if he wasn't the superintendent. As it was, they faded out of his way fast. He was well aware of it. He thought it was a hell of a lot of fun.

Even at this hour, eleven-thirty P.M., there were guards on the ground floor. The metal detector was turned off at night. It was used during the day, when the courts were open and people were coming to trial in Branches 26, 27, 30 and 40. During the day the guards put everybody they didn't know through the metal detector and X-rayed everything big enough to hold a firearm. At night, anybody entering the building was stopped by a glass barricade. A guard asked who you wanted to see, called upstairs, and another guard escorted the visitor up. Nobody was supposed to get loose in the building.

Not that they would have stopped the superintendent at any time. One of the guards dived at the buttons to call the elevator before Bertolucci could reach it, hoping to keep him from having to wait. He wasn't successful, though. Everybody, superintendent or pimp in handcuffs—everybody had to wait while the old elevators in the old building did their grudging thing.

Bertolucci nodded thanks to the guard, but he didn't talk. His mind was someplace else.

The third elevator down the line opened and Bertolucci strode to it. Deputy Superintendent Gus Gimball stepped out wearing his coat.

"Evening, boss," he said.

"Hang on a little bit, will you?" Bertolucci said. Gimball stepped back in the elevator.

They rode in silence up to four. Gus "Bull" Gimball was a tall, slender, slightly stooped black man of fifty-one, the same age as Bertolucci. He had a scholarly air about him and in uniform sometimes looked as if he were in costume. His

nickname did not come from any physical characteristic, but rather from sheer, single-minded, bulldog persistence.

Gimball knew that absent look on the superintendent's face. It meant he was thinking and didn't want to be interrupted. It faded as they got off the elevator, and Gimball said, "Thought you'd left."

"I *had* left. I was a quarter of the way home." Bertolucci wasn't annoyed. It went with the job.

There'd been a late meeting: security for a visiting head of state, Prime Minister Netanyahu, the next three days, with half the force staring at rooftops for crazies, the kind of thing neither Bertolucci nor Gimball liked, but you had to have it right, and several topcops were still here. Bertolucci glanced at Gimball, pleased as always to have him around. Gimball was reliable.

"I just got a call in the car from Mayor Wallace," Bertolucci said. "Wanted me to phone back on what he calls 'the land line' from my office."

Gimball laughed.

Bertolucci had his door open and was at the phone in two seconds. "Sit," he said to Gimball.

There was a single button for the mayor's office. He punched it. "Superintendent Bertolucci!" he said to the phone. Another three seconds passed.

"Good evening, Mayor Wallace," he said.

Gimball listened to the length of the silence.

Bertolucci said, "I'll be right there" crisply, and hung up.

Gimball said, "Crisis?"

"Sounds like World War Three. Why don't you come along?"

"Sure," Gimball said. To say "no" when the superintendent said "come along" was not an option, anyhow—although Gus, Bertolucci's long-time friend, probably could

have asked to be left out. Bertolucci charged down the stairs, bypassing the elevators to save time, Gimball right behind him. Random staffers and officers using the stairs flattened themselves against the wall as they passed.

FIVE

IN THE CAR Nick Bertolucci said, "I wonder what's loose."

"Didn't give you any hint?"

"Crisis. 'Get down here.' Shit!"

"Maybe Prime Minister Netanyahu's been shot."

"Don't even say it," Bertolucci said. Netanyahu was visiting Chicago for an "economic exchange talk," whatever that was. "Couldn't be Netanyahu. We'd have heard."

"Well, maybe he wasn't shot. Maybe he was poisoned at dinner, and they don't want to call a lowly cop, they've got to have you personally do the investigating."

"Then why's he at City Hall? They were doin' dinner at the Palmer House."

"Oh. That's true."

"Maybe it really is World War Three," Bertolucci said. "No, I've got it. The double-domes at the University of Chicago have let loose some recombinant DNA and it's now spreading through Greater Chicagoland and we're supposed to contain it before it turns everybody into hulking, ugly, brutal ree-tards."

Gimball started to laugh. "Lot of that stuff musta got loose already," he said.

Bertolucci snorted. Then he got more serious. "Still—"

He thought for a minute. "I don't know. Hostage situation we'd have heard of. Another brutality complaint?"

"At this hour? Doubt it."

"Flooding?" Bertolucci mused. "Not in November. Something in the water supply? AIDS virus in the water supply?"

"I don't think you can catch it that way."

"It would still cause a slight ruckus in town."

"True."

"Radioactivity in the water? Or—you don't suppose there's a nuclear device on countdown around here some-place? We'd be talking about evacuating the whole city of Chicago."

"Jeez!" Gimball said.

They went in the front doors, waved through by aides who were waiting for Bertolucci but who recognized Gimball too. Ushered across the lobby, waved into the VIP elevator, whisked into the mayor's office, gestured through the doors and into chairs—and the door closed behind them with a thwack as solid as a dozen Cadillacs.

Everybody shook hands.

"Now!" said Mayor Wallace. "Listen to *this!*"

Wallace was a short, barrel-chested black man with a bald top to his head, surrounded by puffs of white hair. His head resembled a brown Easter egg in a nest of white grass. All his gestures were pounces, and he punched on a tape recorder now with a short jab.

"—assist a citizen at 357 East Chicago Avenue."

Both Bertolucci and Gimball recognized the type, if not the exact identity, of a Chicago police dispatcher.

"Eighteen thirty-three. I'm due for lunch."

"Okay, thirty-three. After that job, I'll put a yellow behind you."

Bertolucci and Gimball exchanged glances. There wasn't any problem in all this. So far.

"Eighteen twelve," said the dispatcher.

"Twelve."

"Go find a red Chevy at 211 North LaSalle and tell the guy to turn down his radio. The judge can't conduct his court up there."

Bertolucci cocked his head. A loud car radio outside a courtroom was a crisis? Mayor Wallace said, "Wait a minute."

"—from O'Hare," said the dispatcher.

"I'm at the Michigan–Lake Shore Drive split," said a car.

"Citywide, that was the whole lakefront, Lake Shore Drive from Bryn Mawr south. No traffic."

Bertolucci caught Gimball's eye again. They both knew what it was now. The motorcade in from O'Hare, with Mayor Wallace riding in the limo with Benjamin Netanyahu, two double teams of motorcycles front and rear, and those damn stretch limos for everybody else who was important enough to get into one, and those little flags on the bumpers. Plus the last time somebody got the British flag upside down and Prince Charles' aide had a well-bred British fit. Who could tell which way was up with a United Kingdom flag, anyhow?

But this, Bertolucci could see, was much more serious.

Both cops listened closely, expecting to hear the sound of a shot muffled somewhere in the radio call from a squad car or foot patrol. Still, the motorcade had taken place in late afternoon. It was all over before five P.M. Netanyahu was at the Palmer House in time for dinner. If one of the VIPs had been shot, surely—

"Go ahead one twenty," the dispatcher said. Bertolucci and Gimball tensed, knowing the twenty designation meant a sergeant. Had some sergeant seriously put his foot in the shit?

A voice said, *"Humongous backups on Oak, Chestnut,*

Goethe, all along the lakefront. Can we get somebody at the other end to close 'em off farther back?"

"I'll see what I can do, twenty."

"Eighteen fifteen. I need an RD number for a strong-arm robbery—"

"All cars stay off the frequency for fifteen minutes, except the mayor's fleet—"

"This is stupid!" said a new voice.

"All cars—"

"I'm up to my ass in citizens. And man, they're all pissed!"

"Squad disregard—" the dispatcher said, trying to override the voice with anything he could think of, trying to hint to the man to shut up. No luck.

"—at rush hour! Half of 'em can't get home and I've got an ambulance gridlocked, too. This is a stupid ego trip for the goddamn mayor."

"Who is this?" the dispatcher said. But there was no answer. Somewhere out in walkie-talkie land good sense had reasserted itself.

Mayor Wallace punched the tape off.

"See?" he said.

"Um, yes." Bertolucci said.

"And Prime Minister Netanyahu *may have heard that!*"

"Did he, Mr. Mayor?"

"Fortunately, he was talking at the time."

"Oh. That's good."

"That is not good. What kind of officers are you people hiring down there anyway?"

This time Bertolucci did *not* catch Gimball's eye. He was afraid he'd either laugh or snarl if he didn't keep focused on the mayor.

"Well, I'm certainly sorry this happened, Mr. Mayor. I'll get out a directive in the morning, although they already know the air isn't supposed to be used for—"

"A directive is not going to do it! I want that officer dismissed."

"He isn't identified on that tape, Mayor Wallace. We can't tell who he is. There were hundreds of foot and cars along the route, and he doesn't even say where he is."

Wallace leaned forward and stuck his index finger in Bertolucci's face, right up to the end of his nose.

"Voice-print 'em!" he said.

"What?" Bertolucci caught himself. "What do you mean, Mr. Mayor?"

"This took place at four-seventeen this afternoon. Voice-print everybody who was on duty at four-seventeen this afternoon."

"Voice-print the police officers?"

"That's what I said. Then I want this guy fired."

Bertolucci thought, whoa. We are in deep shit. Gimball was now looking fixedly at the Illinois state flag in the corner.

"Mr. Mayor, with all respect," Bertolucci began, and he hurried on, "this is going to make waves—"

"I don't care, waves."

"It's going to get out, is what I mean. Think about it. This was heard, where? Pretty much the Eighteenth and the First, nobody else is listening and not even all of those. I mean, they were busy. Say a hundred officers heard it, tops. By now they've forgotten about it."

"A hundred!"

"But now say you start calling in everybody it could *possibly* be to voice-print 'em. Coupla hundred, easy. The reason's gonna get out. Some of them are gonna say, 'This is because of what that idiot said about the May—about the motorcade.' " Nearly blew that, he thought. "Then everybody's talking. For all we know, Mike Royko gets ahold of it, next thing it's in the *Trib.*"

The mayor wasn't talking now. This was better.

"Or Beemis gets it and it's in the *Sun-Times.*"

Scored again.

"Whereas," Bertolucci said, warming to his task, "by ourselves we have ways."

"Oh?"

"We'll put it around a little. Get back to the guy. Scare the shi—make him one sorry officer."

"Hmm." The mayor stood and walked to his window. Looked out. Put his hands behind his back for a count of three.

"I'll leave it in your capable hands, Superintendent," he said.

"Thank you, sir."

"Good to see you, too, um, Gimball," he said.

They had been dismissed.

Superintendent Bertolucci stopped by the drinking fountain on the first floor. Gimball, standing next to him said, "That Wallace! What an asshole."

Bertolucci looked around to make sure they were out of earshot of Wallace's hangers-on. "Get us out at midnight for this? The man is genuinely stupid. What we need is a new mayor."

Gimball said. "I can't stand politicians."

"Yeah." They walked toward the doors. "You know, politicians don't have to know anything. They don't have to be able to *do* anything. They just have to talk."

"And look good."

"Yeah."

"You handled him well."

"Shit. What does he think we've got, some cop Mafia that's going to hang this birdbrain on a meat hook?"

"Apparently."

"Wish we had." Bertolucci grinned.

"Actually, we could probably find out. There's grapevines everyplace."

"Oh, hell," Bertolucci said as they ducked toward the limo. "Leave the poor mope alone. I think he was fucking dead right."

SIX

NICK BERTOLUCCI ENTERED the elevator in his apartment building and felt that he was approaching Nirvana. His apartment promised quiet, peace, serenity, nothing like the house he had grown up in. No yelling, no wild riot of cooking smells, no nagging, no clothes on the floor, no wet stockings in the bathroom.

Before taking off his coat, he would call the Golden Onion, the nearest and lightning-fastest Chinese delivery service and order egg rolls, sweet and sour pork, and shrimp lo mein.

He rode up in the elevator, picturing hanging up his coat and taking off his shoes. He would pad around in his socks. His videotapes were alphabetically arranged in a bookcase running from floor to ceiling next to his reclining chair. He would let his fingers do the walking along a row until he came to his tapes of the old "I Spy" television series starring Bill Cosby and Robert Culp. He'd slide one into the VHS with a satisfying space-age metallic gulp.

By that time the doorman would be on the intercom saying he had a delivery.

Nick Bertolucci lived in a high-rise overlooking Lake

Michigan. It was austere inside, all white, and it faced the water. Some people thought it was cold; to him it felt clean. His view of the lake was clean and simple. During the day its colors would be blue, or gray, or silver, or greenish, or blends of them, but it was always simple and pleasing. At night the water was lost in blackness, defined only occasionally by the light of a boat passing. Bertolucci loved Chicago, but he did not want to look at the buildings, the smoke, the car lights, the rooftops, the hassle and the people when he sat in his chair at night.

The only adornment in the living room other than book-cases was a glass-fronted cabinet that housed his gun collec-tion. He collected no particular type of gun. No special period. He bought what he liked or what amused him. He had an 1896 Colt Patterson, the early model with the hidden trigger. A Colt Bunline with the extra-long barrel. A couple of Colt Peacemakers of different years, engraved and nickel plated. There was a German army issue P38. A Luger Para-bellum. A couple of Mausers and Webleys of no special value. He had a small double-barreled derringer .45. There was a Dardik experimental, a gun that had never been widely pro-duced; its claim to fame was a set of different-size barrels that screwed in. As if these days you could run around with half a dozen barrels in your pocket! And he had a couple of black-powder Civil War Colts. They all had some interest-ing or odd feature. He kept them polished to a bright shine.

Altogether the collection was worth some money, but not a fortune—a couple thousand dollars, tops.

The elevator sighed to a soft stop. Bertolucci heard it close behind him while he keyed open his door and stepped into his apartment.

The hall closet was open.

He stood with one foot inside across the lintel and the other still in the hall. The apartment smelled odd, a little bit

chemical, as if a person who bathed in a different kind of soap had passed through his air.

He took one more step and very slowly looked around.

The light in the study made a faint glow on the far living room wall.

SEVEN

"MY GOD, ESTELLA!" he said. "Why didn't you tell me you were coming?"

"I didn't know until today."

Bertolucci had opened both arms in delight when he saw his daughter stride out of the guest room door. But he realized instantly that she didn't want to be hugged. She was tense. Her heels clicked crisply on the floor as she strode to him and kissed him, California style, two inches past his ear.

Well, three years in California . . .

Stella was an assistant district attorney in Los Angeles. She must be good at it, he thought. In three years she'd had three promotions. But it was a high pressure job. He was sorry to see her looking so lean, so smart, so *sharp*, and then he was puzzled that it made him sorry. Why not wish your daughter to be lean and mean and aggressive? But it wasn't that; it wasn't that her cheekbones stood out more, or her lipstick was applied with a chisel-edged brush now. Or that she wore a sleek navy suit for the law courts on a body toned by the handball courts. She looked angry and ready to fight.

"Baby," he said, "sit down here."

"You weren't going to call me that."

"All right, Essie, Estelle—"

"Call me Stella!"

"Whatever you say."

She sat near him on the sofa, though. This was a good thing, he thought.

"Stella," he said, cautiously, as you might address a man with a gun. "Stella—"

She looked him steadily in the eye.

"Stella—you look unhappy."

She jumped up. "I don't know why you say that."

"What's happened?"

"Nothing!"

Time to change tack. "Are you in Chicago for a visit? Or business?"

"Visit."

"Stay here, then. Take the guest room."

"Yes, I was hoping to."

"Is this your regular vacation?"

"Yes. Last year I went to the Russian River for two weeks, but I didn't feel like camping this time. I want to do *nothing at all* for a while," she said angrily.

Russian River? Maybe a love affair gone bad. Come to stay with the old man? No mother to talk to. Or did daughters actually talk with mothers these days?

"You're really okay?" he said, trying to start a conversation. He had been better at this with crooks, better at interrogation back in his days as a detective. More subtle.

"Damn it! Yes, I'm okay! If you don't want me here, just say so!"

"I do want you. Estel—Stella, I miss you, being so far away. I'll love having you here."

She stayed poised, more like a grasshopper about to jump away, than a person having a conversation.

"Stella, I know what," he said. "How about I make you a root beer float?"

She gasped, "You're kidding," ready to be insulted, and then she started to laugh. "You haven't made me a root beer float since I was about eight."

"Okay, you're a root beer float."

She laughed again. Nick remembered that after her mother died, he had forced himself to make her laugh—retrained himself in how to joke, because he was numb and had forgotten how. "Or maybe Chinese dinner?" he said.

She smiled at him and nodded. But whatever was bothering her, he didn't think he had fixed.

EIGHT

THE ROLL CALL at the First District was never going to be a photo opportunity for *Architectural Digest*. No interior designer had a proud drawing of it in his résumé. It could not even be called the most soul-satisfying roll call room in Chicago's twenty-five district police stations. The most you could say for it was that it was warm.

Then again, Suze Figueroa thought, one of the worst things you could say about it was it was too hot. It reeked of recently painted steam radiators, warm shoes on sweaty feet, and hot, slightly damp, wool clothing.

Another thing that galled her as she waited for Sergeant Touhy to call roll, which she would on the very stroke of three o'clock, was that everybody here knew each other too well. They all knew exactly how far to push Touhy, exactly how much she'd take before she blew.

Suze sat next to her partner, Norm Bennis. "Hey, Sarge," Bennis called. "Is the D/C coming in?"

"Yes, Norman," she said with exaggerated patience. Darryl Coumadin, commander of the First District, liked to visit with the troops on Wednesdays. Why Wednesdays? Did his wife spend Tuesday nights at bingo and on Wednesdays he needed human warmth? Then again, maybe Tuesday night was the one night his wife was home, so on Wednesday he liked to come in and order people around.

"All right, group, settle down," Touhy said. "Let's read some crimes."

At that instant Officer Richard Dickenson scooted in the back door, smiling, and slid into his seat.

According to the digital clock it was 2:59:47. Touhy'd started fifteen seconds early and there was no way she could yell at him. He did it on purpose, of course, but she was stuck with it. Let him screw up someday, though, and she'd shrivel him so fast they'd be calling him "Raisin Balls" from now to the next century.

"There's still the problems with the shoplifters at the street market," she said. "Mileski, where are you at with that?"

"Quail'n I spent an hour and a half there yesterday and nothin' happened," Stanley Mileski said.

"See, Sarge," Quail drawled, "we hide around behind the trucks, look at a few squashes, radios, pretend to buy lingerie, you know, we're still pretty obvious, they make us and they split."

"Course, while we're there, nobody takes nothin'," Mileski said cheerfully.

"Plus it's gettin' cold."

"Shouldn't be havin' street markets, this weather," Mileski said.

"It's teenagers," Quail said.

"I know it's teenagers," Touhy said. "We may have to switch this around. The kids're out of school at three-thirty.

Get over there soon's we break. Street manager wants to hide one of you behind the gelati truck and he figures the other one can loaf around in the public toilet."

Mileski and Quail groaned, but softly. Touhy was beginning to lose patience. Both of them hated men's rooms as a place to hang around in. They smelled. Plus people got strange notions of why you were hanging around there.

"If you can't get anything, tomorrow we may have to put Figueroa over there as a clerk. She looks more Italian, anyhow."

Figueroa stared at the backs of Quail's and Mileski's necks, thinking, You two had better do it right. She loved riding in the squad car. She loved the Mars lights and the equipment. She loved getting on the radio. She hated dicking around in some damn marketplace, waiting for something to happen.

Suze thought it would be excellent if she were to become the first woman superintendent of police. She realized Sergeant Pat Touhy probably had exactly the same plans for herself. Unfortunately, Touhy was someplace out in front of Suze. Touhy was a sergeant. Then again, Suze was only twenty-five and Touhy was what? Thirty-six maybe. So Suze had more time.

But how was that going to help, really? If Touhy made superintendent, that would about take care of the CPD's token woman for a generation.

Plus, there were other women to worry about at even higher levels yet. Chicago had a woman at commander level, for God's sake. And where did that leave Suze Figueroa? Best thing, Suze thought, would be for her to make some absolutely spectacular collar, and do it soon. Make the *Trib* and the *Sun-Times*. Picture on page one. Personal risk. Great courage. Line of duty. Against enormous odds. Quick thinking—

"Figueroa!"

Touhy was talking to her.

"We tried," Norm Bennis said, giving her a little time to think.

What had Touhy been talking about?

"We cruised that lot maybe twenty times last night," Norm added. Touhy gave him a glare.

Clued in, Suze said, "Yes, Sarge. There weren't any hookers the whole block. We figure they go into some restaurant along there, get warm, come back out. Plus, there's gotta be some lookout watching for us. Or they wouldn't duck just at the right time."

"Well, you'd better come up with something better than that. The D/C's due in a minute," Touhy said.

She pointed at a dozen officers, including Suze, Mileski, Bennis, Dickenson, Bertolucci and Quail. "You stay for the commander," she said. "The rest of you hit the bricks and clear."

The chair scraping and door bumping had scarcely quieted when the side door opened and a tall man pushing a heavy stomach plowed into the room. White hair stood up all over his head.

First District Commander Darryl Coumadin was a legend.

"Come-Again" Coumadin had picked up his nickname in the old, old days of the mid-1950s when a genuine, no fooling, red-wallpaper whorehouse stood near the corner of Washington and Clark, studiously ignored by law enforcement. Site was a hardware store and juice bar now, condo apartments over.

Coumadin and his buddies would go direct from their tour, and never mind whether it was day or night. The other guys—not one of them still left on the department—would pick a girl, Coumadin too, and retire upstairs. Give 'em an

hour or so and they'd all be back down, mostly talking loudly about going to get dinner. Coumadin would still be upstairs someplace. They'd wait and then they'd get mad because they were hungry and send somebody from management— it was Tessie, usually, and a *big* girl she was—up to tell him get downstairs or they'd leave without him. Which Coumadin wouldn't like, because at the restaurant they'd always make a bet on how many sugar cubes in the bowl, this being the days before the little yuppie sugar envelopes, and for all Coumadin knew he might win and not have to buy his dinner. So he'd come down when they got really impatient. And the girl he liked, Mae, she'd always wave goodbye and say, "Come again, Lieutenant!" This was even though he was just a uniform. So they called him "Come-Again" for one reason and another.

Coumadin stared balefully around at the waiting officers.

"Damn it!" he said, slapping his hand down hard on the table. "We gotta get rid of the stink in the First."

Everybody waited.

"We got hookers in the restaurants, we got hookers on the streets. Hookers out of the posh hotels. Point is, we don't need *that* kind of reputation. We also got a serious escort operation going here. But from the point of view of civilians coming into the district, I mean tourists, what I want out of here are the sidewalk hostesses. Obvious ones. You get me? I want you to move 'em out."

Just push them into the Eighteenth or someplace, Suze thought. But it was cleaning up the look of the First that Come-Again was interested in.

"We got a gentleman runs his stable here, Vice tells me," Coumadin said. "He's maybe fifty percent of the sidewalk action out there. The high class but still mostly streetwalker action. Good lookin' ladies. Goooooood clothes. Not the amateurs, and not the walking wounded, which we move 'em

along easy, and not the secretaries on their weekend stroll, they should make their Porsche payments. This man is the Lord and Taylor of the business. Not quite the Neiman-Marcus, you get me, but not Kresge either. Two bills, say. Tops. And the word is they got a warlord or two. That doesn't affect you.

"What I want you to do is keep records. Their strolls are always real predictable. We're gonna keep track of where they go and who they see and sooner or later one of 'em will lead us to their pimp. Then we're gonna roll up on him. So you see one she's well dressed, I want to hear where she goes, who she meets. You get me? You don't pinch her and you don't even cast a shadow on whoever she's with. I want notes. Places. Times. Descriptions. You got me?"

General murmur of assent. Aldo Bertolucci said, "Boss?"

"Yeah, Bertolucci."

"Maybe cameras? We could take pictures of who they meet?"

"That's not a bad idea." Come-Again thought about it for a couple of seconds. "Still and all, we don't want pictures of the johns. See, you might come up with haffa the City Council." Laughter. "What we just want is who they're working for."

"We could use our best judgment, sir," Aldo Bertolucci said. Coumadin stared at him, in serious doubt about this "best judgment" business. He had a problem with Bertolucci. Bertolucci was a uniform, but his brother was superintendent. His father had been superintendent. And Aldo was a major screwup. Coumadin would have been much happier if Bertolucci wasn't in his district. Still—you played the hand you were dealt.

"I'll think about it," he said.

NINE

AT THE START of their tour, three-thirty in the afternoon, Aldo and Dick-dick were rolling slowly south under the el tracks on Franklin. Aldo was driving.

"I wanna get a Big Mac," he said.

Dick-dick said, "I don't think we oughta do that."

"What are you, some health food nut—"

"No, it's just, you know, Sarge wouldn't like it—"

"Sarge is a *woman*," Aldo said in a voice of total scorn.

"Or Sheehan either. Wouldn't like it. Or Come-Again. I mean, they want us to get out and go get lunch and then get back in. Not sit eating in the car. Plus, it's just the start of the tour. Plus I saw you eat a sandwich before roll call."

"And *now I'm hungry again!*"

"Jeez!"

"I'm goin' over to the Golden Arches, Dick-dick, and I'm gonna drive through, Mars lights and all, and I don't want no lip from you."

"Wait! No, don't—"

"Hey, when I say—"

"Lemme out here. That's a doughnut place. I'll get you coffee and a doughnut. Two doughnuts! And I'll drive after that."

Which he did. By the time they were settled, Aldo eating the two doughnuts which Dick-dick had paid for out of his own money, never mind the old saying that a good cop is never cold, wet or hungry, and never mind the fact that Dick-dick was so low in money that wherever he walked he practically watched the pavement for coins, here was Aldo getting crumbs and sugar all over the front seat and floor (Somebody was sure to notice, Dick-dick thought; never, *never* get the

powdered sugar kind again. Shit!), by then what had been a quiet-air afternoon erupted into activity.

"One thirty-three."

Thirty-three was Norman Bennis and Suze Figueroa.

"Thirty-three."

"Domestic argument, 888 west on Grand. Apartment 1607. Complaint is a Ms. Willo."

"What was that apartment number again?"

"One-six-oh-seven."

"Thanks much."

Aldo, slurping down his coffee, said, "Glad that one's not us."

"Why? 'Cause it's public housing?"

"Right. The elevator's gonna be broken."

Dick-dick admired Aldo's savvy. But he said, "Oughta be fit enough to walk up. Any officer."

Aldo eyed Dick-dick's slender frame and snorted. "Hey! I'm in good shape."

Dick-dick figured agreeing was a good idea here. "That's true," he said.

"I mean, I work out."

Dick-dick said, "I know that."

"Which—" Aldo said, brushing his hands together so hard that sugar and crumbs flew all over, several soggy crumbs landing on Dick-dick's uniform blouse and bouncing down onto his pants. Dick-dick wiped at them fast, thinking that they would get grease on the pants and make ugly spots. He managed to squash them trying to brush them away, and frowned at what he knew would be dark oily streaks.

"—which does *not* mean that I go to one of these simp, yuppie *health clubs!*" From his tone of voice he could have been saying "tuberculosis clubs." "With the rubber plant in the waiting room, and all those space-age machines."

"What, like Nautilus—?"

"Where you exercise *muscle groups!* I mean, Dick-dick, I went to one-a them once, by accident. Some broad comes out and she wants to know, what did I want to develop, my deltoids? My latissimi dorsi? Christ, I nearly said, Lady, I figure I don't need to build up this here Eiffel Tower in my pants. They got a machine, the Gravitron. That sound like 2001 or what?" Aldo clapped a big hand on Dick-dick's shoulder.

Dick-dick could smell the doughnut oil. He didn't want to think what his shoulder looked like. He said, "Gravitron. I see what you mean."

"And all this little yuppie machine does is figure your body weight and it offsets this against what you want to do with your muscles. How much weight you wanna move. I figure, I wanna develop the muscles in my third finger, top side, they're gonna show me a way."

"Well, actually, I think you could do that with—"

"This is *cosmetic* fitness, Dick-dick. Cosmetic fitness. Don't you forget that."

"True, but a lot of people—"

"Plus, you work out, you're thirsty after, what do they serve, these places? Water. Not water fountain water, outta pipes. They got eleven brands of water. At four bucksa bottle. Right? And maybe diet Coke, diet Pepsi, you shouldn't even enjoy your soda pop. I mean, this is not Aldo Bertolucci."

"So where do you go?"

"I go to a *gym!* I go to an honest-to-God gym, by God! This is a place smells like sweat, smells like Clorox, they got a Coke machine by the back door, locker room, two showers, that's it. The whole shebang. Punching bag, that's it. I work out."

"Just on a punching bag?"

"Listen, Dick-dick. I know you used to be a big gymnas-

tics star. That's okay with me. I mean, it's real. You know? It's serious. Took lotsa persistence. I got every respect for you, don't get me wrong."

"Yeah. Yeah, I know."

"But not mosta those people. Anyhow, I hit a punching bag. Little bag, you know, sometimes, keep up my speed, my eye. But mostly the big bag. 'Cause, really, Dick-dick, you get strong, whaddya ever need to do except hit people?"

"Um. I guess that's—um—"

"Just hit people. I got knuckles like rawhide. Tough as a steer. Feel this!" He stuck his fist in Dick-dick's face. Dick-dick, who was trying to maneuver a turn onto Michigan Avenue with three buses and a kamikaze taxi in close competition, figured it was better to turn one-handed and feel Aldo's fist. It did, indeed, feel like hide. Maybe anteater hide, he thought. Something that runs around on its knuckles in the dirt.

"Yeah, that's tough skin, Aldo," he said.

"*Braaakk! Ditditdir! —IRTY-THREE! Zzzz-UNCH!*" the radio said.

"*You're overmodulating,*" the dispatcher said.

"*One thirty-three.*" Suze Figueroa's voice. Gasping.

"*Go ahead thirty-three.*"

"*Can I go to lunch?*"

"*Early for you, isn't it, thirty-three?*"

"*We just walked up to that domestic.*"

"*What? You walked up sixteen flights of stairs?*"

"*Elevator wasn't workin'.*"

"*Yeah. Go to lunch. You need it. Where you gonna be?*"

"*One East Chestnut.*"

"*Okay.*"

There was a thirty-second silence, during which Dick-dick surreptitiously wiped at his right shoulder with his left hand and felt it to be very greasy.

Aldo said, "What'd I tell you. Elevators never work."

The dispatcher said, *"One twenty-eight."*

Aldo groaned.

Dick-dick said into the mike, "Twenty-eight."

"Uh, twenty-eight, get over to the district. Sarge wants to talk with you."

"Ten four."

Aldo said, "What the hell?"

"Yeah," Dick-dick said. "What did we do now?" He figured if he put his reefer on before he went into the station, nobody would notice the grease and powdered sugar on his shoulder.

Sergeant Patricia Touhy was waiting for them practically in the doorway.

"God," Aldo muttered, "we are in some sort of deep shit."

But Dick-dick saw there was a new and different look on Touhy's face. He'd seen rage there, and this wasn't it. He'd seen grim satisfaction, exasperation, exaggerated patience, utter disbelief that any CPD officer could be so abysmally stupid, and a number of other Touhy-type expressions. This was none of those. After a second or two of very fast thinking, Dick-dick figured he had it pegged. Sympathy! Hey! Whaddya know!

"Come over here," Touhy said.

They followed her to a bench along the wall. She said, "Sit," and sat down herself. They sat, too, Dick-dick making sure that Aldo Bertolucci sat next to Touhy.

"Bertolucci," she said, "there's no easy way to do this. We just got a call from your sister. Your father died suddenly. Today. About an hour ago."

TEN

SUPERINTENDENT NICK BERTOLUCCI walked fast down the hall to his office, trailed by his ADS, Lester Grimes. The afternoon topcops' meeting of the deputies and other service chiefs was just over, and Bertolucci reflected only briefly on its compound of competence, failure, ambition, loyalty and treachery—business as usual.

Bertolucci had been able to put Stella out of his mind during the meeting, but she jumped back now, tense, thin and, he thought, angry. He'd left her in his apartment, drinking her fourth cup of coffee. She'd been awake and sitting in the living room when he got up, and he got up early. So she couldn't sleep.

He'd offered her eggs, which she declined. "Too much cholesterol." He'd offered her a bagel. Bran cereal. An apple. "Not hungry." So she wasn't sleeping or eating. Bertolucci felt utterly ineffectual.

Bertolucci heard Grimes puffing behind him. Grimes was a tubby black man in his early forties. He had fat little legs leading up to a fifty-two-inch waistline, and although he bounced cheerfully as he walked, Bertolucci knew Grimes found it very difficult to keep up with him. Bertolucci slowed down, just a little. Grimes had been sent fat-man letters from the department medic for years—cut down, exercise, go see the department doctor—but he couldn't diet, and finally Bertolucci nixed them nagging him anymore. In Bertolucci's opinion, it was better to treat Grimes like a grownup. He knew he should diet; leave it to him to decide.

They rounded the corner into the office complex, Bertolucci straight-arming the door ahead of him. The receptionist in the outer office looked up, then he jumped to

his feet, grabbing several pieces of yellow paper, and headed for Bertolucci. Telephone messages.

In one of the flanking offices, Moffat, the other ADS, and his secretary jumped up too. Both of them grabbed papers from their desks—pink memos, white 8 1/2-by-11 photocopies and yellow telephone slips. In the second flanking office, Lester Grimes' secretary clutched a similar bunch of papers and moved toward her door.

They all converged on Bertolucci half a dozen steps from the door to his private office, and they were all starting to talk. Bertolucci drew a breath.

"Hold it!" he said. "One at a time."

Lester's secretary said, "Yes, but it's *Alderman Spaeth*—"

"The mayor wants you to see his aide at eleven," Moffat said.

Lester Grimes, sweating lightly, said, "I haven't had a chance to tell you, but after the meeting Heidema was all bent out of shape—"

Grimes' secretary said, "There's this strange man keeps calling—"

And the receptionist said, "You're supposed to call Tokyo, and it's already ten P.M. there."

"He's *very* upset—"

"Wallace says they want a position statement by the end of the day."

"She's called every fifteen minutes."

Moffat, a slender white man with pepper and salt hair and a pepper and salt mustache, said, "Wallace's aide is going to be here in ten minutes and you need the background first." It was not a good idea to let the mayor's aide bring up something without the boss knowing what it was going to be. Heads could roll. Moffat overrode the others, with a voice that Bertolucci had always wondered at, it was so much bigger than his body would indicate.

"All right, all right, all right," Bertolucci said to him. "Come in and tell me about it, but make it fast. And somebody make coffee."

Bertolucci's office faced west over the city of Chicago. He glanced out the window. In the far distance a plume of black smoke rose from somewhere beyond buildings beyond other buildings. Nearer, a squad car screamed out of the parking lot. It was a cold gray day, like so many this time of year. He turned back to Moffat.

"It's the CHA murders," Moffat said, referring to the Chicago Housing Authority public housing buildings. Moffat was a trim, vigorous, jumpy little man, who gave off bursts of nervous energy like a metal cup in a microwave. Bertolucci eyed him, aware that despite his appearance, he was not nearly as efficient as chubby Lester Grimes. Plus Moffat had a tendency to panic at big names, like Mayor Wallace. Today more than usual.

Bertolucci said, "Withers is covering that."

"He wants your take on it."

A tinge of annoyance crept into Bertolucci's voice. "Why doesn't Mayor Wallace phone me himself? He'd get a clearer picture. I haven't got time to talk with an aide."

"I don't know. He's always like this."

"True."

Moffat shifted nervously from foot to foot.

Bertolucci said, "Oh, all right. The aide's probably on his way over anyhow."

Moffat scurried back out to his office.

Superintendent Bertolucci thought for a few seconds. There had been three murders of elderly women in a neighboring pair of CHA buildings, all since August. All three women had kept small nest eggs in the apartment. Nothing big. One had $75, one $210, the biggest was $300-some. Withers' report at the morning briefing had warned

Bertolucci that it could be a CHA guard doing the killing.

The CHA had its own police force, but Mayor Wallace wanted the police department to take over patrolling the inside of the buildings, not just responding when there was a call. The CHA housed hundreds of thousands of people. It was like asking the CPD to police another whole city. With the manpower they had—and the budget they had— Bertolucci had told the mayor it was out of the question. He had said so to the media also, seriously pissing the mayor off. Bertolucci remembered the incident with pleasure.

It looked like they were on a collision course, he and the mayor.

Bertolucci allowed himself a half-minute reflection on Withers. He was grateful, for what it was worth, that Withers had been frank at the morning briefing. Information sabotage was the biggest and the easiest way a high-ranking cop could make the superintendent look bad. Keep information from him. Then the superintendent goes to the press and they know stuff he doesn't, which is disaster. Or the mayor calls and the superintendent doesn't know what the hell the mayor is talking about.

The superintendent in the city of Chicago serves "at the pleasure of the mayor." Which doesn't mean the mayor can plug superintendents in and out every couple of months as the spirit moves him. It could look "political." And while everybody knows the city runs on politics, there is a polite convention to pretend it doesn't.

Withers wanted to be superintendent. Mentally, Bertolucci shrugged—not the biggest news story of the week. He dealt with envy on a daily basis.

The important thing was that Withers was still doing his job in a professional way. Either he was content to wait until Bertolucci stepped down in the normal course of things, or he was biding his time until just the right moment. Of

course, Withers would know that if Bertolucci ever caught him manipulating data, he'd be out of there in the time it took to say Eighth District.

So if Withers is gonna make a move against me, Bertolucci thought, it will have to be something big and perfectly timed.

Bertolucci had a mental flashback of the moment—he must have been eight or nine—when he realized for the first time that adults didn't know what they were doing. Just like kids, only they faked it better. There was something his parents were discussing, something they were going to buy, maybe even something as important as a car. And despite the fact that his father was extolling whatever it was, Nick knew, *knew* from the tone of his voice that he was just guessing and hoping he'd be right.

After this epiphany, Nick saw the world with new eyes. At school the next day, he could see for himself that the teachers were guessing half the time how to handle the kids. Or even about some of the material they taught. Just guessing. The janitor didn't really know how to fix the toilet; it overflowed again three hours later. The whole huge adult world was just winging it.

It scared him at first, as if he'd been riding in a car and looked up and there was no driver. After a couple of days, though, he got used to it and it helped him. He got to thinking his guess was as good as anybody's. And as he learned things, he figured if he gained knowledge and relied on his own judgment, he'd *be* as good as anybody.

Grimes came bouncing back in to tell Bertolucci that the mayor's aide was here. "Also, there's that idiot from the *Tribune*." He didn't have to say any more. Bertolucci knew immediately, as anybody in the office would, which idiot it was.

"Send him to News Affairs."

"Also—"

Bertolucci stopped him. "What's the matter with Moffat today?"

Grimes stared at him, surprised. "His daughter had emergency surgery for a leg fracture last night."

"Moffat!" Bertolucci called on the intercom.

"But she's all right, though," Grimes said.

Moffat hurried into the office. "You've got to call Tokyo about the conference," he said.

"There isn't any conference in Tokyo."

"The New Delhi conference. The organizer is in Tokyo."

"Moffat, stop talking. Go home," Bertolucci said. "I mean, go to the hospital. Whatever. But don't hang around here."

"Yes, boss." Moffat smiled.

As Moffat went out the door, Bertolucci caught a glimpse of the man waiting in the outer office. He had hoped the mayor would send Hec Morgan, who was at least a real person you could talk to about the CHA. But it was Carleton Freeman Lynds III. He was sitting on the leather bench, one creased pant leg crossed over the other, a polished top-of-the-line Bally shoe going up and down as he telegraphed his impatience. The gold Rolex gleamed on his wrist, peeking coyly out from the custom shirt with the self-color monogram on the cuff.

"Oh, fuck," Bertolucci said.

After a second he turned to Grimes. "Forget the coffee. See if you can find a bottle of Perrier someplace. And dredge up a wedge of lime."

ELEVEN

AT ABOUT THE time Dick-dick and Aldo Bertolucci were pulling away from the doughnut shop, the mayor's aide finally left Nick Bertolucci's office. First Deputy Superintendent Gus Gimball arrived minutes later with the day's final case summaries. He was trailed by Deputy Superintendent Wally Riggs. Bertolucci was sure Riggs had just attached himself to Gimball, that Gimball had not invited him. Riggs did things like that, afraid he'd miss something.

Bertolucci rubbed his eyes. Gus "Bull" Gimball sank into a chair and sighed. He said, "We have an ethnic group needs attention."

Wally "Wallpaper" Riggs watched but kept his mouth shut. He had been so named for good reason. Wallpaper is stuff that hangs around, doesn't get in the way, looks good, but doesn't help out much, either.

Wallpaper Riggs was the mayor's boy, and probably the mayor's ears on the department as well. Nick regarded him as a cross to bear.

"You know," Nick said, sighing, "sometimes I just get so goddamn tired of ethnicity."

Bull Gimball looked at him over the half-glasses he wore for reading.

"I mean," Bertolucci said, "this ain't a city we got here. We got a loose coalition of ethnic factions."

"Warring ethnic factions," Gimball said.

"And now it's the Vietnamese."

"Tomorrow the Native Americans."

"Maybe Peruvians."

"Yeah, hell, we haven't heard anything from the Peruvians in a looooong time."

Some police officer had been "insensitive" to some Vietnamese person. In a Vietnamese neighborhood! the papers said. As if it would be better to be insensitive to a Vietnamese in a damn Greek neighborhood!

Nick said, "Wally, you can take off. We're outta here in a coupla minutes."

"I can stay if you want."

"Naw. That's okay."

Wally left. Bull Gimball raised his eyebrows at Bertolucci, but said nothing. Bertolucci shrugged.

He stood up and stretched. "I shoulda been a fireman. This job is just a matter of running around putting out fires."

Gus Gimball stood up when the boss did.

Bertolucci's back itched. He wanted to pull out his shirt and give it a good scratch, but he would have to unzip his pants afterward and put everything back together right. Which was another one of the problems of being superintendent. He couldn't go around looking sloppy.

Set a good example for the troops.

Bertolucci settled for backing up to his bookcase and rubbing his back against it. Not too satisfying and besides it made him feel like an elephant rubbing up to a tree. Gus Gimball stuffed his own papers into his briefcase and waited, in case there was anything else Bertolucci wanted to say.

Gimball's hand was on the doorknob when the phone rang. Bertolucci almost didn't pick it up. "I don't *have* to be here every minute," he said.

But he answered it.

"Monica!" he said. There was a pause. Gus Gimball knew Monica was Bertolucci's sister.

"When did it happen?" Bertolucci asked in a tight voice. Another silence.

"All right. I'll be there in twenty minutes."

When Bertolucci hung up the phone, Gimball was star-

ing carefully at the photograph of the Eighteenth District softball team in 1972. He did not want to look as if he'd been listening. Not that Bertolucci would think he could have avoided listening. It was just the way you did these things.

"My dad just died," Bertolucci said.

"Nico, huh?" Gimball replied cautiously, thinking, Now there's a stupid question for you. How many fathers does the boss have, after all?

"Uh-huh." Bertolucci eyed Gimball.

"I'm real sorry to hear that," Gimball said carefully.

"I'd better get moving."

"Um—you okay with this?"

Bertolucci said shortly, "Yeah. Just fine."

Since any other words from either one of them would be likely to open up a can of worms, Gimball made a fist and punched Bertolucci lightly on the arm, the old you-can-make-the-free-throw gesture to a teammate. Bertolucci nodded his thanks.

TWELVE

IN THE CAR, Bertolucci said to Stella, "I'm sorry. You really stepped in it, coming home now."

"Wouldn't I have to come anyway? Will Joey come home for the funeral?"

"I don't know. Your brother doesn't exactly like family events."

"Neither do I."

"That's what I mean."

Stella was silent for about five blocks. Then, unknow-

ingly echoing Gus Gimball, she said, "You going to be all right with this?"

When they got to the senior Bertolucci's house, Stella and Nick could hear the shouting the moment they stepped onto the sidewalk.

"I don't see why!" Monica shouted.

"All my black is old!" her mother screamed. Rose Bertolucci was seventy-two and stood four feet eleven inches, most of it tightly packed into a corset.

"Monica, tone it down," Nick said. Monica was his older sister. She ignored him and said to Rose, "It's hypocritical."

"What's hypocritical about going to Marshall Field's?" her mother screamed.

"It's wasteful to overdo it like that, buying all new stuff, I mean, hundreds of dollars' worth of clothes for the old ba—clothes you'll never wear again, because the next funeral you'll say all *this* is too old and out of style. Or else it's callous," Monica said. "I mean, Pa's lying dead at the parlor. Tonight or tomorrow morning they'll be draining the blood and piping in the formaldehyde or whatever they do and while that's going on, there we'll be in the Better Dresses department!"

"Monica!"

Rose Bertolucci slapped her daughter. Monica screamed and burst into tears. Nick Bertolucci said "Ma, *don't!*" and started to step between them.

"Nicholas, you be quiet!" His mother turned on him, her eyes wide and hostile. But Monica was touching his elbow.

"Never mind," Monica said. He spun away from both of them, knowing that any intervention was only going to make it worse. Bertolucci sighed, caught Stella's eye for a second, and he and she both winked, reminding him of how she had

been as a teenager, irreverent and fun. He was walking back toward the kitchen when the doorbell rang.

He turned around and went to open the front door. Before he had time to recognize the woman standing there, his mother was at his side, gasping an effusive welcome, greeting the newcomer, who stood square and stolid in the doorway. When his mother said "Coletta!" Nick recognized Mrs. Pasquesi. He had grown up with the Pasquesis' son Joe and had visited at the Pasquesi house a thousand times. But this very old woman could hardly be Joe's mother! She thrust out a small hand holding a dish of food covered with aluminum foil.

"Oh, how nice! How nice! Come in," Rose Bertolucci said. "Please come in. Nick is here. Aldo's coming."

"Little Nick!" Mrs. Pasquesi screamed. "Oh-oh-oh, how sad this all is." She ran over and hugged him in fat, soft arms. She smelled like anisette.

"How's Joe?" he asked.

But she was already saying, "I'll just help out in the kitchen for a little while. And she trotted through the living room on tiny feet, glancing avidly at the faces of the family for signs of grief.

Rose Bertolucci watched the kitchen door close. "*Sicilian'!*" she hissed scornfully, giving the word its full Italian pronunciation, staring at where Mrs. Pasquesi's retreating back would have been visible if the door had been transparent. She turned to Nick.

"You didn't *have* to mention Joe," she said.

"Why not?"

"You know he's in prison."

"No, I didn't. I can't believe it."

"In Florida."

"Well, how was I to know that? I don't know who's in the slammer all over the whole country."

"*Sicilian'! Cafone!*" Mrs. Bertolucci repeated, gesturing her contempt at the dish of food. "You watch. This will be *eggplant!*"

"Stella's here," he said.

Rose Bertolucci only said, "Good" as if coming from California was only what Stella owed her, anyhow. Stella took the dish from her grandmother and strode to the kitchen.

Nick touched Monica's elbow. "Come on. Let's go sit on the stoop."

Monica smiled at him. It was such an obvious consolation, the very thing she used to do for him when he was a child and upset. Monica was now fifty-four. She had iron gray strands in her black Italian hair, but she was thin and stylish and medium tall. More like her father than her mother, who was short and plump. And Stella, Nick thought, was much more like Monica than like him. When her little brother Nick had been punished and was crying, Monica would say never mind and take him out on the stoop and give him Necco wafers from her pocket. They were powdery pastel colors, and they tasted chalky. He liked the pale yellow lemon ones, but so did she, so they were usually all gone and he got the pale purple, which were second best. They tasted of flowers.

Monica was combative, like both her parents.

She kissed Nick on the cheek, said "Thanks," but walked in the other direction, away from him into the kitchen, where Rose and Stella had gone with the presumed eggplant.

Nick listened a few seconds.

"Nine in the morning we leave," Rose said loudly. "And you're coming with me."

"Where?"

"First we'll pick the casket—"

"Sure, Ma. I'll come along and save you from excess!"

"Excess!" Rose screamed.

"Like spending too much on the . . ." Monica let that trail off. Nick knew she had been about to say "on the old bastard."

There was a silence. Nick walked toward the front door. He heard his mother say, "And from there we'll go to Marshall Field's."

He walked out on the front porch. It had to be about five P.M. The old neighborhood was darkening but not entirely quiet, car doors slamming a few blocks away—the restaurants on Taylor Street. Someplace a radio. Rock. He couldn't hear any Italian music. Not like the old days.

The old neighborhood wrapped around him. Cooking smells. Tomorrow the neighbors would be over, bringing cassata and dishes of gnocchi and caponata. More Napolitano than Siciliano, his mother would say. He knew there would be signs in the store windows: WE HAVE BACCALÀ. And Easter grass. All year round, green Easter-basket grass.

He let himself slowly down the steps. He could feel his knees creaking. I'm forty years older, he thought, and just for a second he could also feel himself at the age of ten or eleven, leaping down the steps two at a time. No, more—he remembered going through a stage of trying to leap all six of them every time he went out the door. And did. Until his father caught him.

But he'd hardly noticed his knees in those days, had he? Except that they were always skinned.

He sat on the third step from the bottom. One knee popped. Always skinned and always scabby. His mother used to tell him he would have permanently scarred knees. But he didn't. She was wrong.

Then he knew too why he picked the third step. You could rub the lion's head.

He had not sat here in years. You didn't sit on steps as an adult when old Nico lived in the house. Could it really be

that he had not sat on this very step for—what? Forty years? And now he went right to it as if it were yesterday.

He put out his hand. The steps were cast concrete. Cast concrete walls ran down along both sides. They had rounded tops like wood railings and where the railings began, just above the bottom step, were two big finials in the shape of lions' heads. From the third step your hand just exactly fit forward over the head.

Nick felt the lion's heavy, curly mane, almost like cauliflower. He felt down over the nose, which was broad and noble. That's what he used to call it as a kid. Noble.

Then the best part. The lion's mouth was wide open in a roar. You could feel the teeth. When he was very small, he thought the two lions protected the house.

When he was older, his father had said the Italians used lions on their porches because it represented the old saying *Miglio vivere un giorno de leone che cent anni da pecora*—"Better to live one day as a lion than a hundred years as a lamb."

Crap, he thought, stroking the lion's nose. It was better to live. Period.

Nicholas Bertolucci thought of himself as a mature human being. At fifty-one he was far past the age of wondering who he was. He no longer believed that everybody had to like him. He no longer spent any time at all trying to look tough, the way he had in high school, or the way he had as a patrolman. He knew what he looked like—darkish, with a real nose, a nose you could call a nose—and he no longer went through any shit about it. In high school he had spent hell's own time wishing he were American. Blond, with wavy hair—not curly, wavy—short, straight nose, like the movie stars. Tannish, but not this olive skin color. Tall. What he wanted to be was your basic California man.

Fuck it. Now he knew he *was* American, of his own kind.

If he wasn't six feet six, he was at least moderately tall and relatively strong, even now, and he hadn't run all to belly. And anyway, he wasn't in the mating game. After his wife died, that was it. I'm outta here, he thought. He was too busy to go looking.

He and his wife had raised the kids, and raised them well. More thanks to Adriana than to him, he thought, but still he had been careful not to make his father's mistakes.

Stella had gone through law school at Northwestern and then got a job in the District Attorney's Office in Los Angeles. His son Joey had somehow or other become a perpetual student. The kid had a degree in history from Yale. Then he got a degree in psychology. Toronto. Now he was in medical school at Duke. He'd been fifteen years as a college student. So? Better that than prison. Neither of them came home much, until Stella showed up. They talked on the telephone. The children had their own lives. Adult people were allowed to run their own lives. Okay. He could handle that.

And if the department had become his wife and child, he could face that. God knew it had all the elements. It was at one time or another and in one person or another childish, nagging, rewarding, self-sacrificing, abrasive, courageous, annoying, frustrating, enraging and elevating. And involving. It took up all his life. And much of his love.

Nick was aware of "cleaning up" his life, after his childhood with Pa. He might have sterilized it too much, but he didn't think so.

He heard the front door of the house open behind him.

He swung around. Aldo, his brother, stood on the top of the stoop, his big belly looming over Nick's head.

"So?" Aldo said. "Keeping out of the way?"

"How you doing, Aldo?" Nick stood. He was still several steps down. He walked up slowly, to get to Aldo's level, watching Aldo's eyes.

Aldo said, "I got here a little late. I had to go back and change." Nick nodded. "Out of uniform," Aldo said pointedly, as if Nick wouldn't understand. Nick nodded patiently. "Nice to be able to wear that nice suit there to work."

"Mmm."

"See, if I went out and bought a suit like that, they'd figure I was on the take."

All the words he might say ran through Nick's head. Aldo had not needed to do the things that had got him dumped back to uniform. Aldo had had plenty of help from Nick, which he acted as if he deserved, and then he blew it anyway. Aldo had sabotaged his own career.

Nick did not say them.

Their uncle Tony drew up in front in a green Subaru and let out Aunt Mary, Cousin Theresa, and Aunt Frannie. Nick and Aldo helped the aunts inside. Tony came after them, carrying food.

"Nice tie, too," Aldo said to Nick, while their mother accepted the offerings. Frannie was saying, "I would never have thought it would happen. Not Nico! *Never!* I would never have thought we'd lose Nico!"

"Silk, I guess," Aldo said. "Can't afford that kinda thing myself. Salary I get."

"Go to the track less," Nick said, and immediately regretted it. He had told himself not to strike back and how long had that lasted? Three minutes?

"Oh. Oh, we know best, huh?"

But Nick was opening the door again, to his great-aunt and her daughter. They hugged him and shrieked with sympathy. They shrieked a welcome to Stella. Nick shepherded them into the crowd. He was surrounded by relatives.

His great-aunt Rosamarina spied her granddaughter, Nick's cousin Theresa, grabbed her in an iron claw and without preamble explained to her that Theresa's mother,

Rosamarina's daughter-in-law, had been dead wrong in the year 1937. "You put the *prezzemolo*, the parsley, in *after* you take the sauce off the flame! I told her and told her."

"That's Abruzzése," Theresa said. She knew the argument. She had grown up, married, had four children, buried her husband, and buried one child, a son killed in the Korean War, while the argument raged as if it were yesterday.

"Eh?" said Great-aunt Rosamarina. She was eighty-seven and deaf.

"*Abruzzése!*" Theresa shrieked. "Not Basilicata. Mama was Basilicata! They cook the parsley."

"They know nothing! Nothing!" Rosamarina said.

"They have their own customs."

"And then she poured the hot sauce on my foot!"

"It was an accident," Theresa said. Her face said that it was not.

"Well, I guess they'll all be explaining how proud Pa was of his perfect boy," Aldo said in Nick's ear.

Nick spun around.

"Drop this shit," he hissed. "He was never proud of me. I don't suppose he was ever proud of you, either. You know what kind of bastard he was. You can take me off your shit list, because I wasn't born to put you down. I was in the business of surviving. You run your life however you want to, Aldo."

"Ah!" Aldo said happily. "Got to you!"

"Why bother?"

"Hey, what's a good Italian without a vendetta?" Aldo said lightly. But his eyes were blank and his mouth was thin with hatred.

Behind them Mary said to Frannie, "That woman used to serve veiny veal!"

Aldo grinned. "You ever see one of these people forget a slight?"

"Leave me out of it."

Nick stared around the living room for his mother and realized she was the woman that Mary was talking about, who had served the veiny veal. In the mid-1950s for all he knew. He didn't care. He couldn't see his sister Monica, but supposed she was in the kitchen. He thought for the millionth time, *I am not one of these people. I was switched in the cradle. This is all a horrible mistake.*

"Don't hear a word about the old bastard himself, do you?" Aldo said. His lips were pulled tight and his breath hissed in Nick's ear.

"The hell with it," Nick said. "If anybody asks, I'll be back tomorrow."

He left Aldo and beckoned to Stella, who was only too ready to leave.

Nick headed for the door, his hand on Stella's elbow. Stella shot him a grateful glance, and again, for a couple of seconds, he had a vision of her as the child she had once been, happy to see him when he came home from work, giggly and tender.

Nick did not look back. He did not see Aldo watching him.

THIRTEEN

THE DAY AFTER his father's death, Aldo Bertolucci was standing in the street near his mother's house. He was wearing his brown leather bomber jacket that was starting to crack and a pair of boots that could well have been through the evacuation of Da Nang. He'd meant to get his hair cut

two weeks ago, but it was his one day off and the Bears were playing the Lions and he had a hundred dollars on the Bears with a guy who gave him the Bears and three when the bookies were giving a six-point spread. So he stayed home and watched the game. Lost, too. They always know more than the little guy knows. Take advantage, every time.

When Dick-dick was first partnered with Aldo Bertolucci, Officer Hiram Quail had taken him aside and told him important stuff.

"See, cops in Chicago—and hell, for all I know Los Angeles and New York and maybe even *Detroit*, God help 'em—have an image of the Italian police officer. He's the guy who can't stand it if the uniform blouse isn't fitted. Wants to wear shoes with a leaner, meaner, trendier line, even if they don't walk so well. Know what I mean?"

Dick-dick said yeah.

"The Italian cop, these guys say, can't wait to get outta uniform and into something that looks great. Jacket that hangs right. Slim belt, supple, maybe even suede. Real shoes, made in Italy.

"Not that he ain't willing to do his job. May even be a real tenacious officer, a bulldog as a detective, take hold and hang on. But—say he's chasing a fleeing felon down an alley. He's fast, the Eye-tie cop, runs like a deer. Going to be right on top of the guy when he catches him. Little street justice, maybe.

"Big mud puddle looms up. The guy runs through it. The Italian cop looks at it and at his new shoes, shakes his fist and says, 'I'll get you next time, you fucking slimeball!' Now that's a stereotype, right, Dick-dick?"

"You bet."

"Actually," Quail said, "there's two kinds of Italian cops. The second type is like Aldo Bertolucci."

Aldo had parked his car—which had several discarded

Frito, Cheeto and potato chip bags on the floor—half a dozen blocks from his mother's house. He thought he would walk and remind himself about the old neighborhood. In fact, though, he often walked places where he could have driven, and the real reason was that he liked to stroll up on some wino or bum and scare the shit out of him. He liked it fine if some vagrant accosted him and then he sprang his police ID on them and showed them how they'd better act civilized. Clean up the streets, Aldo thought.

Crummy job, but somebody's got to do it.

He never walked in neighborhoods where everybody was well dressed and nobody panhandled. Places like that made him angry.

His mother wanted him to clear out some of old Nico's junk.

"Give it to the Jesuit Fathers," she said.

She and Monica, and probably Nick the brown-nose, were at the funeral parlor greeting relatives. Relatives, brass from the department, plus a lot of old decrepit guys who'd known his father in the old days and hung around and grabbed your arm and breathed denture breath in your face. They'd talk about people who were dead and the Irish ones would say, "He was a lovely man." Couldn't just retire and go away, some of these guys.

Sure, he'd clean out the old stuff, he told her. Let the old lady think he was doing something great. And get out of going to the parlor. He was not in the least aware that he was still afraid of his mother.

He walked the six blocks with a rolling cop swagger that would have alerted any panhandler in his senses to stay away, but there weren't any around to be alarmed. It was too cold. Aldo stopped on the cracking pavement in front of his parents' house. His mother's house now. His hands were on his hips.

There was grass in the cracks where the pavement had broken, grass that might have been green for a few weeks in May but was now seared to gray straw by the cold. The house was four stories high, but very narrow, like all the others on the block. They were all wood sided or steel-colored stone. His mother's was wood with a cement stoop. They all had little peaked roofs over the front stoop, like mustaches over a surprised mouth. There was only five feet of space between each house and the next. Aldo remembered as a teenager trying to see into the bedroom of the house next door. It was almost close enough for him to reach out his window and touch theirs. But the people next door had tan blinds that pulled down by string-covered rings, and the blinds on their side windows were always pulled to the sill.

Next door to his mother's on the other side was the DiNicolas' house, which was stone. Aldo craned around, trying to see whether the DiNicolas still had their shrine. The shrine had been made of an upended white porcelain bathtub, half buried in the earth of the backyard. The exposed part made a perfect Gothic arch. Inside, the DiNicolas had placed a two-foot statue of the Virgin Mary, painted blue, white, pink and gold, and they had surrounded her feet with plastic tulips.

The houses were too close together for him to see the shrine from the front. Aldo was not going to walk around to the back out of sheer curiosity. What did it matter, anyway? Plus, he was going in the front door. Right up to the front and in the door.

He was obscurely satisfied at this, and did not consciously remember that as a child his parents had always made him go in the back. You could go *out* the front, though it was frowned upon, but you had to go *in* the back.

"Don't track in mud. Who do you think you are? Are you Father Mike all of a sudden?"

FOURTEEN

THE OLD CLOTHES in the wicker baskets in the attic were obviously things his father had outgrown years before. His father's waistline had not been this small in decades. Especially not since he retired and grew older and sourer and stouter in front of the TV, hurling insults at the newscasters.

There were uniforms, styles Aldo hardly remembered. One wool coat was so moth-eaten he could see light through it when he held it up to the window.

There were old copies of *National Geographic.* Aldo snorted and pushed them aside. Just the kind of thing the old fart would think was worth saving. Under them a few coloring books. Idly, Aldo opened one. On the left-hand page was a carefully colored picture of a girl in a garden with a watering can. It had been colored in with great precision, none of the crayons ever going outside the lines. The right-hand page showed a boy floating his toy boat on a small puddle. Here the crayons had run wild. The colors were wrong, the water a muddle of red and orange, the boy purple. And the colors had broken riotously through the lines, as if the hand that wielded them knew no bounds. Monica had done the picture on the left. Aldo was sure of it. And she had been babysitting her baby brother, who had colored in the picture of the boy on the right. But which baby brother had she been taking care of? Aldo or Nick?

Aldo closed the book and shoved it aside, too. Underneath was a Donald Duck comic.

Hey! A Donald Duck comic, and it had to be really old by the look of it! The edges were toasted brownish by age, but it had been under all this other junk and protected from light and dust.

Carefully he turned the cover back. In small print at the bottom of the first page, it said 1943.

He closed it even more carefully. This little sucker had to be worth money. Some of these were worth a couple thousand, he'd heard. Hot damn!

Aldo opened the largest coloring book and slipped the comic inside gently. The coloring book would protect it and nobody would see it if the family came home before he was done. He could sneak it out of here and nobody the wiser.

Jeez! This wasn't so bad after all!

Aldo made a pile of the clothes that were so moth-eaten not even the charities would look twice at them. He pushed them with his foot toward the stairwell. Monica could throw them out later.

Back under the eaves there was more stuff that might be valuable. Couple of paintings, couple of metal boxes, a vase with a chip out of the lip.

Aldo went to the larger metal box. He wiped some dust off the handle, but carelessly, not really interested in whether he got dust on his hands. The box wouldn't open. He tried the smaller one, which did open. There was some .38 ammunition, several boxes of .22 long rifle, some .410 shotgun cartridges for skeet shooting. Nothing heavy duty. Nothing very valuable, either. And there were two keys.

The first key fitted the box itself. Guessing from that, Aldo tried the other key in the lock of the larger metal box. It fitted.

At first he thought he'd found something else of real value, an antique handgun maybe, but it was only the poor light in the attic that made him so slow to recognize it. That and the dusty plastic bag around the gun that gave it a grayish look at first glance.

A standard issue .38 revolver. Nickel-plated Colt. Any police officer might have one. Especially fifteen or twenty

years ago. Now that the automatics didn't jam, officers mostly carried them instead of revolvers.

His father's old service revolver, probably. Shit, and he thought it might be worth something.

Keeping it in a plastic bag was odd, though. Seemed like his father never intended to use it again, or he'd have stored it properly. Even odder was the rest of the contents of the metal box. There was a single lead pellet, a .38 slug by the look of it, in a small, clear evidence envelope. Stapled to it was a slip from the Coroner's Office. That put it back before the new Medical Examiner's building was built on West Harrison. Yeah, here was a date, December 6, 1969. The bullet had been removed from the body of one Shana Boyd. From the right frontal lobe. That meant brain. This bullet had killed her.

The name Shana Boyd teased his mind, as if he almost knew it, had heard it long ago.

Under this envelope in the box were two sheets of paper, both of them from Ballistics. Both were copies of photos. The evidence number looked like—yes, it was—the same as the one on the slip attached to the bullet. The other had been run on a .38 with a serial number of 76L2702.

Interested now, he checked the gun. Yes, the serial number was the same. Somebody in the Ballistics department had test-fired a round from this weapon and made a Polaroid photomicrograph of the entire circumference of the bullet.

It had to mean something. Aldo took the first photograph and held it up near the second. He pushed it back and forth until he got the striations lined up.

There wasn't any doubt about it. You weren't supposed to do it this way, you were supposed to stick the two pellets in a comparison microscope, but still there wasn't really any doubt. That spent pellet had been fired from this gun.

What did it mean? Why had his father saved this stuff all these years? Because it certainly was a lot of years. Not one thing here was dated later than December 31, 1969.

So the question was, who was Shana Boyd?

FIFTEEN

FIRST DEPUTY GUS Gimball sat in the VIP section of Holy Name Cathedral, the important and the powerful all around him, and studied Aldo Bertolucci with wonder. Aldo's shirt was coming out of his pants, and the buttons pulled at the fabric over his stomach. He was not a walking ad for the Chicago Police Department. He was a mess.

The priest entered with the thurifer.

Aldo Bertolucci. What was the matter with the man? Fat under his chin. Grudging shaving job. Look at that five o'clock shadow, and it's his own father's funeral. Gimball thought his dad would kill him if he went to *his* funeral like that.

He looked from Aldo to Nick, who was perfectly turned out in his dress uniform. White dress gloves. Jeez, thought Gus, who was also wearing gloves, you never saw so many white gloves in one place as here today.

Nick, with his daughter Stella by his side, didn't look anything like Aldo. Well, the nose, maybe. Otherwise, an inch or two taller, trimmer, perfectly cut hair, face shaved to the smoothness of a baby's bottom.

What was it with a guy like Aldo, who had basically everything going for him? What made him trash it all? And

what did Nick think, sitting here with Aldo just two seats
away?

Nick was not thinking about Aldo. He was trying not to
think about old Nico. He had studied the groined and cof-
fered ceiling, the dark gold on the embellishments of the
ribbed vault, the tall, thin stained glass windows at the end.
   The baluster in front of the choir was golden oak, the
chancel rail also, and even the air high up in the vault shim-
mered dusty gold.
   Monica and his mother had picked a golden oak casket,
too. Nick suspected one of them had chosen it on purpose
because it would look so good here.
   And there he was, his mind back at the coffin and the
body of his father. It was like the old joke—try not to think
of a purple elephant.
   Because he did not want to be glad the old man was dead.
   It wasn't right. Not in a church and not in life. He should
have found a way to reach the old man's heart, not spend all
of the years of life they would have together on earth in this
distant, armed, partial truce.
   Quite suddenly he was seven years old. He was running
in the back door, running home from school, crying, forget-
ting to wipe his feet, but fortunately there was no mud on
them. It was winter and the earth was frozen hard.
   His mother said, "What's the matter?"
   But his father, who was home—must've been on first
watch then, or third—looked up from the newspaper and
said, "Who you been fighting with?"
   "I haven't," he said, trying not to cry, stifling sobs. Crying made his father angry.
   "You tell me, right now," his father said.
   "I was—it was in geography—" He started to cry again,

as the whole thing came back to him, all the indignity and the unfairness of it.

First a kid named Benny, who was always lippy with the teachers, got yelled at by Sister Innocenza. For dropping his books on the floor. And he did it intentionally, too. So that was sort of fair. Then it was another one of the boys, a new kid whose name he didn't know. A new kid who hadn't been in a Catholic school before and didn't know you weren't supposed to clomp your feet around when you had to change position. Fidgeting, it was called. And Sister Innocenza yelled at him, too. Which wasn't so fair. By then she was losing patience. Then Nick had turned to sit the other way in his desk with his feet on the other side of the metal support, and he knocked his pencil on the floor and when Sister Innocenza turned around, he still hadn't got his feet settled. And she came over and gave his hand a crack with her ruler, right on the knuckles.

It hurt so much for a minute he could hardly breathe. And then he started crying, right in front of everybody. And now he couldn't go back to school again, ever.

"I—Sister Innocenza said I fidgeted, but I wasn't, and two other kids did first and made her—made her mad. And she hit *me* and not them!"

"Come here," his Pa said.

Nick was so happy. His Pa would see the injustice, he was a policeman, wasn't he? He understood justice. He would take his side. And what a comfort that was! Someone understood!

He ran to his father.

And Pa seized him up and laid him over his knee and smacked him half a dozen times—spanked him while Nick yelled and begged him to stop.

"That's for being bad in school," Pa said.

*   *   *

Aldo was watching the motions of the funeral mass with only part of his mind. The part that watched was saying, "Goodbye, you old bastard. I had enough of you a long time ago."

The other part of his mind was focused on his find. The gun, the bullet, the ballistics report, the photomicrographs. Because he had remembered who Shana Boyd was.

Shana was the eighteen-year-old black girl killed in the raid on the Black Panther apartment in 1969. The name had come to him less than ten minutes after he discovered the cache, and he should have remembered it immediately. The whole thing had revolutionized the police department and brought down a state's attorney.

He had figured out who had shot the girl. Nick, their Nick, the good brother.

And nobody, nobody in the whole city knew. Nobody but Aldo. He hugged it, turned it over and admired it, played with it this way and that, how he'd use it.

"Thank you, God."

He looked at Nick, just beyond his mother and Monica and Stella in the pew, near the center aisle, wearing his dress uniform. Lookin' good, Nick. Big man. Important. Superintendent Nicholas Bertolucci.

Aldo had always been impulsive, and he knew he had hurt himself more than once by not thinking before he acted. This time he was going to figure it out, plan, then act, because this time it would be the most important move he'd ever made, the sweetest revenge anybody could ever hope for.

And Aldo smiled, thinking, "Wait, Nick. I'm coming after you. Wait for it."

SIXTEEN

NICK BERTOLUCCI AND Gus Gimball joined the Chicago Police Department in the fall of 1964. They were in the same class at the academy, took a liking to each other, graduated together, and hoped they'd get assigned to the same district. It didn't work that way. A cop goes where he's told to go and a rookie has even less say than that. Nick went to the Eighteenth District first and Gus to the Sixth, miles apart.

They had no forewarning then that they were becoming Chicago cops at the most difficult time in the entire history of the department.

They worked briefly in the same district when Gus was transferred to the Eighteenth and both were directing traffic on Michigan Avenue during the Christmas season in 1964. Then in patrol. But by the time they'd had a chance for a few beers after work and a very occasional Chinese dinner on Oak Street, Nick was put into undercover Narcotics. Gus was apprehensive. Nick took enough chances on the job. He seemed to have no fear of physical danger, and Gus was afraid in Narcotics he'd be killed. In his second month he was stabbed to the bone in his upper thigh when a dealer discovered he was a cop because he was carrying handcuffs. But he survived.

In the mid-1960s, Chicago, like most large cities in the United States, was seeing more street violence, and the police were becoming more and more nervous. There was antiwar rioting and civil rights rioting—first, sporadic sorties and small local battles. Harlem, in New York City, in 1964. Then, in 1965, the suburb of Watts in Los Angeles, which went up like dry grass, leaving fifty million dollars' worth of property damage, thirty-five hundred people arrested, nine

hundred injured and thirty-five dead. The long, hot, violent summers of the sixties had begun.

In 1966, Rev. Martin Luther King, Jr., came to Chicago. He moved into a top-floor walk-up apartment on South Hamlin. His goal was to open up the heavily segregated housing in the city.

It was a summer of hundred-degree days. On the 14th of July, in shimmering heat, King spoke at Soldier Field. Forty thousand people came to hear him. Then they marched after him to City Hall, where he nailed his demands to the door. Among hundreds of police officers who lined the route were Gus and Nick, wearing their summer short-sleeve uniforms and their robin's-egg blue crowd-control helmets.

Four days later, in 102-degree heat, some black children were playing in fire hydrant spray. Firemen pulled up in a truck and turned the water off. This act set off three days of angry rioting.

There were housing protest marches into white Chicago Lawn on July 21 and 24. Furious residents threw knives, sticks, bricks, cherry bombs, gasoline-filled bottles and stones at the marchers. White youths tipped over cars and threw cherry bombs into the gas tanks. There were hundreds of injuries.

Gus and Nick missed both of those marches, but Nick was quickly reassigned when all hell broke loose and they were back in their blue helmets guarding the route on August 5 when King and his people marched through Marquette Park.

King had been gone from the city of Chicago for nearly two years when he was assassinated in Memphis, Tennessee on Thursday, April 4, 1968.

By Friday, Chicago was on fire. Businesses shut down. Thousands of rioters swarmed through the streets, smashed windows and looted grocery stores, appliance stores, liquor

stores, toy stores, clothing stores. The Chicago police were overwhelmed.

On Saturday, Mayor Daley called in three thousand National Guard troops to patrol the city. They had orders to shoot if necessary, but nobody knew what necessary meant. Daley issued a directive: "Shoot to kill arsonists, shoot to wound looters," an order that went far beyond the police department's rules for the use of deadly force. Between four and ten P.M. Saturday, thirty-six major fires were burning in the city. All available firemen had been called up and were working twelve-hour shifts. After ten P.M., fire alarms came in so fast they couldn't be counted. There were hundreds of injured people; the hospitals pressed medical students into service. Two thousand firemen with a hundred pieces of fire-fighting equipment were on the streets and could not contain the fires. The Department of Sanitation called out a thousand of its employees to help the firefighters. The night sky was orange with flames and shot with the flashing Mars lights and spotlights of police cars.

By Sunday, hundreds of buildings lay in ruin. Three miles of Madison Street had burned to the ground. Fire hoses laced the city streets and huge rivers of blackened sooty water poured from gutted buildings. Ten thousand police officers, seven thousand National Guard troops, and five thousand regular army troops patrolled Chicago. Some were Vietnam veterans in the Fifth Army Mechanized Division from Fort Carson, Colorado. Others were the First Armored Division from Fort Hood, Texas. They wore full battle dress and carried rifles, grenade launchers and machine guns. They bivouacked in the city's parks.

In spite of the mayor's directive, the Chicago Police Department responded professionally. The death toll in Chicago was lower than in other large cities.

But the country was running faster and faster into civil

insurrection. Chicago police, like others, were stockpiling riot weapons. The Democratic National Convention was scheduled to take place in Chicago just four months later—August 1968. Everybody knew it would be trouble. Nobody guessed how much.

As the delegates assembled to nominate Hubert Humphrey for president, antiwar protesters assembled too. They roamed the city's parks and streets, taunting the police. Finally the police lost their cool.

Pushed beyond their limit of endurance, they charged into mobs, beat reporters, attacked hippies and ordinary bystanders with their clubs, and smashed the cameras of news photographers, even while their commanders screamed at them to stop. Many had removed their identification badges so their names would not be known. Enraged, CBS News demanded an investigation of an attack on their cameraman. Hugh Downs called them "pigs" on the "Today" show. The president of ABC News protested personally to Mayor Daley.

By the time the delegates went home, the Chicago Police Department was a bad name around the world.

In the summer of 1969 the Justice Department set up a special task force on the Black Panther party. Attorney General John Mitchell called the Panthers a threat to national security. Once they were labeled a national security concern, they were subject to wiretapping by the FBI.

Many black leaders argued that the Panthers were a political group, entitled to all the protections of free speech, and also that they were a beneficial force in many black communities. The Panthers in Chicago had set up a free breakfast program for children and a free medical program. To some people in the Justice Department, the FBI and the Chicago police, these programs seemed just a cover for crim-

inal activity. Black leaders acknowledged that some of the Panthers had criminal records, but said that many others did not, and the programs were real.

In Chicago, in an atmosphere of increasing hostility on both sides, Edward Hanrahan had become Cook County state's attorney. Hanrahan's Special Prosecutions Unit, or SPU, headed by Richard Jalovec, created an elite subunit commanded by Sergeant Daniel Groth, who had been detached from the Chicago Police Department for this special duty. The way the SPU was organized, it expanded the prosecutor's traditional role to include very active infiltration of groups like the Panthers.

In the last six months of 1969, eleven young blacks who were not known to be felons or gang members were killed by police in the western part of Chicago. Some of the officers involved were brought before the department's Internal Inspections Division. All were exonerated.

Fred Hampton was chairman of the Chicago chapter of the Black Panther party. He was a young man, twenty-one years old, from suburban Maywood. He'd been a top student and top athlete in high school and was a talented public speaker. The free medical clinic and free breakfast program for children had been his ideas.

Senator John McClellan before a Senate subcommittee called Hampton a felon convicted for a "violent crime." In fact he had been convicted for helping some black youths steal $71 worth of ice cream from a street vendor.

The FBI hired a black man named William O'Neal to infiltrate the Chicago Black Panther party, with particular orders to get close to Fred Hampton. O'Neal became a regular at Hampton's apartment at 2337 West Monroe and before long was able to draw a detailed floor plan of the apartment for the FBI. The FBI passed this along to the SPU.

On November 13, two Chicago police officers named

Rappaport and Gilhooley were killed in a shootout between several police officers and two Panthers. One of the Panthers was killed, the other wounded and charged in the police killings. Rumor was that Fred Hampton was involved.

From then on, the FBI started feeding information to the Chicago police about a weapons stockpile at Fred Hampton's apartment. The FBI gave the police and the State's Attorney the impression that the guns constituted an illegal arms cache.

Through the next couple of weeks, the FBI kept up a constant flow of information to the police about the weapons—they were there in the apartment; they'd been moved out because the occupants were afraid there was going to be a raid; now they were back in the apartment again. Sergeant Groth claimed that he'd been told by an informant that there were three illegal sawed-off shotguns, three stolen CPD shotguns, some rifles, and handguns, and fifty thousand rounds of ammo in the apartment.

The Special Prosecutions Unit, under the command of Sergeant Groth, was assigned several Chicago Police Department officers. They were temporarily detached from the department and appointed state's attorney's police.

Shortly before the raid was scheduled, a highly placed Chicago Police Department officer collected evidence that Fred Hampton had not been involved in the deaths of Gilhooley and Rappaport. He ordered the raid on the Hampton apartment canceled.

Someone in the State's Attorney's Office reinstated it.

The informer, O'Neal, had said that the apartment would be empty of people around eight P.M., because Hampton would be speaking at a meeting and the eight or nine other people who were staying in the apartment would be with him. Somebody proposed that the police go in then, with the warrant, and seize the weapons. There was no chance of

bloodshed in an empty apartment. Somebody else rejected that idea. The final plan was to go in at four A.M., when everybody who lived there would be home.

The raiders studied the diagram of the apartment O'Neal supplied to the FBI. They put on their fur hats and black leather jackets and left from the State's Attorney's Office. Not one of them was in uniform. Although 2337 West Monroe was in the Thirteenth District, they did not inform the District they were on their way until they were within sight of the apartment. This was the first the Chicago Police Department knew about the raid. The neighborhood was bleak, burned out in the riots of 1968.

The raiders stopped fifty yards west of the building. Eight men, under Groth's lead, went to the front door. Three of the eight were told just to stand guard. Six men went to the back.

The back door team went up a flight of seven creaking wooden steps. For a minute they weren't quite sure which of the building's back doors to go in, but then beyond one door they heard banging and shooting. They broke down the door and found themselves in a kitchen, just as the floor plan had shown. The burners of the stove were turned on for warmth.

The next morning one of them described the scene to the newspapers: "As soon as we announced that we were state's attorney's police, a blast of shotgun fire came through the back door. We were both wounded then, but we broke down the door and started firing. Once we got inside the kitchen, we could see firing coming from the hallway and a back bedroom. By this time, other police had broken down the front door and shots were being fired at them, some through the door of another bedroom. It was as if all hell had broken loose."

SPU head Jalovec told *Chicago Today* that one officer was shot in the leg, and as they came through the back door, a shotgun was fired at them by a woman in the apartment.

Sergeant Groth described what was happening at the front door. "The firing must have gone on for ten or twelve minutes. If two hundred shots were exchanged, that would have been nothing." In a later edition of the paper, Jalovec said that after the police announced themselves, blasts of gunfire roared through both the front and rear doors.

Officer Ciszewski said, "The shooting must have gone on for about five minutes, but it seemed like five hours as we fought our way from room to room in the apartment. With all the bullets flying around in that apartment, I don't see how we got out with only light wounds."

But they did get out with light wounds. One officer was injured in the leg, apparently by a shotgun pellet. Another was cut by what was described as flying glass.

There had been nine people living in the apartment. All but three were wounded or killed. Fred Hampton was shot four times, twice in his head. Mark Clark, who had been sitting in a chair near the front door, was shot twice in the arm and through the heart and lungs. All of the survivors were arrested and charged with attempted murder.

State's Attorney Hanrahan announced at a press conference that morning that his raiders had been attacked by vicious, unprovoked, and extremely violent Panthers and had defended themselves. Hanrahan displayed the Panther weapons that he said had been seized. As Sergeant Groth explained, "Our men had no choice but to return their fire."

On December 8, four days after the raid, Hanrahan held a second press conference. He praised the raiders for remarkable restraint, bravery and for "professional discipline" in not killing all the Panthers present.

On December 11 Hanrahan gave an "exclusive" to the *Tribune*. He said that when the police entered the anteroom, a shotgun blast was fired at them through the living room

door, which was closed at the time. He said when Officer "Gloves" Davis entered he saw a woman, Brenda Harris, in bed in the front room. She was reloading the shotgun, and she fired at them. It was not until after this shot that the police fired back.

The officers described calling several cease-fires, but each time the Panthers started shooting at them again.

That evening, at the request of State's Attorney Hanrahan, CBS-TV in Chicago aired a filmed reenactment of the raid. Several of the officers performed the parts they said they had played in the raid. During his part, Officer Carmody of the back door team said he kicked down the door and started to enter the kitchen, when three shots were fired at him from the back bedroom.

Then, under intense media pressure and investigation, the story started to unravel.

Analysts noticed that, for the first few days, the various police officers and the State's Attorney were unable to agree even on which officers were at the front door and which at the rear, and while they all said that they had clearly announced that they were police, they disagreed on whether they had announced it at the front or rear door or both. They also disagreed on whether they got any response from the inhabitants and if so, what it was. Their memories of the response from inside ranged from "scuffling noises" to people asking "Who?" or saying "Just a minute." According to Hanrahan's "exclusive" on December 11, they had got no response at all, and had simply been fired upon. The men were mutually contradictory on a lot of other points, especially who had fired at whom from where.

On December 6, the Afro-American Patrolmen's League, an organization composed of slightly less than half of the

2,100 black police officers in Chicago, announced its own probe, and after touring 2337 West Monroe said they found no evidence that anyone had fired from inside the apartment.

Meanwhile, an attorney for the survivors of the raid and their relatives had hired an independent criminologist, Herbert MacDonell from Corning, New York, to look at the scene. He agreed to do an analysis, as long as it was understood that he would suppress no evidence, no matter whom it inculpated.

On December 11, the Chicago Police Department announced it would undertake its own Internal Inspections Division investigation of the raid. The purpose of the IID as a unit was to investigate alleged police misconduct. Its work was not open to the public. So its reasoning and the nature of its investigation were secret when, on December 19, it announced its findings. It concluded that the physical evidence "fairly established that the occupants of the premises in question fired upon the officers who were in the process of executing the search warrant."

Five thousand people went to Fred Hampton's funeral.

On December 30, the coroner's inquest began. The firearms examiner from the Chicago Police Crime Laboratory, who had examined at least some of the ballistics evidence, testified that two shotgun shells had been fired from Brenda Harris's gun, confirming Groth's account that a woman had fired at him as he entered the apartment. When it was shown that the FBI had also examined the shells and concluded they were actually fired from Officer Ciszewski's weapon, the ballistics expert admitted that was true. Brenda Harris had not fired at all and may not even have been near a gun.

Critics began to tease out of the various accounts other departures from the way things were supposed to be done:

- Hanrahan, for instance, had shown the "seized" Panther weapons to the press and displayed them at a conference before sending them to the crime lab for analysis. No one had kept track of where they had been found.
- If fingerprints were taken at the scene, either they were not preserved or they were being suppressed.
- The bodies of the dead had been removed before the coroner could see them at the scene, as he was supposed to do.
- The autopsy form requires that the coroner make conclusions about the cause of death, primary and secondary, and whether the death is a result of criminal conduct. This was not done.
- Hanrahan's television reenactment of the raid would be likely to prejudice any eventual trial.
- No one seemed to be trying to match the bullets in the bodies to any officer's weapon.
- The raiding officers had not carried the ordinary crowd control equipment, such as tear gas, or lights, or sound equipment, to announce who they were. This suggested that they had never intended nonviolent arrests.
- Officer Carmody had not been hit by flying glass. He cut his own hand on glass from the back window when he smashed the window open with his gun butt.

The controversy did not die down; it grew.

On January 30, 1970, the living occupants of the apartment were indicted on a total of thirty-one counts. All of them were charged with attempted murder and armed violence, and most of them also with unlawful possession of firearms.

Then on May 8, 1970, all the charges against all the sur-

vivors of the raid were suddenly dropped. This took place one week before the prosecution was due to respond to the defendants' request for disclosure of informants, surveillance, and other official actions against the Panthers that led up to the raid. There was speculation that the state's attorney and the FBI did not want the information revealed.

Also in May the federal grand jury, which had been working on the case for months, issued its report. Among other facts, they found that between 83 and 100 shots were fired that night in the apartment. Of those, only one was fired by a Panther weapon. That was the slug fired by Mark Clark, who had been sitting in a chair near the front door. The 82 to 100 other shots included 7 fired from revolvers, 12 to 25 from shotguns, 19 from the carbine and 44 to 48 from the Thompson submachine gun. Forty-two of these were fired blind, through the living room wall into the front bedroom. Of the shots fired blind through the wall, 18 went on all the way through the front bedroom into the rear bedroom. The officer with the submachine gun had simply sprayed the entire wall back and forth with .45 caliber machine gun fire.

The grand jury report found an "irreconcilable disparity" between the accounts of the officers and the physical facts.

As for the Internal Inspections Division, which claimed its proceedings had considered the physical evidence, the grand jury found no evidence that it had ever interviewed neighborhood residents, performed ballistics analyses of the officers' weapons to compare them to the spent pellets found at the scene, or taken details of the statements of the officers. It had not even visited the scene.

The grand jury asked police captain Ervanian whether it would be unfair to describe this as a whitewash, and he said, "The way you describe it, no, sir."

The grand jury had also considered the testimony of the firearms examiner who said that the two shotgun shells he

had examined had been fired from Brenda Harris's weapon. These were the shots that the FBI examined and concluded were fired from police officers' guns. The firearms examiner admitted that he filed a report full of errors because to do anything else would have cost him his job. He said that he was under daily pressure from the State's Attorney's Office.

The grand jury report called the IID investigation "so seriously deficient that it suggests purposeful malfeasance." As to the raid itself, the grand jury called it "ill-conceived." Whatever the purpose of the raid, the state's attorney's police had used excessive force.

By now the story of the Panther raid had gone from one in which the Panthers fired hundreds of rounds at the State's Attorney's Police in a wild firefight ranging throughout the apartment, to one in which only one shot could even be traced to a Panther weapon and up to a hundred were fired by the raiders. Indeed, the police most of the time were apparently shooting at each other. But the State's Attorney's Office had a new position now: what was really important was that the Panthers, or to be specific Mark Clark who was in the chair near the front door, had fired *first*. Whatever the raiders did in response was therefore justified.

Herbert MacDonell, the criminologist hired by the survivors of the raid, had been to the apartment, had studied and photographed the surfaces—walls, doors, ceilings and floors—and had constructed a model to trace the paths of the bullets fired.

The shot fired by Mark Clark was easy to trace. It was a "deer slug" fired from a shotgun. Its course went from the chair where Mark Clark sat, through the living room door blowing fibers outward, across the entry hall, through a partition, and across the stairway that led to the upstairs apartment, where it struck the wall and fell to the floor. The

trajectory was determined by drawing a line from the chair through the partition to the impact point on the wall. Then the door was moved until the hole in it, with the wood fibers blown outward, was fitted into that line. Thus, MacDonell determined the position of the door when the shot went through it. Similarly, a slug fired from the hall had struck the living room wall above the hassock. This slug contained wood fibers consistent with the door. By drawing a line between the position from which the police officer outside the door was standing to the hole in the living room wall, and placing the second hole in the door, with the fibers blown inward, in line with it, the position of the door at the time of the shot could be determined. Both police and survivor testimony had the first shots coming close together while the raiders were breaking in. MacDonell's result: the door was almost closed when the shot from the outside hall was fired into the room; the door was farther open when the shot from inside the living room was fired. It was most probable that the police fired first.

MacDonell turned up some previously ignored data that might explain some of the confusion. There was evidence that one shot was fired in the entry hallway into the east wall of the entry, for no apparent reason. There was no target there. It was probably the weapon of one Officer Jones, as the wads and shot pellets were consistent with the weapon Jones was carrying and the place it was discharged was consistent with where he was standing at the beginning of the raid. Two of the survivors said they heard a shot outside the door at about the same time as the pounding on the door. MacDonell thought this shot was an accidental discharge, and it may have startled Sergeant Groth, causing him to fire into the room as the door was broken open. The two together may have triggered Mark Clark's response shot at the now almost fully open door, and caused the rear door team

to come crashing into the apartment. In other words, the Panthers may have fired not the first or even the second shot, but the third.

On August 24, 1970, a grand jury indicted fourteen officials for conspiring to obstruct justice, including Cook County State's Attorney Edward Hanrahan, Assistant State's Attorney Jalovec, a deputy police chief, two police sergeants, a crime lab specialist, and seven other raiders.

Two years later, on October 25, 1972, Judge Philip Romiti found the evidence against them not sufficient to prove conspiracy. But that trial did not try to fix blame for the raid or ask whether the Panthers' rights had been violated.

The relatives of the slain and injured Panthers sued. After ten years before the courts, the City of Chicago offered to settle by paying them one million, eight hundred thousand dollars.

The controversy has never died.

No one ever knew, or at least no one ever proved, who shot Fred Hampton. The evidence was that the fatal shots had been fired at him point-blank as he lay unconscious on the floor. If this was true, it was murder. The bullets that went through his skull vanished. The officers' weapons, by and large, vanished. But AVENGE FRED HAMPTON has lived ever since; it is still being written as graffiti on Chicago buildings.

The IID was disbanded. The Cook County state's attorney is no longer permitted to "borrow" police officers as special state's attorney's police.

Gus Gimball had been in the Eighth District during the raid on the Hampton apartment. He was entirely uninvolved.

Nick Bertolucci's part in the raid was largely ignored by

the media, since he was just a backup in the team, recruited at the last minute, and he never went farther than the living room. In early 1970, he became a trainer at the academy. The department was just developing methods to help police officers resist insults and name-calling by taunting them methodically during special training courses. The department was also teaching trainees to step back from confrontation, to take the fire out of a dispute rather than attack. It was a new world and a new department.

Old Nico Bertolucci despised the new techniques.

Nico had been first deputy superintendent at the time of the raid; he became superintendent a month later. Then his involvement in the coverup leaked out. The mayor replaced him. Nico went into the General Support Division, where he was nicknamed "jockstrap of the department." A year and a half later, he retired.

Nick and Gus took the detectives exam at the same time. Both made detective. In two years, they took the sergeants exam. Both made sergeant.

At first Nick was in Area Six detectives and Gus was in Area One. Then Nick was transferred to Area One. Together, Nick and Gus caused many Chinese dinners to vanish.

Both were promoted. Because of his father, Nick moved a little faster than Gus. Old Nico still had friends.

In 1982, Nick became chief of the Detective Division. He made Gus his second-in-command. When Nick became deputy superintendent of the Bureau of Investigative Services, Gus Gimball moved to chief.

When Nick became superintendent of police, Gus Gimball became first deputy.

SEVENTEEN

ALDO BERTOLUCCI SAT in his study, which was a back room in a small house he owned a couple of blocks west of Addison. Outside the narrow, dirty window, the alley was dark, the distant glow of a street light scarcely illuminating the pavement. The study was off the kitchen, just inside the back door and had been intended as a mud room by the builder. Aldo's wife, Regina, had used only half of it as a mud room, with hooks for the kids to hang up their stuff when they came in from outdoors. The linoleum near the door was still scuffed from the constant depositing of their boots in the winter and muddy shoes in the spring and fall. Unlike most kids, they actually had left their coats and shoes in the mud room. They had been afraid of what their father would do to them if they didn't.

The linoleum on the other side of the room, where Aldo sat, was of almost pristine gloss, though the green color was faded by the years.

Regina Bertolucci had called the far side of the room the sewing room for ten years or so, until Aldo noticed that she never sewed anything and took it over himself. Regina had actually used it to get away from Aldo. By the time he took it over, he was coming home as little as possible anyway, so it didn't matter much to her one way or the other. And when she thought about it, having him in the mud room and herself in the living room was probably better than having her in there and him in the living room.

So Aldo sat in a swivel chair facing a wooden card table. He had a brass floor lamp at his left, and two old melamine bookcases flanked the window. The shade was half drawn, as it always was. In the corner farthest from him were a dress-

maker's dummy in a size ten, a size Regina Bertolucci would never be again, a sewing machine, a canvas knitting bag with a wooden frame, stuffed with fabric scraps and yarn and odd-size needles stuck into pieces of paper to keep them from getting separated.

Aldo hunched over papers and objects on the makeshift desk.

The door burst open. "Why didn't you tell me you were home?" Regina said.

"Get out of here! Close the door!"

"What?" she said, genuinely surprised.

Aldo had slipped a sheet of newspaper over the stuff on the desk and was now getting himself composed.

"I didn't tell you I was home because there was jets of steam coming out of the bathroom door and the hair dryer blowin' like mad." He shuffled a corner of the newspaper farther over the center of the desk. "Now leave me alone, I got work."

Regina eyed the table but didn't refer to it. "You have to meet me at the hall after you get off tomorrow night. It's Lonna's twenty-fifth."

"It'll be over by the time I get off."

"Oh no it won't. They'll go to three A.M."

"Hell."

"Not that I plan to stay that long. You're off at eleven. You can get there before eleven-thirty."

He would have liked to hit her. But her head was covered with metal rollers of an indestructible 1955 vintage, and he'd sure as anything cut his hand. He half grinned at the thought of the headline: WOMAN SAVED BY CURLERS, CITES BEEHIVE HAIRDO AS FACTOR.

"What are you grinning about?"

"Nothin'. Leave me alone."

"Eleven-thirty. Don't go to the Furlough. The twenty-fifth is silver. We've bought them a cake knife."

"With my money."

Regina turned and left. He got up and slammed the door.

He went back and sat down in front of the tent of *Chicago Sun-Times* that lay over his treasures. Slowly, savoring the revelation of the objects, he pushed the newspaper back.

The bullet in its little clear envelope, the piece of paper documenting the autopsy, and the gun in its larger plastic bag, all lay in front of him in their great beauty. He had not taken either the revolver or the spent pellet out of their bags, not once. He was too smart for that. The last thing he wanted to do was screw up those striations on the bullet, even a little bit.

He rested his hands on the tops of the two bags, though, just enjoying them. Then, for the seventh, the eighth, the dozenth, the hundredth time, he smoothed out the autopsy report. It had been only partly filled in by the coroner.

Beautiful! There was just one more thing he needed now. It was the report of registration to Nicholas Bertolucci of this particular sidearm, with the serial number 76L2702, the whole ball of wax in black and white. He knew where it would be. It would be where all sidearm registrations were always kept—in the Personnel Division at headquarters. It would either be in Nick's personnel jacket in the main file, or it would be so old that it would be in a box of retired papers in the personnel storage files.

If the shooting of Shana Boyd had ever become a legal case, of course, the gun registration would have been assembled with these things as a link in the chain of evidence. A smoking gun, he chuckled. But just the opposite had happened. The whole affair had been wiped clean, everybody's part in it, even the leaders. Old Nico must've just grabbed

PATHOLOGICAL REPORT AND PROTOCOL
CORONER, COOK COUNTY, ILL.

NAME Shana Boyd   DATE OF DEATH Dec. 4, 1969, 4:30 am
ADDRESS 2337 W. Monroe   AUT. yes   CERT... no   INQ.
IDENTIFICATION uncle   EXAM Inst. of Forensic Pathology
William F. Boyd   BY Dr. R. Hoffritz M.D.

EXTERNAL EXAMINATION
RACE Negro   SEX female   AGE 18 yrs   LENGTH 5'3"   WGHT 112 lbs
HAIR black   IRIS ____   SCLERA_   PUPILS ___

Musculature _____	Skeleton:	Slender _____
Pigmentation _____		Medium _____
Edema _____		Powerful _____
Decubitus _____		Deformed _____
		Amputations _____

SIGNS OF DEATH:
Cornea: Cloudy __ Turbid ____   Decomposition: Skin-slip ____
        Dry __ Shrunk ____   Tissue gas ____
Body heat _____   Discoloration ____
Lividity _____   Dehydration ____
Rigor mortis _____   Putrefaction ____

HISTORY OF CAUSE OF DEATH:
Decendent was removed from the above stated address, pronounced dead at the scene. Diagnosis: Supposedly gunshot, brought to the morgue by star #77193 of the 13th District. This is a 13th District case.

IN MY OPINION THE SAID_____Shana Boyd_____death was
Part I: IMMEDIATE CAUSE bullet wound of brain_____
Part II: OTHER SIGNIFICANT CONDITIONS CONTRIBUTING TO DEATH BUT NOT GIVEN IN PART II:
Date: Dec. 5, 1969.

"The body was placed under fluoroscopy and one bullet was seen and recovered from the medial aspect of the left temporal lobe. The brain was in all other aspects unremarkable. . . ."

this stuff from the lab, and it vanished into nowhere, just like all the other bullets and guns had turned invisible and the toxicology reports had altered themselves.

Aldo couldn't walk into Personnel and ask for it, of course. Personnel guarded its files carefully. There was always somebody there during the day and the doors were locked at night. Aldo couldn't walk in with any requests at all, he was fuck-all as far as these people were concerned. And Commander Cole hated Aldo's guts, thought he was a screwup, which was no big deal anyhow, because Aldo hated him first.

Aldo worked in the building where the First District was, at Eleventh and State, and still he couldn't just walk up to the Personnel Division, which really pissed him off. Go in with his hat in his hand when he needed something specific, otherwise it's what do you want? And he surely couldn't rummage in the files. Not only couldn't but shouldn't, because he didn't want it remembered later that he'd even been near them.

If all went well.

Because he was beginning to get an idea about how he might get that gun registration. It would be the last piece of the puzzle. No, that was wrong. It would be the last piece of the proof. It would be the firing pin for his weapon.

Aldo Bertolucci stared off into space, lost in a glowing golden daydream. He held the bottom left corner of the autopsy sheet with his left hand. He moved his right hand from the lower left corner of the sheet up past the top right corner, then repeated the motion over and over. The paper did not need smoothing. He was stroking it, feeling it, gloating over it, petting it. He loved this sheet of paper.

EIGHTEEN

THE GANG AT the Furlough Bar saw that Aldo Bertolucci was not his usual self. Aldo not being his usual self could only be an improvement. He looked like a man who had lived fifty years with migraines, a bleeding ulcer and hemorrhoids, and suddenly somebody waved a magic wand and he was cured. The transformation was evident in his walk as he came in at the end of the tour. It was in the way he said "Beer!" to the bartender instead of hunkering himself down on the stool, waiting until the guy asked if he wanted a beer, and then snarling "Unnnh" as if how stupid could the guy be, he always drank beer, always came in here for a beer, what could he possibly want but a beer?

It was also in the more buoyant step of his partner Dick-dick. God knew the job had to be easier for Dick-dick if Aldo was in a good mood.

"S'pose it's because old Nico Bertolucci has been lowered to his final rest lo these many hours?" Stanley Mileski whispered.

Bennis said, "Must be. He must've been some kind of nasty."

"S'matter with you guys?" Aldo said.

"Bad tour," Bennis said.

Suze Figueroa said, "We apprehend a serious speeder—right in the middle of State Street. So he wants to argue. Plus all sorts of pedestrians standing around. These people ten minutes ago they're saying this man coulda run me down. Right past my kid, practically over her shoes. Now that the guy is arguing, they feel sorry for him, we got police brutality."

"Like that's new," Aldo growled.

"Plus three alarm systems malfunctioning, one end of the beat to the other. We're beginning to feel like yo-yos."

"Someday we're gonna find a real alarm," Bennis said, "with real bad guys and serious firearms, streetsweeper and all that shit, and we are *not* going to be ready for it."

"Then there was this hooker on LaSalle."

"Bennis," Figueroa said, "don't talk about that."

"Sent Figueroa walkin' down the alley, see if she could slide up on the lady's pimp, as per Coumadin's orders."

"Bennis—"

"So the hooker says to her, 'What's your name?' Suze says Suze and the hooker says, 'I'm Sabrina.' Then she says, 'You ever wanna give up that cop shit, girl, I can get you serious money.' "

"Bennis—"

"Says, 'Tits like that, make you a fortune, fast.' "

Everybody laughed. Suze said, "I'd make more money, that's for sure."

Bennis said, "So then we get a call, accident with injuries on Michigan Avenue, citizen called it in. Directly in front of the *Chicago Tribune* building. Paramedics are on the way. We're there ahead of the paramedics, figuring what can it be, busy street, somebody's fender bender and a cut forehead."

Suze said, "We get within eyesight of it and Norm says, 'Oh, wow.' He jumps out of the car before I even have it stopped. I get the car locked and I'm out and I'm yelling 'Stand back!' at the civilians."

Norm Bennis said, "This Tennessee Cadillac with a plow blade must've decided to pass a stopped CTA bus. The blade clipped a very large man who was coming around the front of the bus. After hitting the man, the driver must have panicked and swerved right, mowing down another half-dozen people waiting on the corner.

"So I get on my radio. 'We've got seven down, and four look critical.'"

Suze said, "So Norm, with his gloves on, is putting some direct pressure on a deep gash in the buttocks of one of the pedestrians. The Tennessee Cadillac, a rusty pickup with an attached plow blade, had careened on over the down pedestrians into a street light. The light is bent, the plow blade is unscathed, and the driver, smelling like beer, is sitting on the ground with his head in his hands. I think of cuffing him, but some first aid to the others seems more important, so I just ask for his driver's license and stick it in my pocket. Then I run to the large man who had been hit first. He's thrashing around in the grip of a couple of civilians. I run over yelling, 'Let him alone.'

"One says, 'Hey, we can't. We're trying—'

"But the other one backs off. I get hit by a spray of blood across my chest. I look closer. The man's right hand is cut off clean by the plow blade, and the man, way beyond reasoning, is trying to run away. If he runs, he's gonna bleed to death. The two pedestrians were right trying to hold on to him. The hand is nowhere to be seen.

"I drop back and tackle him, pin both ankles together. He falls. I yell 'Hold him down!' to one of the good Samaritans. The other whips off his necktie, and I twist it around the man's arm, just above the stump of the wrist.

"I get back on the radio and yell, 'Tell the EMT's to bring ice or whatever they use for severed human parts."

"Then I go looking for the hand.

"Bennis and I look under the bus. No hand. We look along the gutter. Now there's people with cameras coming out of the *Tribune* building. Reporters. Shit! Plus, somebody has a videocam. The ambulance sirens are getting close. I figured great! Let those guys take over. You do one wrong thing on film and they forget everything you did right.

"But I run over to the plow. I go around to the front of the plow and there, next to the edge of the blade, impaled on a protruding bolt, is the hand. I grab it off before something worse happens to it. Like some weirdo steals it for a souvenir."

"Hey, what'd it feel like?" Aldo said.

"It was limp and warm. Felt lumpy, like a lot of marbles inside a glove. So I jog back to the scene. Norm's gesturing to the two units of emergency vehicles that had arrived. The cameras are flashing. One of the medics, this self-important type with large pink ears and a short haircut and a spiffy white shirt, brushes Bennis aside. He yells, 'Stand back now! I'll take over.'

"And Bennis says, 'Give that man a big hand!' "

Suze said, "I coulda killed him. If that gets in the paper, Bennis, you're a dead man."

Bennis said, "Hell, my man, they won't use it." He grinned. "Kind of a pity, too."

"By that time, the driver of the pickup gets nervous," Suze said. "Bennis sees him getting his jacket and looking around like which way is best to rabbit. Bennis says 'Whoa!,' anchors him, and by then I'm asking them to run his license, social, the whole bit. Turns out this is not his first vehicular no-no, plus he's got a sheet. Plus, if I know anything about it, he'll come back with a blood alcohol of .20 easy."

"So naturally, when all that turns up," Bennis said, "we're the rest of the night in the station on the paper."

"You can tell alcohol just like that, huh, Figueroa?" Aldo said.

"Sure. Like you're .07 right now and rising," Suze said.

"It runs like that, some nights," Mileski said. "I mean, we had nothing but domestics tonight, one end to the other."

"We had that kid—" Quail said.

"Yeah. Suspected child abuse. Neighbor called it in. But

I say that's domestic, too. I mean, we are really social workers, not police officers. Know what I mean?"

"Yeah, that's true," Quail said.

"Very true," Bennis said.

"Hey, Dick-dick! Why so quiet?" Mileski said.

"Oh, I don't know."

"Whatsa matter?"

"I'm just so goddamn broke."

"You make what I make," Mileski said.

"Yeah. Yeah. But I'm *really* broke."

Hiram Quail said, "Jeez, Dick-dick, you know I'd piss on a live spark plug if I could make you rich. Maybe you just oughta stay away from the women for a while. Go fishin' with me. I'm goin' to Wisconsin two days."

Mileski said, "Yeah, Dick-dick. Save up a while."

Bennis said, "Or either that or take 'em to McDonald's instead of the Cape Cod Room."

"I don't take 'em to the Cape Cod Room," Dick-dick said.

"Nightclubs is worse," Mileski said. "You got your cover, you got your minimum. Hey, even take her to a Cubs game, you got parking, maybe eight-ten bucks, you got your tickets at twenty bucks, you got your beer over three dollars each and who's gonna want less than three maybe four? Then you gotta feed her after. Hell, you can't move these days without dropping sixty bucks. So you basically just gotta keep your pants on here a week or two."

Dick-dick said, "Yeah." He thought for a couple of seconds and added, "How?"

Suze glanced at Aldo. He was staring at Dick-dick intently, his jowly face like a toad that had just swallowed a fat shiny fly.

NINETEEN

NICK BERTOLUCCI WAS northbound on Michigan Avenue, going home, driving more slowly than usual. The death of his father had left him feeling mortal. Not fearful—in some way almost serene. Not depressed, but resolute.

To Gus this afternoon, he had said, "I'm going to make some staff changes."

"Such as?"

"Gus, someday I'll be retired and maybe you'll take over—"

"Don't say it."

"You'd rather have Wallpaper Riggs?"

"Oh lord. Riggs? Anybody would be better."

"Point is, I am not going to leave things the same as when I came in. We need big changes. Look at the stuff we really *have* to have. A new building. A new communications system. And the technical people say they can't install a new communications system in this building anyhow, we need the new building built to certain specs, so the two problems interlock. It's going to take money and the city doesn't want to cut any loose."

"Mayor Wallace?" Gus said.

"Exactly. I'm about fed up. If he doesn't get us what we need, I'm going to take it right to the media."

And that, thought Gimball, would be war.

Nick went back to staffing. "First, if we want to persuade 'em, we have to show them we can cut costs."

"I agree."

"I'm gonna put Professional Counseling under Personnel. That'll eliminate a deputy chief. And a deputy chief's salary."

"Oughta work."

"And I'm gonna combine Neighborhood Relations and Senior Citizens. Lobowitz is about to pull the pin, so it's not gonna reflect on him."

"Oh, hell, Nick—" Gimball paused.

"What?"

"Bennie Riggs has been hanging around there for fifteen years, figuring he'd get it when Lobo stepped down."

"Well, he can figure again."

"He's Wallpaper's nephew!"

"I know that. We've got too much nepotism as it is."

"Oh c'mon, Nick. You know how department politics work. You get in a job, you bring in people you can trust. You know what Farragut used to say when he was superintendent."

"Yeah, yeah. 'I'd rather have 'em loyal than smart.' "

"Yeah."

"Well, we need 'em smart now."

Gimball sat quietly. He was well aware of the danger Nick could be placing himself in. And what made the whole thing difficult for Gimball was that what Nick wanted to do with the department was exactly what Gimball thought ought to be done. He wanted to tell his old friend to be careful. And at the same time, he wanted to say, "Do it! Give 'em hell, Nick."

Gus said, "You brought in people when you came into office."

"Couple. You and Kluger. Phipps and Zucker. But not the others. I don't like Heidema or Withers and they don't like me. And I kept them because they do the job."

"I don't know, Nick. Wally Riggs was never your man at all. Mayor Wallace owns him. You give Riggs this pop in the chops and you could be in serious shit."

"Hey, Gus. Riggs will never be my man no matter what I do."

"An insult is something else."

"Look, what we got here is a unique window of opportunity. The mayoral election is right around the corner. Wallace is sixty-two. Opposing him we got Elmer Atkinson, who is forty-one and a reformer, both Democrats, plus he and Wallace are both black so we don't have a factor there." Nick said, "Point is, I haven't publicly leaned either way yet, Wallace or Atkinson, but I can."

"I know." The superintendent of police was one of the two or three most powerful jobs in the city after the mayor's. Certain times, it could be kingmaker. "On the other hand, Wallace could replace you."

"Wouldn't dare. Rock the boat with the election coming up? No way."

"Later."

"Forget later. We make the department's needs known *now*, and we pit Wallace and Atkinson against each other—"

"Which they are already."

"Then we see which candidate comes in behind us. Then I push for him, and that's all she wrote."

"But they can make all the campaign promises they want."

"No, not really. Atkinson is chairman of the Finance Committee in the City Council. We've got a couple of things pending, including the new building development plans, that he can break the logjam on. So can Wallace from the mayor's office. And *we'll* know who helped us and *they'll* know we'll know, and I'm gonna make it goddamn clear that the one that helps us gets my shoulder to his fucking wheel. See?"

"I'm for that."

"I've reached the stage in life," Nick said, "where I'm becoming gut-deep aware that I only go around once." He thought, but did not say, that he would like to leave office having made Stella proud of him.

Gimball nodded.

"And Gus, I don't intend to be a place-holder. I'm not in this job for its ceremonial aspects, even though God knows I spend half my time having to deal with 'em. I'm not here for the glory, either, even though—"

Gimball finished the sentence. "—it sure is nice." It was a joke between them. They laughed.

"Gus, I'm going to bring this department into the twenty-first century or die trying!"

Gus said, "I'm with you. And I think it's gonna work."

"With your help."

"With my help. Although God knows it's risky. Takes balls of titanium."

Nick lifted his hand, made a fist, and aimed it slow motion at Gus. Gus met it knuckle-to-knuckle with his own.

TWENTY

When Nick got home, very late, he was amazed to find Stella still awake and reading in his big armchair. A tall stack of books stood next to her on the floor. He wondered whether it was the "to read" pile or the "finished" pile.

"Did you have dinner?" he asked her.

"I found your Chinese restaurant phone number on the corkboard."

"Two minds with but a single thought."

"Mmm." She was curled on his sofa with a book called *Scientific Evidence in Criminal Cases.*

"Stella, should I call you when I'm not going to be home for dinner?"

"I'm a grownup."

"You know, that's what your mother used to say to me."

"She may have said it, but she didn't mean it."

"What? Didn't mean what?"

"Well, she may have meant that she didn't worry, or that you didn't need to call, but she worried a lot anyway."

"Why?"

"She thought you were trying to be Clint Eastwood. You know, taking chances. She thought you'd get yourself killed."

"No, she didn't."

"Yes, she did. You took risks. You were shot twice."

"It just happened. It's the job."

"Not really, Dad. Most police officers go their entire career and never fire their gun except on the range."

"I know that."

"She said you were being brave because it was the opposite of being a bully. Like Granpa."

Nick was stunned. "She never once told me."

"I know."

"But—"

Stella cocked her head at him. He felt a great urge to take care of his child.

"Stella, what is it? You seem to be having a retreat here. You never go out."

Instantly she bristled. "If I bother you—"

"You do *not* bother me. Don't say that every time I ask how you are. I get the feeling you want to talk about something, but then you stop halfway and decide not to. Do me the favor of at least realizing I care about you."

"Right," she said.

"Is it possible that I could help?"

She sighed and closed the book.

"Yes, Dad, to a certain extent I am hiding out here. Not *from* anything. Or anybody. Just to think for a while."

"Is it a problem with a boyfriend?"

"Oh god!" Stella jumped up. "Wouldn't you just think that? That's what your whole generation is like!"

"What? What did I say wrong?"

"A man problem, right? What else would the nice little daughter worry about?" Her feet were planted wide, her arms thrown out angrily, her face fierce and drawn.

"Stella, please, I'm just *asking*. Humor me."

She didn't say anything.

He said, "Look, I care about you. What's so wrong about that?"

"It's a work problem. Just like you have. Work. The job. Okay? And maybe I'll tell you and maybe I won't!"

TWENTY-ONE

DURING THE LONG, cold, end of November of that year, when Come-Again Coumadin was getting more and more upset about the blatant hookers in his district, Sergeant Patricia Touhy heard from an alderman that a large number of colorfully clad, unescorted young women took dinner at the Iba Japanese restaurant on Monroe Avenue. In fact, the alderman reported that they would have a snack there, leave, then come back and snack again.

It occurred to Touhy that the alderman might have a

point; the women were within a stone's throw of several world-class hotels when they were in the Iba, and if they were getting messages there, or if the Iba was in fact a call girl operation cleverly disguised as a restaurant, it was time the First District had a close look at it.

She took the theory to Lieutenant Mike Sheehan, who agreed, and who then took it to Commander Coumadin. Sheehan reported back that Coumadin said to proceed; in fact, he advised Sheehan to nail their ass, so that afternoon when the third watch arrived at the locker room, Touhy asked Mileski and Suze Figueroa if they had any decent clothes with them.

Stanley Mileski got huffy, saying he was already dressed decently, but Suze actually did keep a set of pretty decent clothes in her locker. She sensed a prize coming and nodded agreeably.

When it turned out that they were to go to the Iba and spend the evening drinking sake and eating dinner at the department's expense, Hiram Quail offered to go instead of Mileski if he didn't have any good clothes, and Dick-dick wanted to go but didn't ask. Nobody even thought of Aldo; too slobby, too rude.

Of them all, only Norm Bennis and Dick-dick had ever been to a Japanese restaurant. Norm was so sophisticated that the type of cuisine he hadn't tasted has not yet been invented. Dick-dick had gone to one because he would do anything to impress a woman, and one woman he'd been squiring the spring before wanted Japanese food.

Bennis told Mileski, a cold-beer drinker exclusively, that the sake would be warm, but that didn't discourage Mileski.

By the time he and Suze were all silked out—Mileski having had to slide on home for a white shirt—it was five o'clock. Touhy said that was not too early. People left work

and went someplace for drinks was her theory. Plus lots of the ladies of the evening took care of men on the men's way home from work.

"Linger," Pat Touhy said, smiling. "Gaze at each other. Have an absolutely lovely time."

Stanley said, "Um."

Suze said, "Why sure, boss."

"There you go. Now be good little yuppies," and she sent them out into the city of Chicago.

Norm Bennis dropped them three blocks from their destination, grumbling about being left out, although, he said, if he were actually *going* to a Japanese restaurant tonight, the Iba would not be the first on his list.

"Third, maybe. Fourth. Like that."

"Good night, Norm. Happy ten ninety-nine."

Two-man cars acknowledge assignments with "ten four," one-man cars with "ten ninety-nine." The distinction lets the dispatcher know immediately how many officers are in the car, which affects to some extent the assignments the officer will be given.

"Ninety-nine indeed," Bennis said. "I will carry the torch as if there were two of me."

When Mileski and Figueroa walked into the Iba, there were quite a few people there, as Touhy had predicted. Many were Japanese-American businessmen, some were visiting Japanese being treated by American hosts. An equal number, though, were non-Japanese Chicagoans.

The sushi bar was at one side. Forty feet long, it was flanked by cushion-topped stools. About half of these were already occupied.

The hostess was a Japanese woman in a chrysanthemum-print dress. She pointed at some tea tables and said something to Mileski that he didn't understand and Figueroa couldn't hear. There were ten or so of these low tables,

arranged on a raised platform at one side of the room. Each was a small, semiprivate area, separated from its neighbors by a bamboo and rice paper divider. Because the area was raised, Mileski figured they would have a good view of the rest of room.

"Uh—sure," he said.

She led them to one, as centrally located as Mileski could wish.

There was a low square wooden table, lacquered black. Placed around it were four square red cushions.

Mileski stood still as if terrified. Suze, however, had observed the other diners as they passed. She slipped her shoes off and placed them next to her and back a bit, as they had. She was grateful she had changed out of her police issue shoes. No, give credit where it's due. Touhy had ordered her to.

Suze caught Mileski's eye and telegraphed, "Take off your damn shoes." He did. She sat on the floor and folded her feet up under her.

Mileski, who was six feet six, sat and put one foot next to the table. This pushed his knee up in front of his nose. He put his other foot next to the table, which left him looking across the table at Suze from between two knobby knees clad in moderately clean chinos.

He stuck one leg out straight and knocked the table out of line.

The hostess tittered cheerfully and gave them menus. Then she went away.

"Shit, Figueroa," he said. "This thing is lower than my coffee table!"

"Pretend it's a picnic."

"I don't picnic at my coffee table! My damn three-year-old couldn't sit comfortably at this thing. This table can't be more than sixteen inches high."

"Be quiet. We're supposed to be on a date."

"Date! I'm in pain."

"Well, try to look happy. Better yet, try to look like you're in love."

"Oh god!"

Suze studied the menu, knowing she'd have to order. Mileski'd be too shy.

Mileski scooted his ass around on the cushion. He couldn't get comfortable. He tried folding his legs, Indian-fashion, like the Japanese diners to his left. But when he folded his legs, his knees didn't go down very far, and so he couldn't get close to the table. If he pushed them down and squeezed under the table, they wanted to lift the table up. Plus he groaned that it made his hip joints ache.

Meanwhile the waitress, a smiling Japanese woman, arrived to take their order.

"Sake, please," Suze said.

Mileski said his sacroiliac was going to crack. Pains were starting to shoot up into his shoulder blades. "Move your feet," he said. Suze slipped her feet to her left, her knees to her right. Mileski stuck his legs straight out under the table, all the way over to her side, where his big smelly feet clad in red socks stuck right up next to her thigh. She looked away from them, around the room.

"Look," she said, leaning her head slightly toward the dining room.

Mileski swung his head around.

"Not like that," she said. "Be subtle."

"I can't be subtle sitting on the floor."

"Look."

Mileski saw two really excellent-looking women—lots of leg, good bodies, *serious* hair—at a table in the center of the room. One had just stood up.

"Why do they get a table and we don't?" he groaned.

"Because. Watch the blonde. She just came back to the table."

One of the women was black, very young, very slender, and wore a saffron yellow dress. The other was white, not as thin, voluptuous. She wore a cherry red dress. She picked up a purse, said something to the other woman, and went out.

"Oh," Mileski said.

"First she went off to the women's room or whatever, now she's leaving."

"Doesn't prove anything."

"I know. Point is, we'll see if she comes back. Or if the other one leaves."

The sake arrived. It was in a warm ceramic bottle. It stood on a lacquered tray flanked by two tiny cups.

"Why such small cups?" Mileski asked.

"Because. Try to feign a romantic interest in me, Mileski. You don't want people getting suspicious. Try hard."

Mileski tasted the sake. "Not bad. But they need bigger cups."

The sake went fast, little cups or no little cups, and Mileski ordered a second round. By then the black woman had gone to the back of the restaurant, then returned to her table, then left.

"Hmm," said Mileski.

"Are there phones in back, or what? Are they getting assignments from somebody out there? Or they could be—"

"—calling their answering machines from a pay phone."

"So don't they have cell phones?"

"Go see if they're in the ladies' room."

"Hey! Why don't you pretend to go to the men's room and hang around in the hall?"

"Because."

"Mileski—oh, never mind." Suze got up from the table in a lithe manner that was an affront to Mileski. She was gone three minutes.

"There are phones in back," she said.

"Shit. They could be independent contractors."

"Plus the women haven't come back yet."

The waitress was heading their way.

"You'd better order dinner," Mileski said.

"Sure. No problem."

Suze smiled at the waitress, very much as if she knew what she was doing. "Kitsune udon," she said. That was noodles. Mileski couldn't complain about that. "Sushi and sashimi. The sampler." She'd always wanted to try sushi. On the table was a plastic folding chart in full color of the different types of sushi and sashimi. It gave their names in Japanese and then a translation. When the food came, she would be able to identify the items.

"And another sake," Mileski said. To Suze he said, "For the pain in my back."

That was when the blonde in the red dress came back.

Without asking, the hostess brought her a Perrier and a glass.

Mileski said, "She might be carrying a beeper. Which we couldn't hear from here."

"Or they could set the beeper to vibrate."

"Then they call back and find out where to go next."

"Mmm. Smile at me or something, dammit!" Suze said.

"Well, the longer we sit here the more stuff we get to eat and drink at the department's expense." Mileski folded one leg and knocked the wooden table several inches in the air. Suze caught the sake bottle as it slid toward the edge. The blonde looked at Mileski and smiled.

"Huh," said Mileski.

He folded his other leg while looking at the blonde and knocked the table sideways.

"Do that again," Suze said, "and I'll shoot you."

"Jeez. I'm trying. But I'm in pain!"

"Fake it."

Mileski produced a ghastly smile.

Just then an exceedingly thin man in a blue velvet suit appeared at the far side of the restaurant. He walked with a loping stride to the blonde. The skinny guy looked angry.

"Hey, Mileski!" Suze said.

The skinny guy gestured angrily to the blonde. She took a cell phone out of her purse and shook it, shaking her head.

"I'll follow him," Suze said.

"No, I will."

Mileski and Suze lurched to their feet, but Mileski knocked the table into Suze's ankle. She stumbled against him.

When she turned, both the blonde and the skinny man were disappearing through the front door.

Suze skirted other diners, reached the door, looked both ways, but didn't see them. The restaurant was between two alleys. She ran to one and looked down it. Nothing. She ran to the other and looked. Nothing. Too late. Mileski skidded to a stop behind her. He said, "Damn!"

Back at the table, he added, "Of course, it's not definite. We'll hang around a while and see. Quite a while."

"Well, sure. We'll eat a while. Order more food. Drink more. Act natural. All that good plainclothes stuff."

The udon noodles arrived, and the sushi and sashimi on wooden trays with wasabi, slices of spicy pink ginger and scalloped green garnishes. The tekka maki was wrapped in seaweed, the sashimi was made of a dozen different types of fish. The waitress poured soy sauce into little ceramic dishes, placed the trays and left.

"What's this?" Mileski said pointing at some orange balls on a seaweed and rice slice. "And that." He pointed at a spongy pinkish-coral material wrapped in seaweed.

"The orange balls are ikura, salmon eggs. That's uni, sea urchin, that one's raw squid, and that's anago, sea eel."

"Raw squid, Figueroa! Sea urchin! Eels! Shit! I wouldn't touch that crap with a ten-foot pole!"

"Well apparently," Suze said, "I have to."

TWENTY-TWO

BACK AT THE Furlough Bar sometime after midnight, Suze explained how she had eaten a Japanese dinner with a Ten-foot Pole.

"The food was great! I loved it! Not that"—she cocked her thumb at Mileski—"he did. Plus, then two other women came in. I mean, these were bookends. Pale white skin, black hair, red lipstick. Ladies of the night! These were vampires of the night."

"They can suck *my* blood," Aldo said.

"They were beautiful. But just—eerie."

"Auugh!" Mileski groaned.

The Ten-foot Pole looked more like a folding ruler. He was hunched over his beer and his knuckles were white as he gripped it.

"What's the matter?" Hiram asked.

Stanley Mileski said, "I can't get up."

"You never could," Aldo said.

"Hey! Stop clowning around. I mean it. I can't stand up. Something's wrong with my back!"

They all looked at him. He wasn't kidding.

Hiram Quail said, "Get his other arm," and took the left. Norm Bennis took the right.

"Ooowww!"

They got him off the bar stool, but he stood folded forward, breathing through his mouth. The veins bulged out on his forehead. He *really* wasn't kidding.

"Can you drive home?" Suze asked. "I can take you in my—"

"Yeah, yeah. I can drive. I drive sitting down, like most of us!"

"Don't get crabby. Give Dick-dick your keys and he'll get your car out of the lot."

Mort the bartender, who hardly ever spoke, came around the end of the bar with two white tablets and a glass of water.

"Funny," Quail said, "I didn't think you served water in this place."

"Chaser," Mort said. He handed the tablets to Mileski. "Aspirin. Can't hurt."

Mileski took them with the water.

"This is unquestionably a job-related injury, my man," Norm Bennis said. "Be sure you put in for it."

They got him into his car and waved him off with as much ceremony as if he were going on the *QE 2* to spend six months in Brussels.

"Shit!" Aldo said as Mileski disappeared into the distance. "I gotta leave. My goddamn wife is at a goddamn anniversary party."

Because of his back, on the next afternoon when the third watch reported for work, Stanley Mileski was not among them. Sergeant Patricia Touhy wanted to partner Dick-dick with Quail while Mileski was gone.

But Aldo said, in a voice of hurt and outrage, "You can't take away my little buddy!"

The entire room stared at him. Aldo was so totally unsentimental and so totally lacking in most of the basic evidences of friendship that the whole room was silent in wonder. Dick-dick glowed with pleasure.

"Oh hell," Quail said, "I can go alone. No problem."

Sergeant Touhy didn't like to be given directions by the troops. However, she thought this would be a nice time to exhibit flexibility and generally be a "good boss." She said, "I guess. As long as we've got you both out on the street it doesn't matter."

Suze Figueroa stared at her feet, but her brain was revving like anything. Aldo was not exactly Mr. Sociability. Since when did he care whether he rode alone or not? And why with Dick-dick especially? Until just a couple of days ago, Aldo had showed every evidence of being just as annoyed with Dick-dick as he had been with every other member of the unit. It didn't make any sense.

Then again, it wasn't her problem. Neither she nor anybody else in the room realized they were seeing Dick-dick's last chance pass by.

So Dick-dick rode with Aldo again.

TWENTY-THREE

"YOU WANNA POP for doughnuts, Dick-dick?" Aldo asked.

"Um. I'm not too hungry right now, matter of fact."

"How about I buy 'em?"

"Well, sure, if you wanta."

"Dick-dick, you broke?"

Dick-dick looked at Aldo reproachfully.

"All right, you're broke."

"Yeah."

"How broke?"

"Quite a lot. Hey, leave me alone, Aldo."

"I'm tryin'-a help, you know. Dick-dick, you ain't into the sharks, are you?"

"N-no."

"I don't even mean mob, just the shys, the sharks. Are you?"

"I don't want talk about it."

"Oh shit! Dick-dick, you can get your ass creamed. Christ, you don't even gamble, like I do. You just goddamn spent it all, huh? What'm I gonna do with you?"

Dick-dick didn't answer.

"See, maybe I could help you," Aldo said.

"Hey, nobody can help me. This is just sorta cruel, saying you can help."

"No, I'm not kidding. I got a job I can't do. I'll pay for it. Five hundred bucks."

"What job?" Dick-dick said suspiciously.

"See, Dick-dick, you got your gymnastic background, plus you're *svelte*, which, God knows, I'm not."

"What job?"

"It's easy for you. And no come-backs. I mean, do it, nobody knows."

"What job, Aldo?"

"Well, see, I want you to go up the outside of the building and into the Personnel office and get me a piece of paper."

"*What!*"

"It won't be any sweat at all for you. You go outta the washroom onto the roof of the annex and you're two floors below the Personnel Division windows. Five minutes, tops. You just go up the drainpipe hand over hand, Christ I could do it if I was twelve insteada fifty-two, and they don't even lock the windows, ordinary double-hung, no problem, because who's gonna break in from the department? I went in today, asked for my days off accumulated, looked around, it's a piece of cake."

"Are you *crazy? Break into the department!* No, I'm not gonna do it! Larry Cole runs a tight ship."

"I don't *care* Cole runs a tight ship! He's a desk jockey! The place is not Fort Knox!"

"I'm not gonna do it."

"Nobody'd ever know. Do it at night, nobody's there."

"No. What do you want, anyway?"

"Oh, just something out of a file. An old file nobody cares about anymore."

"Why can't you just ask for a copy of it?"

"Because it's not *my* file."

Dick-dick stared at Aldo a couple of seconds. "No," he said. "No, no, no, no!"

Aldo let him go for the time being. They finished the tour and went for beer at the Furlough. But Aldo knew Dick-dick's answer wasn't a real, final no. As soon as Dick-dick had said "What do you want, anyway?" Aldo knew that he wasn't a hundred percent against it. In fact, he knew Dick-dick wanted that money badly, but was too scared at the idea to say yes and go get it.

Which, as far as Aldo was concerned, just meant that he needed to offer Dick-dick more money. Aldo stopped by his bank the next afternoon on the way to work and checked his

account, which was $314.99. First he was angry, because that meant his wife had to have taken out a couple hundred. Then he smiled, because it was sort of a joke on him—he couldn't have paid Dick-dick $500 anyway.

TWENTY-FOUR

RICHARD "DICK-DICK" Dickenson grew up on a farm in Iowa. It was a small farm, by Iowa standards, eighty acres and a few chickens. The farmhouse was small and so gray it could have belonged to Dorothy's Aunt Em. It was so depressing that Dick-dick (at that time called Richard) could only hope and pray that a cyclone would come and carry him off.

It never did.

They farmed the eighty acres as two forty-acre pieces, one in corn each year, the other in some cover crop intended to enrich the soil—red clover, Dutch white clover, rapeseed or flax. From the time Dick-dick was eight or so he helped in the fields.

There were no small tillers available back then, not that they could have bought one; his father couldn't even afford a plow. His mother would not work in the fields. She threatened a nervous breakdown if the subject even came up. So Dick-dick and his father cultivated the corn by hand.

On a forty-acre field, if you start at one end of the first row with a hoe and work all the way down one row chopping and hacking at the weeds, back up the next row, down the third and so on, by the time you get to the end of the last row,

ten days or so later, it's time to go back to the first row and
start over.

They did it all June and July, up to the time that the corn
was tall enough to shade the ground so the weed seeds didn't
sprout.

About then it was time to turn over the fallow field and
work the clover or whatever into the soil. For this, they
rented a horse from a neighbor.

In high school Dick-dick (now called Rich by his friends)
discovered gymnastics. He was strong from field work, slender and not too tall, and fearless about falling. A natural. He
led his high school team from the day he came on as a fresh-
man. He went to every conference, tournament and competition in Iowa, then the Central States, then the Nationals. In
his last year the school took up a collection to send him to the
Olympic trials. He qualified and went to Barcelona, but finished out of the money.

Even so, from May through early September he worked
in the fields.

When he graduated from high school, he worked two
years at a feed store, lived at home, saved his money, bought
his father a used riding tractor, and then moved to Chicago
intending never to return to the fields. In Chicago he took
two terms of college courses, mostly secretarial and accounting, while he got old enough to apply to the police.

At twenty-one, he applied. Took the tests. Took the psy-
chologicals. Was interviewed by the shrink. At twenty-two he
was accepted. At twenty-two and a half he was in the academy and loved it. Lots of the other recruits complained when
they thought they drew hard duty. He said, "You want to
hear about hoeing corn?"

At twenty-three he was on the street.

They actually paid him for this. He had never had a job
before that he didn't consider temporary. This was a lifetime

thing. He had never had money coming in regularly before, never really had any money at all before, so he spent it.

Then they paid him again the next week.

He was in hog heaven, they'd have said at home.

Happy? *Loved* it!

TWENTY-FIVE

THE BANKER WAS an extremely smooth man. His hair was combed flat against a lot of shiny scalp. His face was shaved to a polish. Even his skimpy eyebrows looked combed. All the hairs went in the same direction.

Aldo shook the man's smooth, soft hand.

"Call me Henry, Aldo," the banker said.

"Sure thing, Henry."

"What can I do for you?"

"I see your ad over there." Aldo pointed to a showcard describing "trouble-free mortgages" with "expedited" paperwork.

"But we hold your mortgage now, don't we?" Henry said.

"Yeah. It was eighty thousand originally, and it's paid down to forty, about that."

"So what would you like to do with it?"

"Well, Henry, I'd like to raise it back to fifty thousand and get the ten. We got this family emergency."

"Well, Aldo, that's what we're here for."

Henry punched up the data, saying, "Now, you know you can't just raise a mortgage. You'll need to refinance it, which amounts to taking out a new mortgage in the amount of fifty thousand."

"Why can't I just raise the one I've got?" Aldo asked, trying to keep the desperation out of his voice. Regina would never sign a new mortgage, and she certainly wouldn't sign without knowing where the money was going, and if she knew she *certainly* wouldn't sign it!

"No, no, we've got regulations, you know. You wouldn't believe the regulations in banking today. This won't take long, though, you know. You don't have to worry about that. You're a customer already and what we mean by expedited is *expedited.*"

"Well—"

"See, this works for the bank and for you. Did you know, Aldo, that when a bank gives you a mortgage, for the purposes of the bank's own accounting it enters the whole first year's payment as the payment of all the interest owed, which naturally goes down as profit for the bank. But when the bank fills out its tax report, it enters only the percentage of the money that is represented by the total mortgage interest divided by the number of years of the mortgage—one-twentieth in the case of a twenty-year mortgage like yours. So when we refinance a mortgage, the new figure of the remaining interest goes down on our bank accounting as the whole mortgage interest figure again, so we look fine on our profit-loss statement. This is the way it's supposed to be done, strange as it sounds. So basically, you know, refinancing the mortgage is good for you and good for us!"

Aldo, while wishing he could hit the man between the eyes, was trying to keep from looking like he wanted the money instantly. He nodded as pleasantly as he could.

When Henry said, "Let's get this paperwork ready, shall we?" Aldo nodded harder.

Papers in hand, Aldo went to work. He put them in his locker in the district while he went out with Dick-dick for the

night's tour. He made only one reference to his proposal, saying to Dick-dick, "I might be able to get you more money than I thought."

He let it go at that, pretended not to notice when Dick-dick shook his head.

Let it work. Let him think about it.

When he got home that night, he took out the mortgage papers, signed his name on the line where he was supposed to sign. Then he took out several canceled checks that Regina had signed. All her signatures were slightly different. He knew that one way forgeries were detected was that they were written too carefully, or written too slowly, by tracing a genuine signature of the person being forged. He was not going to make that mistake.

He changed pens to one with a wider tip than the one he had signed his own signature with. It was a black fibertip; he had used a blue ballpoint.

He copied Regina's signatures over and over, all the different ones in turn, as close as he could get. Aldo was no artist, but he copied and copied, remembering never to write slowly, until he got it pretty good.

Then he took the mortgage document and in one quick movement wrote Regina's name.

It didn't look bad at all. In fact, it looked pretty good.

Then he took all the practice sheets, tore them in tiny bits and flushed them down the toilet little by little, which took ten or fifteen flushes, by which time Regina was at the door saying, "Aldo? Are you sick?"

"No."

"Do you have diarrhea?"

He said, "Yes, dammit! Go back to bed."

TWENTY-SIX

SUPERINTENDENT NICK BERTOLUCCI came around the end of the hall and into the anteroom outside the small meeting room on the fourth floor. He saw an overweight uniformed officer inside lumber to his feet ponderously but fast to open the already half-open door, but Bertolucci motioned him to stay seated. Outside the door he stopped.

Everybody was already there. Bertolucci liked everybody in place before he walked in. Kept him from having to waste time making small talk.

Inside the conference room were four deputy superintendents, including Wally Riggs and First Deputy Gus Gimball. Also somebody from Legal Affairs, somebody from News Affairs, and somebody from OPS. Riggs was talking loudly beyond the door. Bertolucci knew immediately that Riggs was telling a story to Bradley Heidema, because it was a religion story, a Protestant religion story. Heidema was very religious, very strict. Heidema had occasionally reprimanded other officers for going to dances, drinking alcohol at departmental parties, or gambling, even including the Illinois State Lottery.

Wally loved telling jokes that involved the target's religion, race or physical appearance. Bertolucci had hinted that he might not be making friends, but picking up on hints was not Wallpaper Riggs' major talent. Riggs said, "People like to show that they're good sports." Bertolucci figured Riggs was an asshole and might as well act like one.

". . . gets to heaven," Riggs was saying, "and he meets Saint Peter. Saint Peter is showing him around, all the sights. He's showing him the meeting rooms where people in heaven can get together and have fun. They come to one

meeting room, they can hear the singing and laughing all the way out in the hall.

"Saint Peter says, 'That's the Presbyterians. They're having a sing-along.' And they go on a little farther. There's another meeting room and there's a lot of laughing and some people calling out happily and shouting and all. So the guy says 'Who're they?'

"Saint Peter says, 'That's the Catholics. They just had a picnic and now they're playing bingo. They have a lot of fun up here.'

"So they walk on a little farther and they get near this big room, which is absolutely silent. Saint Peter says, 'Let's tiptoe past this one.' So they tiptoe past, and the guy glances in and sees all these people, but they're not making any noise at all. Just sitting there stiffly. And when they're past, he says to Saint Peter, 'Who are they?' Saint Peter says, 'Those are the Christian Reformed.' And the guy says, 'Are we being quiet because they're so conservative and quiet and they'd be mad if we disturbed them?'

"And Saint Peter says, 'No. We're keeping quiet because they think they're the only ones up here.' "

Everybody inside the room laughed except Heidema. Kluger laughed loudest because he thought Heidema had a major asshole problem. Bertolucci chuckled to himself and walked in the door. Heidema smiled at the superintendent, but he was holding himself stiffly and looked pissed off.

Wallpaper strikes again, Bertolucci thought.

Everybody put up with him, and all for the same reason. Why get on the mayor's shit list?

Bertolucci sat, with First Deputy Gus Gimball on his right.

Next to Gimball was Hans Kluger, the deputy super in charge of the Bureau of Administrative Services. Kluger had the face of an angel, round-cheeked, with rosy lips and blond

curly hair. And he had the thickest Chicago accent anyone had ever heard. The man could not say "th" if his life depended on it. When he was a kid at the academy, instructors would say, "Hey, Kluger, say 'them,' say 'these,' say 'those.' "

And Kluger stolidy would say, "Dem, dese, dose."

"Hey, Kluger! What if your name had been Thayer? Or Thigpen? You'd say Digpen."

"How about Hans Kluger III? You'd say 'Hans Kluger da Turd.' "

Deputy Super of Investigative Services was Charles Withers, a black man young for his job at forty-seven, but with twenty-six years in.

Bertolucci studied the five deputies. When the time came for him to be replaced, chances were one of these would take over. Not impossible that somebody another level down would get it—but not as likely. Ordinary the department proposed three people to the mayor and the mayor picked one.

The scariest would be for the mayor to pick Riggs. And Riggs was the mayor's boy, too, so it wasn't impossible.

Kluger wouldn't be the best bet, either. Kluger'd risen as high as he should. He was more cop than administrator, which was no bad thing, but he had no talent for mediating. He was a scrapper, not a peacemaker.

Withers? Well, maybe. But Withers and Heidema were conservatives. If something was new, it scared them. Unless it was glitzy new equipment, and sometimes even then. Gus Gimball would make a great superintendent. Too bad the existing man can't appoint his successor . . .

"All right, let's get started." At these morning briefings, the divisions reported in order. Then they took up general matters.

News Affairs said, "We're getting questions on the CHA murders."

Withers described the search. He seemed to have done everything right, and after ten minutes they went on to Heidema's report on the computer-aide dispatch system. Heidema'd done his homework.

The biggest current problem was Alderman Spaeth's ward, which was riddled with drug and gang wars and drive-by shootings. Anything effective would require a lot of police presence and for a while the ward would look like a police state. This triggered a heated debate.

Finally, Bertolucci said, "Enough! What we're gonna do is this. We're just quietly gonna take back the urban environment in Alderman's Spaeth's ward. We're gonna borrow five hundred officers from other districts, and we're gonna flood the area with cars and put a cop on every other street corner."

Gus Gimball said, "That'll strip the other districts."

"What this will do is enable us to arrest the people in that ward who are hard-core criminals. It'll start the ward off a lot cleaner after a couple of weeks, and the district oughta find it easier to maintain. Ultimately, we need more police officers. The budget hearings in the City Council start this week."

"Where they'll tell us to make do with what we got!" Withers said.

"Hold it. Where we're going to make a real case for increasing manpower."

"And *then* they'll tell us to make do with what we got!"

"All *right*, Withers!" Bertolucci snapped. Withers froze. The other four deputies wished they were lying out in the tall grass somewhere. Bertolucci had the power to make Withers' next post out someplace where God lost His sandals.

Bertolucci got up. Pacing around the table, he said, "This is one we're going to win. We need three things from the City Council. First, the new building. And what happens on

that—who votes us the cash—is gonna tell us who our friends are. And who our enemies are."

Bertolucci glanced at Riggs to see if he was getting it. He was challenging Mayor Wallace directly, and it might as well get back to him.

"Two! To hire regularly, not off and on whenever they agree to cut us a little loose change.

"Three! We need to increase the size of the department. We may have to ask for five thousand more to get five hundred, but we're gonna do it.

"We are going after the best damned recruits we can find, and we're going to be able to get them because what we pay is competitive in the job marketplace. The Council is gonna give me a regular recruit budget or else, and we're gonna take in regular class groups on regular dates. Otherwise we've got no hope of keeping the best people. What we got now is an average of *two years* between when a person applies and when he gets called in for testing. Anybody with more than three neurons between their ears not only got a job in that amount of time, they've been appointed CEO!

"The CPD hasn't grown by one officer in fifteen years— actually we're down in numbers—and unless we get what we need the city is basically cutting us off at the knees."

"We've said it before," Kluger said.

"Right. But this time I'm going to say it over and over again to everybody, every TV reporter, press rep, every casual bystander *if I have to*, until I get some action."

Kluger said, "Wallace's gonna be furious."

"Let him. Or let him help us. I'm taking this, as they say, to the court of public opinion."

Gimball said, "Good."

Bradley Heidema, of all people, said, "Maybe it's about time."

Kluger said, "Amen."

"If I don't get results, I'll give interviews to the *Trib* and the *Sun-Times* and *Chicago* magazine and *People* magazine and Channels Two, Five, Seven, Nine and Thirty-two, and radio and I don't care what the hell all else. I'm going to make a coast-to-coast stink out of the situation if I don't get action. And if you don't think that's possible in the present climate of opinion—"

"I think it's possible," Gimball said, helping out.

"And I think we'll get results," Bertolucci said. It was time to throw a little sugar toward Mayor Wallace. Carrot and stick. Bertolucci was laying his career on the line, but he and Wallace could both come out ahead, if Wallace chose to play.

"Mayor Wallace wants a safe city as much as we do," Bertolucci said. "I don't like not being able to do my job right. If there's one thing I'm going to do while I'm superintendent it's bring the Chicago Police Department into the twenty-first century."

Kluger nodded. Gus Gimball silently raised his mug of coffee in a toast.

Bertolucci walked downstairs afterward to take a car to the academy. He was going to spring a surprise inspection. Gimball, Heidema, Legal Affairs, News Affairs and OPS got into an elevator. Withers and Riggs took a different elevator from the other topcops after they left the meeting. They happened to have one all to themselves.

"Seeing Wallace tonight?" Withers said.

Riggs said, "Dinner."

"Remind him of the problem we got here."

"Sure. What do I say?"

"Tell him it's worse."

TWENTY-SEVEN

"HEY, DICK-DICK, COME on," Aldo said. "It's bucks for boogers!"

"No. No."

"There's nothing to it."

"It's nothing, then *you* do it."

"Be serious. I weigh two hundred and thirty. I'd bring down the whole pipe. Plus I never could shinny up anything. Even when I was a kid."

Later, Aldo and Dick-dick were on South State. A man had come out of a restaurant and seen his car, a white Mercedes, turning the corner heading south without him in it. The dispatcher said, "Go with lights and sound," which they did.

Their lucky night. Not only did they intercept the guy, smooth as silk, turned right across the street when they saw him coming, no other car on the street to confuse things, also the guy stopped instead of ramming them, but another squad, coming up behind the guy, got there the same time and wanted the pinch, so they didn't even have to do the paper and they'd get credit for being Johnny on the spot.

"Sometimes everything goes right," Aldo said.

Aldo and Dick-dick's adrenaline was up from blowing through all the red lights with the siren on—their blood pressure had to be up, too, and you're feeling like you're ten feet tall, so Aldo figured this is the time to get Dick-dick when he's feeling invincible, so he said, "Hey. Eight thousand dollars. I'll pay eight thousand dollars."

Aldo had intended to offer five thousand first and ooze on up to ten, if he had to. But now that he actually had ten thousand dollars that Regina didn't know about, he wanted some

of it for himself. Go to the track his day off, which was Wednesday, make a serious killing. Aldo felt seriously good. This was gonna be easy. No danger to him, nothing traceable to him, no comebacks to anybody.

Dick-dick stared at Aldo. Dick-dick's tongue was gripped between his teeth and his eyes were frozen open in surprise.

Aldo just repeated, "Eight thousand dollars. It's a personal thing to me. Nobody else cares about it. No skin off anybody's nose."

He let that hang a few seconds and said again, "Eight thousand."

The night was cold, but not unusually cold for late November in Chicago. Forty, forty-five degrees maybe, Dick-dick thought.

Rather think about that than what could go wrong.

He stood on the roof of the annex to the police department, a building next to the department itself, built separately, but completely connected internally. You could walk between the two on every floor, but there was a difference in floor heights, necessitating ramps.

He'd walked up from the First District area to the sixth floor of the department, and gone out the washroom window from the department onto the roof of the annex. This was the point where he stepped into danger. Up to here he had been just an officer in the washroom. Now he was where he shouldn't be. And where he couldn't think of any good reason to be.

If somebody caught him, could he call it a dare? Climb up the wall as a dare? Be Spiderman? If he tried that, would he be fired?

Jeez, he should never have let Aldo talk him into this.

He half-turned around to go back in the bathroom window. Tell Aldo it couldn't be done, there was somebody in

the Personnel Division. That wouldn't work, Aldo'd just put it off to tomorrow.

Tell him he wasn't going to do it?

But eight thousand dollars was just way, way too much money to pass up.

Dick-dick held his body still while he methodically studied every window that overlooked the spot where he stood. Of the three dozen or more he could see from where he was, only two were lighted. One of these was frosted, so nobody would see him from it anyway. The other was partly blocked by a bookcase, and there was a sickly-looking plant on the sill. Probably whoever was in that room never looked out the window anyhow.

The three windows of the Personnel Division were all dark.

He took a deep breath. There was a downspout next to the Personnel Division windows that ran from the top of the building all the way down to a sewer opening in the cement on the ground. There were also several large conduits carrying wires running across and down the building. Also, the windows had sills and overhangs.

"Shit," he whispered. "Might as well be a ladder!"

He was a gymnast, not a burglar. He couldn't climb wearing gloves, but that was all right, for two reasons. The pipe would be cold, but he was so fast it wouldn't matter. Also, he didn't want to wear gloves in case he was caught. He wanted to be able to claim it was a dare. Looking like a burglar was certain catastrophe.

There was no moon. But Chicago was never dark. He'd be seen if anybody looked out.

He jumped, seized the downspout, and swung up onto the seventh-floor windowsill. Piece of cake. You had to laugh, really.

He grabbed the pipe again and vaulted to the eighth-floor windowsill.

There he was, looking into the darkened offices of the Personnel Division. No movement inside. He took hold of the mullions between the panes of the old windows and pushed up. Nothing happened. Shit! What if they were locked? Why would they be, nobody up here?

He planted his feet together on the sill, crouching, and pushed again. There was a rending screech and the window shot up. He caught it just in time, before it crashed against the top of the frame.

Stupid window probably hadn't been opened once since the summer.

There was still no movement inside the room. He checked carefully before he stepped in, making certain that he was not going to dislodge anything on the inside sill, or anything on anybody's desk inside. His goal was to come and go like a shadow, moving nothing that would give away the fact that he'd been there.

He stepped down onto a chair that stood beside a desk. Then he closed the window to within a quarter of an inch, so that nobody seeing it from any other window would notice it was open and investigate.

Now what? There was a frosted glass pane in the door that opened onto the eighth-floor hallway. But Personnel was at the end of a long hall. And anybody in the hall would see a light. The elevators were in the middle of the hall, thirty, forty feet away, so it was not likely that anybody from any other office would even glance at the Personnel door. Still, he'd better not hit the lights.

When did the cleaning people come through? Damn, how was he to know something like that? He'd just have to keep an ear out.

Dick-dick almost started to laugh out loud. Keep an ear out? He was so keyed up if he dripped a drop of sweat on the floor he'd probably jump out of his skin at the noise.

Now all he had to contend with was where to find the file.

The most obvious bank of files was along the inner wall.

Dick-dick got the flashlight out of his jacket. When he reached the front of the cabinets, he covered the lens of the flashlight with his hand, then turned it on. Then he moved his hand just enough to let light fall on the letter designation on the front of the file drawers: A—AMM, AMN—BRI.

That was the one he needed. He turned off the flashlight while he pulled open the file drawer. Pulled it open as silently as grass growing. The one sound of that window going up had been enough for him.

With it open, he put his hand back over the flashlight and turned it on. Then he let just enough light fall into the drawer to pick out the names on the tabs. He guided his wedge of light carefully back through the drawer.

BERTOLUCCI, NICHOLAS.

Okay. He felt shaky, seeing the name like this.

Next problem—how to go through the file without taking his hand off the front of the flashlight.

Should he take the file out and read it somewhere else? That would chance his being caught if anybody came in. If he left it in the drawer and read it in the drawer, he could shut the drawer and hide if somebody came.

But if he read it inside the drawer, he would be positioned so that light in the room could be seen from outside the main door of the department.

He was proud of himself for acting so decisively. He took out the file, shut the file drawer in case anybody came, and took the file onto the floor behind a desk to read, where his light would not be seen from the hall.

If he heard a key at the door, he'd be out the window with the file. Someday somebody would find it missing, but they'd blame one of the people who worked there for misplacing it.

Which served them right, desk job, anyway.

The paper Aldo wanted was not in the file.

Nick Bertolucci's stuff went back only to 1975. Somebody'd cleared everything out prior to that.

He'd never worked out with Aldo whether he'd get paid if he went through with the thing but didn't find the paper. He should've. Crap!

But if there was one thing he knew for sure, it was that Aldo did not go in for charity.

All right. Maybe they retired old papers past a certain date. Made sense. But did they throw them out? He'd hate to think he went through all this for nothing.

No, they wouldn't throw them out. Lose them maybe, but not throw them out. Bureaucracies never threw things out.

What they did do, Dick-dick thought as he replaced the file in the drawer, was clear things aside when there was an inspection. The "Omigod, the superintendent's coming in ten minutes, everybody *clean up!*" kind of thing.

Sure, and there in the far corner was a humongous stack of boxes. Let them be labeled!

TWENTY-EIGHT

BEO—CHR WAS THREE boxes down from the top of a stack. But Dick-dick was careful again. He took off the top three, removed BEO—CHR and put the others back. They weren't in order anyway, so if he had to get out quick he could put the top one back and nobody the wiser.

He was so pleased with himself he didn't hear the key in the door until it was turning.

Christ!

He put the box on top of the pile, but there was no time to run.

Dick-dick stepped behind a coat tree where somebody had left a raincoat. The door swung open. A man entered.

I'll run into the hall and escape if he sees me, Dick-dick thought. I'll go down a few flights of stairs and then pretend to be coming back up for something and I'll describe somebody running past me, I'll say he had red hair and was—

But he knew it wouldn't work. The man who came in was Commander Larry Cole, not one of the overweight, sluggish desk officers. Cole was tall, slender and quick. He'd be on him like a hawk on a rabbit.

Cole had not turned on the lights. This was his office, and he knew his way around. He went into the far room, which was his private office. Dick-dick heard some rummaging around, the sound of paper being shoved away. Then Cole came back out, carrying three books.

Dick-dick's hopes rose. Cole was going to leave.

But Cole stopped. He was now two feet from where Dick-dick waited rigid behind the coat tree. Dick-dick could smell a chocolate bar Cole probably had in his pocket. Which made Dick-dick pray that he himself was not wearing

any noticeable aftershave or had picked up any stray street smells during his tour that evening.

Cole's head came up as if he noticed something wrong. He sniffed the air.

Dick-dick saw his job, his pension and maybe even his freedom go out the window. His teeth were chattering, but he kept his mouth shut and hoped they couldn't be heard beyond his own straining ears.

Commander Cole walked over to the slightly opened window and closed it. He looked around the room. Paused, thinking. Then he walked out and locked the hall door.

Dick-dick sank to his knees behind the coat tree. After a couple of seconds, he settled back on his ass and gave himself over to a minute of shaking.

When his heart was back in running order and his eyeballs stopped throbbing from the rush of terror, he went back to the pile of boxes. He said "Eight thousand dollars" to himself, sat down because his leg muscles still didn't feel right, and opened the box.

"Goddamn cops who take classes anyway!" Aldo said. "I mean, I am suspicious of cops who think they have to go on taking classes. Can you imagine coming all the way back to the office at this hour for a couple of *books!*"

"Mmm." Dick-dick could imagine it all too well.

"I say there's nothing worse than an intellectual cop!"

"Guy gets to be a commander, you'd think he'd stop taking classes," Dick-dick said, still weak, but pretending to be as calm as a politician in a bribery hearing.

Aldo was talking him into a better mood, while walking him to the Furlough. When they got there, Dick-dick headed straight to the bar. There was a quaking feeling under his diaphragm that no amount of reasoning with himself could fix.

"What took you so long?" Norm Bennis said.

Quail said, "You weren't late car, were you?"

"Extra paper," Dick-dick said, as they'd arranged, and practically fell into his beer.

But Aldo couldn't stand it any longer. He went into the men's room and opened up the envelope Dick-dick had given him. There, where he had enough light to really see it—it was the right paper! And it was beautiful.

It was a registration-of-firearm record for Officer Nicholas Bertolucci, dated March 6, 1968. It was for a .38 Colt revolver. The serial number was 76L2702.

TWENTY-NINE

"HEY, BOSS," WALLPAPER Riggs said. "What was the very first thing the two pink flamingos did right after they got married?"

Nick Bertolucci actually tried to think. It had to be an ethnic joke, given Riggs' mentality. Italian ethnic joke, for that matter, since he was asking Bertolucci. But what? He looked over at Gus Gimball. Gus just raised his shoulders.

"I don't know," Nick said patiently. "What *did* the two pink flamingos do right after they got married?"

"They bought some plaster Italians to put on their front lawn."

Nick laughed. So did Gus. Then Nick said, "Hey, Wally. You'd better get the survey results over to the beat rep."

"Oh. Yeah. See ya."

And Wally was out of there.

Nick sighed. "Oh lord."

Gus nodded.

Nick stood with Gus at the window of his office, facing out over South State Street. It was 2:45 P.M. As they watched, Nick's brother crossed the street with another man, both apparently heading in to the First for work.

Seeing him, Nick sighed again.

Gus said, "Aldo?"

"Mmm-hm."

"How's he doin'?"

"Who knows? Never tried for sergeant again."

"How long's he got to pension?"

"Year and a half. I tried to help him, once upon a time."

"You never told me exactly—"

"Well, yeah. He came on the job in 1978. By then I had fourteen years in. So, coupla years later I got him a good assignment, he makes sergeant, everything looks just fine. I figure maybe Aldo's got past the difficult age. Then they're having a party in the district, party for the lieutenant, birthday, I think. This particular lieutenant isn't one of our leading lights. There's a rumor he's tied into protecting some heavy pimps in his district and one or two of them got busted by accident and it comes out there might be this connection. So it's not impossible there could be a prosecution. Rumor is the guy's going to jail. But anyway, they're having the birthday party. Somebody's brought in a big cake. So they're cutting the cake, the lieutenant is, and he cuts down into it there's something hard. He digs it out. It's a metal file."

Gus laughed.

Nick said, "Well, yeah, it was funny. It was funny to everybody but the lieutenant. I mean the guys all laughed their heads off because they weren't so fond of him anyway, and if he wound up in the slammer, okay.

"But he was furious. He's yelling 'Who did this?' and Aldo's laughing harder than anybody, so right away he

knows. Asks Aldo and the silly putz admits to it. Stuck the file
in and smoothed the frosting over the hole. So he gets busted
back down."

"I never heard about that."

"No, you heard about the other one."

The other one was not funny. It was so unfunny that Gus
had not mentioned it specifically. It involved a fistfight between Aldo and a supervisor who had told him to quit gambling in public. Aldo was in Narcotics and by then Nick was
chief of detectives, and even so it was all he could do with all
his clout just to keep Aldo from being fired.

Nick had always been considered real heavy, because at
the time Nick entered the academy, his father was already a
deputy superintendent. By the time Aldo came on the job,
old Nico Bertolucci had been first deputy superintendent,
then he was raised to superintendent right after the Hampton case first broke, got himself into political trouble when
his part in the coverup came out, and had sunk to a lesser
post in General Support, where he served out another few
years checking on squad cars until retirement age. Even so,
he had friends on the job who thought his political troubles
were actually signs of strength on his part; he was for the
department against the world, and they were willing to act as
clout for his two boys.

Aldo would therefore have seemed heavy from the moment he went to the academy, but people soon got the sense
that he was not. He was thirty-three when he came on. It was
clear from the first that he was a source of trouble, trouble
for himself and everybody around him.

"How come Aldo came on the job so much later than
you?" Gus asked.

"I came on after I got out of the army. You and I came on
in '64. Aldo was discharged in 1965. So first he gets into this
thing where he's gonna make a million dollars selling these

glass refrigerator containers door to door. I mean, somebody really did a number on him, convincing him he could make a fortune."

"He's not a salesman type anyhow."

"No. No, he surely isn't. Then one time, early one November, Aldo thought he got this great deal on frozen turkeys. For Thanksgiving. Got them one-quarter what they were selling for in the stores. Tried one, cooked it; it was great. It was some warehouse going out of business. Like that. So it was one of those freezing cold Novembers. A lot of snow, fifteen degrees. He gets the truckload of frozen turkeys delivered, a thousand of them, puts them in the garage, and goes around the neighborhood taking orders. Half-price turkeys. People say, okay, they'll take two or three or six, they're real cheap. About two days before Thanksgiving he plans to deliver them. The day before while he's out there's a change in the weather. You know Chicago. It's eighty by noon. He comes running home, tries to get people to come and get their turkeys. Runs around in the car taking turkeys to people. But have you ever tried to move a thousand turkeys? Plus people aren't home, they changed their minds, they want them day after tomorrow, whatever. The turkeys defrost and then they start to spoil. By the next day, some of them are exploding from the gases and the garage smells like hell. He had to hire three guys to help him get the rotten turkeys into a dumpster and pay to get them out of there. He wound up maybe two thousand dollars in the hole.

"Then he went into a used car lot. Can you imagine! In 1975 or '76 this must've been. A used car lot!"

"Had to be five hundred of 'em in Chicago."

"Easy. But he and his pal thought they were gonna take over the market."

"Sad."

"Well, in two years or so he and his partner had lost their

shirts. And his partner skipped town with the $370 or so they had left in the bank. By that time Regina was pregnant, so it seemed like they oughta get married and Pa said he'd better find a real job, meaning the CPD, of course—"

"Which I imagine he wanted for Aldo all along." .

"Oh yeah. Oh yeah. You can say that again. He screamed at him to do it. And which is also probably why Aldo wanted to try anything else first. Poor schmuck. Never had a chance. He couldn't save enough money to do anything else with. I mean money went through his hands like a dose of salts through the hired girl, as my mother-in-law used to say."

"Sometimes I'm glad my kid Jeff was able to tell me he didn't want to come on the department. I wouldn't have wanted him to feel like he was cutting my heart out."

"Yeah. Hey, Gus, are you all right?"

"Sure, why?"

"Your hand's shaking."

"Nothing," Gimball said. "I must be tired. Happens mainly when I'm tense or something. I'm taking a half day off tomorrow."

"Good."

And going to the doctor, Gimball thought. "I'd better get back to work. The specs are on your desk."

"Thanks."

Bertolucci had asked for the specifications the department electrical, engineering and communications specialists had come up with for their ideal building. He was going to a retirement party tonight for the oldest member of the Chicago City Council. He'd see Elmer Atkinson there. And take him aside, and just run a few numbers past him. See if he was mayoral material, from the department's point of view.

As the door closed behind Gus, Bertolucci looked back

out the window, but of course Aldo was long gone. He thought of Aldo as he had been forty-five years ago, a fat little boy. Earnest and anxious. Aldo was a year older than Nick, named for his mother's father. But Nick had been the one with sense. He had known, almost from earliest childhood, that his father was dangerous, and he had known how to avoid him. Usually.

Aldo, poor blundering chubby child, had not. Aldo was punished, and punished again. When Nick carefully never showed his father any fears he had, Aldo just couldn't help it, and was punished for them, and then was more afraid of the punishment than whatever the original thing was, and his fear and clumsiness enraged old Nico and made everything worse.

There was the time Aldo, maybe all of six, had refused to go down to the cellar to get something their mother wanted, canned green beans most likely, because the bulb had burned out and it was dark down there. Old Nico roared at him— was he afraid of the dark?

And Aldo, cringing, said he wasn't. So Nico told him to go down and get the green beans. And Aldo wouldn't. *Couldn't.* Couldn't move. So Nico picked him up and called him a mollycoddle and said, "No son of mine is going to be a sissy." He took him to the basement, handcuffed him to a steel support pole and left him in the dark.

Nick, a year younger, had known how he would have handled it. He was more afraid of the cellar than Aldo, he believed. But he would have gone down, terrified, bumped into a few things, and tried to find the jars of beans. No matter what.

Poor, blundering Aldo.

Or was it *because* of Aldo that Nick knew what to do? Was it because he could watch Aldo make the mistakes first that

he could pick his way through the minefield that was his father?

Nick looked out at the city of Chicago. He felt inexpressibly sad, and wondered why. The sun was low in the sky—nearly four o'clock in November. A few vapor trails were dragged over the pale lemon wash of dying sunlight. There was no warmth in the sunsets this time of year.

We're all over fifty, Nick thought. Aldo and me. Gus, too. Getting on toward the end of our lives. And you can't fix anything that happened in the past.

Best thing you could do is forget about it. If you could.

THIRTY

ALDO AND DICK-DICK got to the Furlough Bar earlier than usual that night. Hiram Quail, Mileski the Ten-foot Pole, and Norm and Suze were already there. Mileski had recovered from his little back problem.

Except he didn't think so. He asked for water for his Extra-Strength Tylenol.

Mort the bartender said, "Hey, I don't sell water here, Mileski."

"Then gimme a beer with a water chaser." And he took two Tylenol. "Shit, riding in that car brings back the pain."

By that time Dick-dick, triggered by Mileski's remarks, was ordering his second whiskey with a beer chaser.

"Suddenly you got money, Dick-dick?" Bennis said.

"Little bit."

When he got to his fourth whiskey with the fourth beer, Suze said, "You sure are rich!"

Dick-dick said, slurring slightly, "Sometimes friends help you out, you do them a special favor."

Aldo slid his gaze slowly toward Dick-dick.

About the same time, Nick, wearing his dress uniform and becoming more and more uncomfortable, was thinking of leaving the City Council party. But he wasn't quite done with his job. He'd talked with Wallace. And not been too happy. Wallace had been real cute, not once uttering the word "money." Nick had now separated Atkinson from the herd.

Atkinson was in a dinner jacket, and despite a thickening waist, he wore it well. Carmine DeContini, eighty-seven years old and now about to lay down his City Council gavel, looked terrible in a tux. His skin was yellow—not because of his age, it always had been yellow—and it went badly with black. He was stooped, and the dinner jacket bunched up its shiny lapels like the bow of a ship, even when he was standing. But he still had his loud laugh, and lame duck or dead duck, whichever, he was surrounded by dignitaries, including the governor and a representative of the president of the United States.

Which took the focus away from Nick and Elmer Atkinson.

Which was what Nick wanted.

"I agree," Atkinson said. "In fact, one of the reasons for a technologically superior police force is that you have more accurate crime data and therefore fewer brutality complaints."

Now get him to stop talking like a candidate, Nick thought.

"Well, the videocameras in the squad cars are just one thing . . ."

He let it hang. On the whole, he was favorably impressed with Atkinson. When he heard the reform candidate was

going to be Atkinson, who was the chair of the finance committee, Nick had thought maybe the guy would be a numbers person, with no people skills. He hadn't known Atkinson personally, not beyond budget hearings, and hadn't been able to guess what kind of candidate he'd make. Now he thought the man had a chance.

Atkinson was a good-looking man, but very medium—medium height, medium weight, medium brown color, and at forty-two in medium early middle age, all of which might have added up to serious boredom for the voters. But Bertolucci thought he was not as ho-hum as he might have been. He was quick, and he had a good smile. What interested Bertolucci more was he seemed to have balls. There was an incisive edge to his voice.

"You're talking about the building," Atkinson said.

"Everything—well, a lot of things—stay on hold until we get the building. We need a totally new dispatch system. Which can't be installed in the existing building. Come see our communications room sometime. It looks impressive because you've got lights and maps and action, all the bells and whistles you could want, but if you look closely, they have to find out where each squad car is by *asking* the car! Now a lot of other cities already have a mechanism that shows the position of the cars by lighted dots on the maps the dispatcher is looking at. You can imagine in a crisis, you got a fleeing gunman, you can save minutes—"

"You can save minutes when even seconds are precious."

"Yes," Bertolucci said, surprised. After a couple of seconds, he said, "It all boils down to money."

And Elmer Atkinson flat out said, "You need more."

"Damn right we do."

Bertolucci glanced over at the luminaries clumped around DeContini. He did not want Mayor Wallace to see

him in lengthy conversation with Atkinson. Atkinson noticed the glance.

He said, "I might just come and look at that communications room someday soon."

"Good."

"How's tomorrow?"

"Fine."

"I take it"—he paused just long enough for Bertolucci to know he meant business—"that you want to know for *sure* who your friends are, before the election."

Bertolucci paused too, then deciding to take the risk said, "Yes. It'll make all the difference to us. And maybe a difference to the candidate."

"Well, hell, that's fine, then. Let's get some of that shrimp and champagne!"

THIRTY-ONE

BENNIS AND FIGUEROA were rolling south on Canal Street near where it crossed the Amtrak rail lines.

"Definitely not a savory neighborhood, my man," Bennis said.

Suze said, "Definitely a place where the gritty underbelly of Chicago shows its—um—gritty underbelly."

The radio said, *"One sixteen."* Not them.

Some car answered, *"Sixteen."*

In a deep and portentous tone, the dispatcher said, *"Burglary, unlawful entry, no force. One eighteen South Dearborn."*

"Ten four."

"That's the Voice of Doom," Suze grumbled, referring to the dispatcher. "What's he gotta be so gloomy about? He's inside, bathroom breaks whenever he wants them."

"Is that so? I thought—"

"I don't know specifically about the bathroom, Bennis. I mean, he's inside, warm, dry. No heavy lifting. He can get coffee without having to park. Lock the car. You know."

They were off the tracks area now, where the car had bumped and danced, rattling everything on top, including the Mars lights, rattling everything inside including Figueroa and Bennis. So when they felt a bump at the front, Bennis stopped.

"Better see what it was."

"Okay."

"Listen," Bennis said. "It could of been a dog. Mad dog. Like that."

"Yeah. We'll both go look." Suze knew that Bennis, absolutely fearless when attacked by knife-wielding undesirables, was pretty much afraid of dogs. That was okay with her. She had things *she* was afraid of, sometimes even knife-wielding undesirables, and Bennis would back her up. Neither went around telling everybody else in the district the private things they learned about each other during their long tours.

Bennis crept uneasily around the driver's side. Suze marched briskly around the passenger side, but she had her hand on her sidearm. Injured dogs could attack you.

"*That's* no dog!" Bennis said.

"Unless they got a new yuppie model."

"With a naked tail."

"Not a bad pet for an apartment," Suze said.

"Yeah! Eat anything you don't want."

"Live in a small space."

"Don't pull your arm off, you walk it on a leash."

"Cute little curved teeth."

Bennis reached down to pick up the rat. It was dead.

Suze said, "No! Don't touch it!"

"Why not? I handled rats before."

"You'll get fleas. You'll get a disease."

"Hey! I'll get the AIDS gloves."

Bennis came back with one of the packages of disposable plastic gloves they were supposed to wear whenever it looked like they might be handling blood. He slipped them on and grabbed the rat by the tail. The back half was squashed, but the tail was clean. The rat hung limply, like a sack of peas on the end of a string.

"Let's put him in a bag."

"Not in my car!"

"It's not your car."

"Are you out of your mind, Norman! What do you want it for?"

"I was just thinkin' about Coumadin and the stink in the First."

"What are you talking about?"

"I thought maybe we get back tonight—you ever notice the air duct goes over the locker room and from there into Coumadin's office?"

"Noooo . . ." Suze said slowly.

"Well, you should. It does. Personally, I'm always real careful what I'm sayin' in the locker room just in case. Anyway, there's a vent grate in the locker room ceiling. So if a person pushed the grate up and threw this little sucker a couple of feet into the duct, so he wouldn't smell up the locker room when he gets ripe, what do you figure would happen?"

Suze stared at Bennis. She could see him pretty well in the orange sodium-vapor street lights, even though they

made him look like a victim of liver disease. Both started to grin widely.

"Plus, we're late car tonight," Bennis said. "Shouldn't be anybody there hardly when we get back."

THIRTY-TWO

BENNIS AND FIGUEROA got to the Furlough a little late that night. They were giggling and nudging each other with their elbows when they climbed onto the bar stools, but nobody else much noticed. Stanley, Hiram and Aldo were at least two beers ahead of them already, and Dick-dick maybe three.

Everybody had another round when they got theirs.

"Hey!" Norm Bennis said. "You all do your part to take care of the stink in the First?" He laughed uproariously.

"Yeah, sure. We was the eyes of the community," Stan said.

Dick-dick said, "Us too. Couldn't take our eyes off 'em."

"I got Dick-dick on a short leash, this assignment," Aldo said.

"Yeah, well, there's other times you stick me way out twisting in the wind, Bertolucci," Dick-dick said.

Norm glanced at Dick-dick, but that was all he was going to say. Norm chuckled. "Well, I can tell you gentlemen that Figueroa and I have done our part."

Dick-dick got to his feet and walked to the men's room. He listed slightly to the left and had to make a half circle to compensate.

Suze hunched over her beer. Some of the excitement of

planting the rat in Come-Again's air duct had worn off, leaving her with the exhaustion that followed a long eight-hour tour. She had to get home, set the babysitter free. Maybe put in a load of laundry.

Sometimes Suze got a little depressed at these after-hours bar sessions. She was part of the team, they liked her, all but Aldo. Norm respected her. But still she knew that they would talk differently when she left. They would talk easier. They'd throw around comments about women and sex and generally engage in their male-bonding crap.

Sometimes it really pissed her off. She didn't want to be one of the boys, exactly. But she sure as hell wanted to be one of the guys.

Damn, she thought. I deserve it, for that matter.

Lot of evenings she'd leave early. Well, fuck 'em, she thought. Tonight she'd make somebody *else* leave first.

"Yeah, well, I take care of my partner," Dick-dick said, slurring his words.

Aldo snarled, "Hey, Dick-dick, you drink too much."

Since Aldo could be crabby or possibly even halfway pleasant in the same tone of voice, and since nobody wanted to know about it if he was intending to be crabby, nobody continued this line of chat.

Along about midnight Aldo said "Jeez, I'd better go. What's the matter with you, Figueroa? I usually just wait until you're tired and leave and then I figure I'm gonna be tired in an hour."

"Tired? You kidding? I don't *get* tired. What I'm leaving for is I get up at six to get JJ up. Make the brown bag lunch. I stay here till twelve, by the time I get home I get five hours sleep."

"Sure, but what do you do after he leaves and before you

come over here for the evening?" Mileski the Ten-foot Pole asked. He leered at Suze and moved his eyebrows up and down, thinking he looked quite a bit like Groucho Marx.

"Screw you, Mileski," Suze said.

"No, hey, what do you do?"

"Get groceries, so there's something to eat when he gets home. Laundry. Clean the house. I mean, the excitement just never ends. What do you expect?"

Quail said, "You oughta go fishin' with me, you get a weekend off. Get outta the city. Complete change."

She said, "Thanks. But I got JJ to take care of." Her son was seven years old, and not easy to give to a sitter for long.

Aldo said, "You gonna leave, Dick-dick?"

"I'm getting wasted here," Dick-dick said. He spoke very, very carefully. He got off the stool and stood very, very straight.

"You are seriously pissed," Stanley said.

"You, sir, could be right."

"Ah, hell," Aldo said. "I'll walk you as far as the el. My fucking car's in the shop."

"Mmm. A gen'leman," said Dick-dick.

Aldo shrugged big shoulders into his coat. Dick-dick had a black leather jacket. "That isn't gonna keep you warm," Suze told him.

"Don't get like a mom," said Mileski.

By that time Aldo and Dick-dick were out the door. "What's with those two?" Hiram Quail said.

Suze waited fifteen minutes, just to make her machoness obvious. Then she left, heading for the CPD lot and her car. Aldo and Dick-dick were out of sight.

THIRTY-THREE

THE NIGHT WAS crisply cold. It was so cold all the crud in the air must have frozen and fallen down, Aldo thought, because the stars were bright and hard.

There was a sugary drifting of snow along the sidewalk, most of it lodging in the cracks. It crunched under Aldo's feet. Less so under Dick-dick's, because he shuffled some.

They came to the stop for the Ravenswood el. There were stairs leading up to the platform.

"Suppose I could go on the el as far as Clybourn and take a taxi," Aldo said.

"Yessir," Dick-dick said, concentrating on putting one foot on the first step. He got that right, tried a foot on the second step. That worked out, too.

"What I mean," Aldo said, following him up, "you think there's taxis there this time of night?"

"Where?"

"Clybourn."

Dick-dick was doing pretty well now, one foot after another, climbing the steps. Up, step, other foot up. In fact, he was doing so well that he got in the habit of it and when he got to the top, unaware, he went on stepping up. The lack of a step where he expected one upset him completely, and he staggered forward, nearly falling on his face. Aldo caught him.

"Aha!" Dick-dick said.

There was nobody else on the platform. Even though it was not a windy night, it was colder up here, just from the passage of air. Air sucked around the metal girders, making the structure sigh softly.

It was an old, rusted el stop, the kind with pillars that

crowded the tracks and supported a metal roof and three metal walls, which kept the worst of the weather off the passengers. Some of the girders were pierced in decorative patterns like cloverleafs and strings of beads.

Somewhere far away the train was coming toward them, because the tracks started to sing faintly. There was more motion in the air. The sound was like a bird, a large bird, flying some distance overhead.

Then the light of the train caught the roof, flicked over it, down, and along the girders as the train rounded the curve from the south. Aldo and Dick-dick were shivering now in the cold. The train came sweeping around the bend, still not visible itself, only a splash of light on the metal structure across the tracks.

The vibration was on them, though. The train was close.

Aldo nudged Dick-dick. He staggered. Aldo gave him just a gentle, light shove in the small of his back. He wavered, lost one foot over the edge of the platform, then, turning sideways as if to try to get back on the platform, saying "Oh?" in a puzzled voice, he dropped onto the tracks just as the train entered the station.

THIRTY-FOUR

DAMN! DAMN THAT stupid Dick-dick, putting him in this kind of position, Aldo said over and over as he walked casually but fast down the metal stairs from the el platform. God damn him!

Could have been so simple and easy. No problems, no

come-backs. Stupid fuck, all he had to do was keep his mouth shut!

Aldo hit the sidewalk before the screeching from the train brakes stopped shivering the night air.

Damn!

The engineer hadn't seen him, he was sure of that. The enclosure part of the el station was shaped like a long box with one side missing. Trains drew up along the open side. When a train approached the station, the boxed-in end hid the people on the platform from the train.

And as soon as Dick-dick started to tumble slowly backward, Aldo was out of there. Down the stairs and out.

Stupid shit Dick-dick. Now Aldo had to take the damn bus home. Unless he went back to the CPD lot and got his car.

No, that was too dangerous. One of the boys might see him. One o'clock in the morning, hardly gonna hide in the crowd. This way, at the very worst he could say he forgot he'd driven to work. Stupid Regina wanted the car half the time anyhow—stupid St. Cecilia Society, or shopping.

It was Dick-dick's fault. A nothing job, all he had to do was keep his mouth shut. Aldo counted on his fingers, *four* days he'd given that idiot to shut up about it, talked to him on the job, okay he was going to be cool. But get three-four drinks inside him and there he was dropping hints all over the place all over again. Aldo hated people who couldn't hold their liquor. He should've shut him up a week ago. That very night. Saved himself a lot of worry. Saved his breath, too. Some people you just can't talk to.

Saved his money, too, if he'd gotten rid of him right after he got the paper.

Aldo heard sirens in the distance.

Engineer probably called from the train. EMTs. Who

would respond from the First? he wondered. Fiddleman, maybe, first watch, or that congenital idiot Reilly. Sangucci?

What difference did it make? Drunk kid falls on the tracks, all they'd find out.

His bus was coming. Aldo climbed up tiredly, his legs starting to feel it now, the seeping away of the adrenaline rush. He shoved his money in and plopped down in a seat.

As the bus trundled away, he could see some Mars lights coming up in the distance. They took a turn toward the el stop.

THIRTY-FIVE

STARVIN' MARVIN WAS one of the very few downtown pimps who were Jewish. Born Marvin Medved in Skokie thirty-eight years ago, he just never settled down to suburban living. Lawns, lawnmowers and in-ground sprinkler systems were not charmin' to Marvin. He now had a stable that kept him in style. It consisted of virtually every ethnic group in the Greater Chicago area. Marvin was an equal-opportunity employer.

Starvin' Marvin had always been thin. Not just thin, skinny. Not just skinny, skin and bones. It was the way he was.

These days, people meeting him for the first time shied away, thinking he had AIDS. But Marvin was perfectly healthy, vigorously healthy, even though he had not been plump since early infancy. He was a five-foot 65-pound seventh grader. He was a six-foot 118-pound high school senior.

And he was now a six-foot 121-pound thirty-eight-year-old pimp in a midnight blue velvet suit with a white brocade vest in a midnight blue Cadillac.

Marvin wanted a Mercedes, but hadn't gotten around to it, what with one thing and another.

Marvin's purpose at this hour of the night, past one A.M., was to see if one of his women was on the job. Unlike a lot of people in his line of work, Marvin did not really enjoy being on the street. Especially this weather. Marvin got cold easily. No fat on his bones.

Of course, the heater in his car was seriously excellent. However. Point was to see if Annette was at the corner. Sometimes these days Annette wasn't where Marvin thought she should be. Either she was doing some work on her own, or she had another man.

Starvin' Marvin knew that getting a lech for one of his own girls was not smart. But what was he supposed to do? Marvin was well aware of the oddity of wanting her to work but not wanting her to have another man. Well, it would be odd to the citizens; in his world, people would understand.

Marvin had taken several slow circles east on Jackson, across State Street, south on Michigan, west on Congress, north on Dearborn and back around again, since he couldn't be sure when Annette would be on the sidewalk. Then he parked near the el stop. She could've gone into a bar. Most hotels would ask a girl to leave if she sat around in their bars too long. Speaking of which, he might have to set up a little fund for a couple of the bartenders, see if he could make things easier all around.

The el train above him braked with an unusually loud shriek of metal. Marvin was surprised when he saw the fat cop come down the el stairs. Starvin' Marvin knew all the cops in the First by sight, he thought. Most of them, he knew

their names. And Aldo Bertolucci worked third watch. If he'd changed, first watch went on two hours ago. Why's Aldo coming to work this late?

Not that it mattered. Some kind of stupid cop emergency.

Marvin looked back toward the corner for Annette and didn't notice that Aldo turned north, which would take him away from the First, not toward it.

THIRTY-SIX

THERE ARE TWENTY-FIVE district police stations in the city of Chicago. The uniformed police officers work out of the districts. They patrol on foot and by car and respond to incidents as requested by their dispatcher throughout their tour. The First District is unique in that it is housed in the same building as the command offices that control the entire police force of the city. The others have separate district stations of their own.

Detectives, however, work out of six area centers. Area One at 5101 South Wentworth covers the First, Twenty-first, Second and Third districts.

When the operator of the elevated train realized he had struck a man, he radioed emergency. The call went into the 911 system and both the paramedics and the police dispatch system were alerted.

Reilly and Fiddleman, the two First District men Aldo expected to catch the call, were sliding along their car's beat, which covered the north part of the First District, when the

call came in and they were sent over to the scene. By this time the EMTs were responding also.

The job of the first uniformed officers on the scene is to find out what's happened, and if it's an unexplained death, shut the scene down, keep everybody out, and call the technicians and detectives.

Fiddleman got up the el stairs faster than Reilly, who was a fat, pink-colored white man of forty-five.

Fiddleman approached the stock-still el train, on which a few dazed night workers sat. He guessed there were maybe six people on the train, at what was now 1:17.

Three of the passengers, as well as the train's engineer, had got out. A middle-aged man in a camel hair jacket was throwing up at the far end of the station, which was only fifteen feet away, not nearly far enough.

An elderly woman, easily seventy-five, wearing carpet slippers with slits cut for her corns despite the cold weather, was looking down at the tracks. Fiddleman was about to take her gently by the shoulders and move her away from the horrible scene when she said, "Christ, and I just had liver for dinner."

Fiddleman hoped she was speaking from some sort of civilian shock. Then he thought in an instant's flash of remorse, how do I know what sort of life she's had, she's here on the el at this hour, this weather? At her age.

Then he looked down at the track and understood what she meant.

He said, "Everybody go back on the train and sit down, please. This won't take long."

The three civilians and the engineer turned around.

"Not you, sir," Fiddleman said to the engineer.

Fiddleman saw Officer Reilly's head slowly appearing up the stairs.

"Hey, Reilly, save yourself a step," Fiddleman said. "Go back and tell the dispatcher to call Area One." The area was five miles away. It would take them a few minutes. "And tell the EMTs there's nothing to hurry up for."

"Thanks a lot," Reilly said.

"And string some barrier tape down there. We don't want a lot of foot traffic up here."

"Traffic? At this hour? I take it we've got a body, hot shot?"

"Yes, we do."

Fiddleman turned back to the track and studied the situation. His primary job was to make sure nobody messed up any evidence. Still and all, you can't help looking. Fiddleman figured he could have been a detective, he just wasn't all that good at taking written exams.

He walked to the very edge of the platform. The body had been rolled as it passed under the cars, but was basically in two pieces. Fiddleman studied the torso, then looked again at the face of the corpse.

"Holy shit!" he said, not believing.

He crouched down and looked closer. An image flashed into his mind—him opening his locker at the district, getting out his stuff. Next to him, Dick-dick slamming his locker door, cocking a grin at him, saying, "Have a nice tour."

"Crappy tour," he had said, but said it smiling. Dick-dick seemed an okay kid.

Fiddleman got hold of his walkie-talkie. Catch the detectives and warn them before they leave the area. Must be something unusual you do in a case like this, even though he wasn't sure what it was. Call the street deputy? Probably.

Like vibrations in water, news that a police officer had been killed spread almost instantly. Once the Area knew about it,

the District knew about it, then the other districts picked up the vibrations.

The spread was not as fast as it might have been if an officer had been killed on duty. But the street deputy was there in minutes, about the same time as the techs, plus a sergeant and lieutenant from the first watch at the First, and some brass from Area One.

It was pretty clear that, not only had Richard Dickenson not been killed on duty, he had not been killed in any job-related incident, like trying to stop a mugging on the el. In fact, it was worse. It looked like he had been drinking to excess and had fallen drunk to the tracks.

Fiddleman, asked the question directly by one of the detectives, admitted that when he went to look at the body he smelled beer and hard liquor, maybe scotch.

"Well, sure, cut him in half like that, it all comes spilling out," the detective said. His name was Ray Moses and he was a very small man. He was the smallest police officer Fiddleman had ever seen.

"Mostly gone now," said Moses' partner, sniffing the air.

"Well, sure. Drip through the tracks. Plus, there's a little breeze."

Fiddleman turned away and waited for instructions, if any.

The first watch sergeant, O'Byrne, called Sergeant Touhy at home to ask who Richard Dickenson would have been hanging around with. She said Figueroa, Bennis, Quail, Mileski and Bertolucci at the Furlough Bar more than likely. She added that Bertolucci was his partner.

"Bertolucci," O'Byrne said, heavy with dismay. "Nick the Bear's brother?"

"Yeah. Sorry about that."

So O'Byrne called Aldo at home. Aldo had been half ex-

pecting the call, told the guy yeah, Dick-dick had been drinking. The sergeant asked Aldo to come in to the Area, tell them what he could. Aldo said hell, why not? He'd never sleep now anyway.

THIRTY-SEVEN

"WELL, YEAH," ALDO said to Detective Ray Moses. "He was a little under the weather."

"*Very* drunk?"

"Well, yeah. Not falling down—I mean, he could walk. He'd had a lot, though," Aldo said, knowing they'd do a blood ethanol, get the alcohol level anyway, so he'd better be as accurate as possible. "Probably four whiskeys and chasers. No, maybe five. That was why I walked him to the train."

"Put him on the train?"

"Naw, just walked him to the stairs."

"Didn't go up with him?"

"No need."

"Why'd you walk him?"

"Well, crossing streets or whatever. You know. I should've got him driven home. But he seemed to be doing all right by then."

"Okay," Moses said, standing up. He stuck out his hand. "Sorry about your partner."

"Yeah." Aldo shook the guy's hand, which was half the size of his, fitted into his as if it was a doll's. Moses had to be under five feet four. Had to have come on, Aldo thought, after they started taking women, dropped the height requirements, all that bullshit.

"Can be tough," Moses said.

"Shit, yeah," Aldo said. "I can hardly believe it. He was just a kid, too, Dick-dick."

"Who?"

"Oh, Dickenson. We called him Dick-dick."

"I see. Thanks for coming in."

Detective Ray Moses reported to his boss at Area One. His boss reported to Deputy Chief Ken Lovici, who was chief of detectives, Field Group B, which was all of the city south of Division. Lovici reported to Deputy Superintendent Charles Withers, who headed the Bureau of Investigation Services, which included the Detective Division, along with Organized Crime, Youth and, for some reason, Auditing.

Charlie Withers was not a fan or a friend of Superintendent Nick Bertolucci, but he knew what he was supposed to do. He went to First Deputy Gus Gimball first thing in the morning and told him that the superintendent's brother's partner had been killed during the night.

"I'll tell the boss," Gimball said. "Anything else?"

"Dickenson was drunk. Aldo Bertolucci seems to have walked him to the el stop."

"It'll be rough on Aldo, then."

"I guess so."

"How long'd they been partners?"

"Oh, ten months on and off, they tell me."

"Okay. Thanks, Charlie. I'll tell the boss."

THIRTY-EIGHT

Sᴇʀɢᴇᴀɴᴛ Pᴀᴛʀɪᴄɪᴀ Tᴏᴜʜʏ "handled" roll call.

She wanted to give the troops a serious lecture on how hanging around in bars until you were too wasted to get home safely didn't look good for the department. However, she thought it would look heartless. And while Touhy already had a reputation for tough-mindedness, which she carefully nurtured and maintained, this would be too much.

"Officer Richard Dickenson is dead," she said. She realized they had all heard about it already; they were whispering when she came in and dead silent after they sat down. But this was how you did things. "He fell in front of an el train. That's all we know so far." Touhy was not into mushy verbiage. Her bald announcement of Dick-dick's death was accompanied among the crew by shuffling feet and glances at Aldo. She said, "Bertolucci, Quail's gonna ride with you tonight. Mileski can go alone."

"That's okay, Sarge," Aldo said. "I'm all right. I'll miss Dick-di—Officer Dickenson, but I don't need anybody."

"Bertolucci!"

"Yes, boss?"

"Quail is riding with you tonight!"

"Yes, sir, ma'am."

Bennis and Figueroa were at most ten minutes out of the CPD lot when Bennis pulled the squad car to the curb.

"All right, Figueroa, what's wrong?"

"What's wrong? Dick-dick is what's wrong!"

"Well, it's sad. It's more than sad. Such a young guy—"

"Norm! You noticed as much as I did—"

"That Dick-dick and Aldo were acting strange? Sure."

"Not just strange. They were acting like Aldo had gotten Dick-dick into something."

"Well, yeah. So?"

"Don't you care?"

"Of course I care, but what's the connection?"

Figueroa was stumped. *Was* there a connection between the sly remarks Dick-dick was making and his death?

"I don't know, Norm. But it's too much of a coincidence that one minute he's talking about coming into money and the next minute he has a peculiar accident."

"How peculiar is it to fall in front of a train if you're wasted?"

"Plenty. *Plenty* peculiar. He wasn't that drunk and he'd been riding that train forever."

"So? You think he was pushed?"

"No, maybe. I don't know—"

"You think Aldo got him into gambling or in with some rough people?"

"Suppose Aldo and he gambled, and he won. That was why he had money. Then he gambled more and he lost and wouldn't pay?"

"Nope. Not enough time. He was all high about having money last night after work. Walked out of the Furlough and fell in front of the train. When could he've lost the money?"

"Oh. You're right. But Norm, there's something else."

"Well, what? Come on, this is your buddy here."

"His car was in the lot."

"Dick-dick's car?"

"No, Aldo's. When I went to get mine. They'd been long gone by then. Aldo said he'd walk Dick-dick to the train because his car was in the shop."

"That's right," Bennis said slowly. "I remember."

"So he lied."

"Shit." Bennis was silent a few seconds. "Not necessarily. Aldo was putting away a lot of beer. Maybe he just forgot."

In the old days, if an officer's partner was killed, the officer was expected to just plain tough it out. "Be a man" about it. Gradually, it got obvious that having a seriously stressed-out officer on the street did nobody any good, least of all the department. Police officers whose partners had been killed on the job got sent to counseling whether they thought they had a problem or not. Nowadays even if your partner died off the job, you knew you could go to counseling if you wanted to.

If you showed any signs of acting weird, your supervisor would send you to counseling whether you liked it or not.

And not everybody liked it. In fact, some fought it. Especially because if your partner was killed on the job—shot, for instance—you could be taken off the street for a specified period of time, put at a desk or whatever. And while some officers lusted for a desk more than sex, others did not want to leave the street for the whole remainder of their natural lives.

The Furlough gang saw Aldo this way. So that night when they all got to the bar and Mileski asked if he was going in for counseling, nobody was surprised when Aldo said, "I ain't goin' to no shrink."

"It's not a shrink, my man," Norm Bennis said. "It's a counselor."

"A counselor is a shrink."

"A shrink is a psychiatrist. A psychiatrist is an MD. The counselor is a psychologist. They aren't MDs."

"Hey, why do you know so much?" Aldo asked.

"Well, it's true."

"Don't matter," he said. "I'm not goin'."

The Furlough gang figured Aldo was toughing it out. Mileski said in a whisper to Suze at one point while Aldo

was in the john, "Two days ago, Aldo was sayin' he couldn't ride without his little buddy."

"Yeah, they did seem to be getting along lately." She didn't know whether to tell Mileski about the car. She didn't know whether to tell the detectives. Tell on a fellow cop?

Aldo and Dick-dick had both seemed happier. Suze admitted that. But thinking about it, wasn't that last week? This week Aldo and Dick-dick had moved into a weird kind of third stage in their relationship, something that included an element of caution on both sides. Of course, that wasn't utterly unheard of. Odd couples got paired up in squad cars all the time and just had to work things out. There weren't many other jobs like this, where you spent maybe eight hours a day in the company of one other person, in a closed space, and where on top of all that, you occasionally had to defend the other guy against attack. It was no wonder if relationships got explosive.

But she was terribly afraid that wasn't it. Aldo walked Dick-dick from the bar. Aldo was not a helpful character. Aldo's car was in the CPD lot. Why didn't Aldo drive Dick-dick home, if he wanted to be so helpful? Why didn't Aldo drive himself home?

The memorial service was tomorrow, after which Dick-dick's body was going to be shipped back to Iowa.

THIRTY-NINE

IN THE MORNING Aldo went out and bought a fresh pack of Polaroid film. He went from the film place to a store that sold home computers, typewriters with memories, laptops

and other stuff. It was crowded. A salesman came by, but Aldo barked at him that he was just looking and the man went on to greener pastures.

Aldo took a manila envelope out of his pocket. He was wearing gloves, which was not too noticeable, since it looked like snow today anyhow.

He took a white envelope out of the big manila envelope and rolled it into one of the typewriters on the display shelf. On the front he typed:

First Deputy Superintendent Gus Gimball
Department of Police
1121 S. State St.
Chicago, IL 60605

Personal and Confidential

Then he put the white envelope back in the manila envelope and left the store.

He stopped at a copy place, took the gun issue form, the photomicrographs of the striations on the pellet and the test pellet, the gun registration and the autopsy report, and photocopied them.

Back home in his study, he laid the nickel-plated Colt .38 revolver and the spent pellet in its plastic envelope on a sheet from the *Chicago Sun-Times*, fed the pack of film into the Polaroid camera his son had gotten for Christmas in 1979 and only used for two weeks, and photographed them. Patiently, he sat there and watched the image appear—beautiful, he thought, like the sun coming up on a new day.

Still wearing his gloves, he put the photograph and the copies into the white envelope.

He sealed it using a wad of toilet paper and water from the sink, because he knew they could blood-type saliva. Even

DNA if they wanted to spend the money on the test. He used the wet wad of paper on the stamp, too.

Aldo had given everything a lot of thought. He was a year and a quarter to pension. If the department found out he'd burgled the Personnel files, he'd be out, in which case he'd lose his pension. Aldo had no savings. If he lost his pension, he'd lose his house. Also his wife, probably, which might or might not be such a bad thing, but with community property she'd get half of whatever pittance the house netted out as.

Basically, he'd be ruined.

He'd thought about waiting a year and a half before sending the stuff to Gimball. Thought about it, but never seriously. He couldn't have borne waiting that long for his revenge. Couldn't. It would eat him up and kill him in six months, sitting on it and not using it.

Which was basically why Dick-dick had to die. Dumb shit. Keep his mouth shut, no problem. Some people just didn't know what was good for them. And whatever came to them was their own fault.

He was sure they couldn't get him for Dick-dick's death. Guy was drunk. Plus, there was no motive. Enough said.

Aldo had considered sending the evidence to the media. They'd eat it for breakfast, lunch and dinner. But that kind of publicity—after all, it would splash all over him and Monica and his mother and his children. He could be generous, couldn't he? If and only if he got what he wanted. As long as Nick lost the thing he loved most. Aldo believed himself to be a street-smart, savvy kind of guy who knew how the world worked. But not a bad guy. Why not be able to think well of himself?

As it was now, Gimball would probably think that old Nico had kept all this material together all these years. Gimball might have doubts about the gun registration, because he

knew the way the department operated, and would realize that the shooting had never got to the level of becoming a case. But even if he wondered if the gun registration had been in the CPD files, he couldn't prove that it had.

He'd know that whoever sent the stuff was somebody who hated the Bertoluccis, and with old Nico being the kind of guy he was, there had to be a lot of haters out there.

Gimball would know immediately that the stuff was genuine.

Aldo put all the stuff away in his locked box. Then he posted the envelope at a place five miles away from his house, on his way to work.

FORTY

NORM AND SUZE started their tour peacefully. It was cold, eighteen degrees but no sign of snow. About five hours into things, after they'd eaten eight P.M. "lunch," the heater quit. They called the dispatcher, asking to go into the District, but he wanted them to stay on the street.

Norm said, "I need hot coffee. Get on the air and see if we can take ten minutes."

"Good idea," Suze said. "I'd like to talk with you. Quietly."

" 'Bout what?"

"What we're gonna do." Stanley Mileski, Aldo Bertolucci, Hiram Quail, Norm Bennis and Suze Figueroa had gone to the memorial service for Dick-dick and then the Mexican place on East Chestnut for lunch. Suze had studied

Aldo, not letting him see, but just being aware of his facial expressions and body language.

"Norm, I watched Aldo today. This is not a man who's saddened by the death of his partner. There's more spring in his spine than I've seen before, ever."

Norm nodded. "Yeah, I saw that too."

"Aldo is energized. Aldo—believe it or not—is happy. Suddenly, Aldo is acting like a man with a future."

"So?"

"So, do I tell the detectives?"

Suze reached for the mike to tell the dispatcher they were taking a coffee break. Before she could touch it, the radio said, *"One thirty-three."*

Norm said, "Oh, hell."

Suze answered, "Thirty-three."

"See the man at 1703 West Polk regarding, um, suspicions about the tenant in apartment thirty-one."

"Did they say what kind of suspicions?"

"No. The janitor and the landlord are both there, in the lobby, he said. Caller was the janitor, and they don't want to enter the apartment without a PO there. They're suspicious."

"Oh. Ten four, squad."

The long, drab brick building was four stories, looked like twelve apartments per floor. There were two men standing in the lobby, one in overalls and one in a three-piece suit.

"Thanks for coming," the suit said, as if he had doubted they would and was pleasantly, if grudgingly, surprised.

Suze said, "What seems to be the trouble?"

The man in overalls answered, but addressed his remarks to Bennis. Suze was accustomed to this. A lot of people figured the woman on a team is some sort of secretary in uniform.

"Lemme show you," the man said.

Suze said to the suit, "You're the owner?"

The man nodded.

"Do you live here?"

"No," the landlord said, as if she were nuts. Why would he live in this dive?

"How do you happen to be here?"

"Mr. Feenstra called me."

"What makes you think there's a problem?"

"Um," Feenstra said. He had a way with words.

"All right," Bennis said. "Show us."

The building had been built the height it was because any higher and the city code would have required elevators, so they trooped up the ill-lit stairs single file. Feenstra led, followed by Figueroa, then Bennis, then the suit. They trooped down a tan hall with a cocoa brown carpet until Feenstra stopped at a door, causing Norm and Suze to come to an abrupt halt. The suit had already stopped several feet back in the hall.

"There," Feenstra said.

Bennis and Suze stooped down to look. There was a small pool of glistening dark stuff seeping out from under the door. Norm and Suze exchanged glances. It surely looked a helluva lot like blood.

"She's been fighting with the husband," Feenstra said. "About another guy. For weeks. Haven't seen her the last two days, though."

Bennis nodded. He knocked hard on the door. The sound made both Feenstra and the landlord jump. No response from inside the apartment. Suze said to Feenstra, "Open the door."

Feenstra took out a string of keys and unlocked the door. After this, he backed up.

Bennis turned the knob. He stepped in, Suze after him,

both careful not to step in the fluid. "Wait out here," he said to the men in the hall, unnecessarily—they were already backing away. Suze closed the door.

Protect the scene. Just in case.

All the lights were on in the apartment. There was some strange shiny bluish blackish long stuff and a piece of paper on the floor of the hall. Suze saw what she was looking at perfectly clearly, but it didn't exactly register on her mind. Bennis's mind either. He said "What's that?"

They stooped and stared at a piece of paper, not touching it. It said, "You wanted her—you find her."

There was a pool of blood and body fluids and the piece of paper near the door. Leading away from them was a trail of—that strange stuff. Bennis and Suze stepped carefully, following it.

The entryway was short, maybe four feet, and the thing followed it, then turned right, past a living room door. What was it? Twisted rope? No. Like sausage, Suze thought, knowing there was something wrong with that idea.

In the next second she realized what the rope was and gagged. Christ! Oh god! She was not going to throw up here and foul up the evidence, she thought. She'd strangle first. She faintly heard Bennis gasp and knew he had realized what it was at about the same time.

The trail was ten feet of large intestine, which they followed around the bend, where it became small intestine, going down a hall past the living room and kitchen doors. The hall had to be twelve feet long or so.

"We shouldn't go in," Bennis said in a rasping voice.

"We're supposed to find out if they're dead first."

"Are you kidding?" he giggled nervously, then caught himself.

"We're supposed to check," she insisted.

The trail of intestine led around into a bedroom off the

hall on the left. Careful not to touch anything or step on anything but the apparently bare floor, they turned the corner.

The body was sprawled on its back. It was a woman, naked, with a severely bruised face. Her abdomen lay open from pubis to breastbone. The last part of the intestine was still attached, disappeared, in fact, into a pool of fluids in her belly and probably ended at her stomach, where it was supposed to.

Suze groaned.

"That dead enough for you?" Bennis asked.

It was right then that they realized they were holding hands.

"Jeez," he said.

"Let's shut it down and get on the air."

FORTY-ONE

"CHRIST!" SAID BENNIS to the guys at the bar. "He'd left it—the body—perp was probably the husband, near as anybody knows now—he'd left it like a treasure hunt."

"No," Figueroa said, "like a maze. One of those things where you follow around the bends with your pencil to get to the prize. 'You wanted her, you find her.' " Her voice sounded hollow.

"If he couldn't have her, nobody would. That kind of thing," Bennis said.

"How many feet of intestine does a person have?" Mileski asked. Everybody made retching noises.

"Eight or ten feet of large, twenty-five feet of small," Bennis said.

Quail said, "How come you know so much?"

"On-the-job training, my man."

Suze said, "Jeez, Bennis!"

"Then again," Hiram Quail said, "Aldo here has a good thirty feet of large, hundred feet of small."

"Hey," Aldo growled. "Someday you too'll be old and fat."

"You haven't said much, Aldo," Suze said.

"Ah, hell," Aldo said.

Suze was well aware that Aldo didn't like her. She wasn't especially put off by it. Aldo was known to hate Hispanics, blacks, women, Asians, the rich, the poor, lawyers, doctors, and particularly intellectuals. Everything considered, she thought, being hated by Aldo put her in good company.

Tonight, though, she wasn't interested in company. The tour had been too much. After a couple of minutes more, during which Aldo and Quail said they'd gone back to that Mexican restaurant where they'd eaten after the memorial service, had a nice wet burrito, big as your head, she realized she was weary and sad. She said, "Well, I'm outta here."

There was a chorus of farewells, of which Aldo's voice was not one. Norm Bennis walked her to the door.

"You okay?" he asked.

"Oh sure. All in a day's work, huh? You okay?"

"Yeah. Hell, I like people with guts."

But he wasn't really okay. He joked about it like they all did, but Suze could hear the tension in the lack of timbre in his voice.

Bennis punched her on the arm. She punched him back and went out the door.

When she got home, she realized it had been a couple of

hours since she had thought about Dick-dick. She'd meant to go by the el stop where he died, too, just to see if she could turn up a witness. Maybe resolve her doubts. She'd really meant to. But not tonight.

FORTY-TWO

AT THE FURLOUGH, Aldo still wasn't talking.

Quail said, "Hey, c'mon, Aldo. Cheer up."

Thinking he would test Aldo, Bennis said, "Being sad's not gonna bring ol' Dick-dick back, Aldo."

"Yeah. Time marches on and all that crap."

Aldo said, "Leave me alone," at which point he farted.

"Shit!" Hiram Quail said. "Aldo, did you have to do that?"

Bennis said, "No problem, my man. Pure methane. Harness it and you could light and power the city."

Mileski said, "Hey, Aldo! You ever light a fart?"

"Get lost."

"No. I'm not kidding."

"You can't light a fart."

Bennis said, "Sure you can. Like I said, it's methane. Like swamp gas."

"What makes you know so much?"

Mileski said, "He's right. It's like sewer gas."

Quail said, "Well, gee, that surely makes some sense, don't it?"

Aldo said, "I still don't think you can do it."

"Hey whaddya think, Mort," Mileski said. "I mean bartenders know everything, don't they?"

"What?"

"Can you light a fart?"

"How should I know. Want another beer?"

"Yes."

Bennis said, "No, he's had enough. Let's try it."

Mort said, "Well, you're not going to try it in here!"

"Didn't say we were, my man." Bennis stood up.

"Hey! It's orange!"

Bennis, who was lighting Aldo, said, "Why isn't it blue, like a gas stove?"

Quail said, "Contaminants."

Aldo said, "You watch your mouth."

"I'm watching your ass," Quail said.

"Here goes another one."

Bennis held up the Bic lighter.

"Wow!" everybody said.

The back room at the Furlough was full of cases of beer. There were a couple of old wooden kegs, empty, and a couple of new aluminum kegs, full, that Quail and Mileski were using as seats.

Mileski said, "My turn."

He had his pants around his knees, said "okay," and Quail came up to hold the lighter because Bennis wanted to quit for a while, saying it was "intensive work."

Mileski was all ready to go, when he straightened up suddenly.

"Wait! Wait!" Mileski screamed and started hopping away across the floor, with his pants around his ankles.

"Wassa matter?" Quail demanded, hurt.

"Don't do it!"

"Listen, I'm not gonna singe you. This is Mister Careful, here."

"No, it ain't that," Mileski said, standing in the far corner, trying to get his pants back up.

"What then?"

"Jeez. I'm fulla gas, Hiram."

"So? That's the point."

"Hey, no. I'm serious. Suppose you light me and it goes all the way inside and I *blow up!*"

Hiram Quail fell all over laughing. So did Aldo and Norm Bennis. "Hey, that can't happen," Quail said.

"Sure it can't, you moron," Aldo said.

"How do you know?"

That stopped them.

So Bennis gave it a try instead of Mileski.

"That was yellow, not orange," Aldo said.

"No, it was yellow-orange."

"Cadmium yellow medium," Mileski said.

"How do you know that?"

Mileski suddenly realized that he knew it because cadmium yellow was one of the colors he and his wife used for touch-ups in their china-mending business and he didn't want to talk about that. Somebody who was going to be nicknamed Iron Balls someday had to be careful.

"I don't know, but I like the orange ones," Mileski said.

Bennis said, "No, the lighter the color the purer the gas."

"Oh. That's probably true."

Quail said, "It's the longest flame that really counts, though."

Mileski said, "We've got to figure out a way to quantify this. Yeah. Otherwise you can't tell who's best."

Aldo said, "Hey, you're being too competitive."

"Oh, yeah?"

"You Poles are too competitive."

"Oh, yeah? Well, I'm not. I'm the absolutely least competitive person I know."

Bennis laughed. "We gotta direct the flame. Maybe straws," he said.

"Straw burns."

"Not that kind of straw. The kind you drink out of."

"Oh, *right.* That's not a bad idea."

FORTY-THREE

AT ROLL CALL next day, Norm Bennis leaned over to Mileski and whispered, "I just figured it out."

"What?"

"Tiparillos!"

"What?"

"Just the tip, naturally."

Suze Figueroa leaned over from his other side. "What are you talking about?"

"Nothing. But Suze, my man, I don't think Aldo's a killer."

"How would you know?"

"Character study. Shows no guilt."

It was the afternoon for Commander Darryl "Come-Again" Coumadin's weekly inspirational visit with his troops. Lieutenant Sheehan lounged near the flag in slim fighting trim, barbered and tailored and muscle-toned. Sergeant Touhy was just starting to read some crimes, when Coumadin himself burst into the roll call room twenty minutes early.

His face was flushed. His wattles wiggled back and forth. His jowls jiggled. His dewlaps danced. His beady little eyes protruded from under shaggy white eyebrows that undulated like hairy white caterpillars.

"Hey!" he said.

Sergeant Touhy stopped talking. Lieutenant Sheehan froze and looked blank. The rest of them watched with bright interest.

"Commander—" Touhy began.

"This district is dirty!" Coumadin said. His white shirt pouched out over his pants. His belly was hopping up and down in rage.

"What?" Touhy said involuntarily.

"This district is dirty!"

"Sir!" Sheehan said calmly—he was proud of always being calm in any crisis whatsoever—"Sir! There's been no hint at all of such a thing."

"We haven't had any suggestion of any unprofessional behavior on the part of any officer," Touhy said, thinking that this was not the kind of thing you talked over in front of the troops. You discussed it privately first—

"Or any payoffs," Sheehan said.

"I'm not talking about that," Coumadin said, growing purpler in the face. His nose was the color of a ripe plum. "Payoffs! Shit! I'm talking dirty!"

"Sir?" said Touhy. In her career she had learned a hundred inflections to put on the word. This one was "You'd better explain," with a light sprinkling of "You're the boss."

"*Dirty!*" he screamed. "I'm talking about the district station! The district! Dirty! Dirty! Dirty! Stinking! Unclean! This is a disgrace! Come in here a minute."

Coumadin charged back to his private office, trailed by Sheehan, then Touhy, then as many of the officers as could fit through the door, Mileski, Quail, Bennis, Bertolucci and

Figueroa included, all jammed in the doorway like olives in a jar.

"Smell this, goddammit!" Coumadin shrieked.

They sniffed the air. Sniffed again.

"Oh," Touhy said.

"Yes, sir," Sheehan said. "That surely smells bad."

"What do you suppose it is?" Bennis asked innocently, not catching Figueroa's eye.

"Peeyoooey!" Mileski said.

Suze whispered in Bennis's ear, "I think he smells a rat."

"That's strange," Touhy said. "This is the only room that smells this way."

"Well, get the janitors! Get the maintenance people! Get the Property Management Division!"

"That's Commander—"

"Get the chief operating engineer! And do it now! This is a disgrace!"

"Yes, sir," Touhy said, grimly. She turned and saw the First District officers crowding around her rear.

"And you people hit the bricks and clear! Out!"

That night in the Furlough's back room, Bennis said, "Okay, now, we got length of flame, color, and predictability. Okay?"

Quail and Mileski said okay. Mileski said they oughta have odor suppression, but nobody took him up on it.

"Light me," Aldo said.

Bennis got out the Bic and lit up. Aldo took off.

"Wow!"

"Not too bad!"

Bennis, Quail and Mileski flipped their notepads.

"9.1"

"8.7"

"9.4"

"Well, let's see," said Bennis, taking out his pocket cal-

culator. "That gives you a total averaged score of 9.066, best so far."

Quail said, "Next nearest score is Norm Bennis with an 8.95 lifetime achievement total."

Bennis said, "I've been highest in predictability."

"Well, I," Quail said grandly, "actually achieved a light lemon yellow."

FORTY-FOUR

GUS GIMBALL DROPPED the envelope he was holding, jumped up from his desk, ran to the wall and slammed his fist into it as hard as he could.

"Aaaaah!" he gasped with the pain, yelled "Shit!" and fell back into his chair. There were four knuckle dents in the wall paneling.

By then his ADS and secretary were falling through the door.

"Are you all right?"

"What happened?"

"Are you hurt?"

"I'm fucking great! Leave! Close the goddamn door!"

They didn't move at first. Gimball rarely swore. There were some serious swearers in the department, some world-class cussers. Gimball was a nonswearer. He was a semilapsed Baptist, and he definitely tried to control his swearing. He almost never lost his temper. They stood staring a couple of seconds.

"Close your mouths! You look like fucking fish!" Gimball

yelled. They backed out and pulled the door closed as gently as if it were nitroglycerin.

Gimball reached for a glass of water he had on the desk and poured some over his knuckles to cool them. He grabbed a batch of tissues and patted at the water. Then he left the wet tissues in place on his hand while he sat back down, breathing hard. His hand throbbed. He was just as glad that it did; the pain distracted him somewhat.

It was early afternoon. On his desk was the day's mail, and in the middle of it an envelope he had just opened marked *Personal and Confidential.* His aide knew he dealt with these himself. Gus figured it was the honorable thing to do.

Gimball got a manila folder out of his bottom drawer and opened it out flat on the desk with his uninjured left hand. The folder flopped closed again. He threw the wad of wet tissues into the wastebasket, where it made a dead plop. Then he flattened the folder with both hands.

He had opened the envelope in the same way he opened any others, without particular regard for fingerprints, Gimball now took the first sheet carefully by the tip of the upper right corner and lifted it onto the manila folder.

It was the photocopy of the registration to Nicholas Bertolucci in March 1968 of a .38 Colt revolver, serial number 76L2702.

Then Gus took hold of the Polaroid by the outside margins and shifted it also to the folder. It was a picture of a nickel-plated Colt revolver. He wondered whether there was enough detail so that he could bring up the serial numbers with a magnifying glass. But he was pretty sure it wasn't necessary.

Next he shifted the autopsy report into the folder. Shana Boyd. He'd known the name instantly, before he even read the date. Good God!

And the photomicrographs and ballistics report. As icing on the cake.

For just a few seconds Gimball toyed with the idea that they were all forgeries. After all, these were only photo copies of the real papers. There was no way to examine the quality of the originals themselves. Judge how old they were, for example. Or compare the paper quality to the paper the department used in 1968. Or check the actual signatures of the pathologist or ballistics man against their known signatures.

But this really was just wishful thinking. Looking at the documents, his years as a detective stood behind him and laughed in his ear: "Forgeries, Gus? Are you kidding?"

If somebody forged these, he was the Wehrmacht's all-time forger, kept in a bunker under Berlin all these years practicing his craft. Nobody could duplicate the headings, the department forms, the crabbed style of filling in the documents, the bad typewriters, the misspellings. These were forms they hadn't used in fifteen years or more; the formsets were much more detailed now. These leaped out at him from memories two decades old. Nobody could know this stuff—

—except somebody in the department! Holy *shit!*

Somebody who wanted to get rid of Bertolucci, who detested Bertolucci, who would wait with this shit until the time seemed ripe. Somebody who could step in and pick up all the chips?

Bradley Heidema or Charles Withers? Not Riggs. He didn't have the brains.

Neither Heidema nor Withers was an idiot. They did not drive out of the yard without all four wheels on the car.

Gus thought about the cruelty of Heidema or Withers sending this material to him, knowing he was Nick's friend. Or maybe that was the reason. The friend of my enemy is my enemy. Nick should have transferred Withers and Heidema

when he took over from Enrique Lopez. It made no sense to keep people on who would be after your scalp, however well they did their jobs.

Heidema or Withers? Which one would have had the balls to do this? At first blush, Withers. He was less hide-bound than Heidema. Less cautious. But then, Heidema? — Gus had always felt that the man was sneaky.

Christ, what a goddamn mess this was going to be!

And finally, after all the other emotional underbrush had been cleared away in his mind, Gus Gimball faced the basic problem. His friend Nick had shot a girl. And then covered up, or permitted a coverup.

If he had known about it at all.

Was Bertolucci a closet racist? Had he been eager to go along on the raid? Or did his father force the assignment on him? Practically everybody else involved in that raid was either retired now, quit, transferred, had gone to prison on some other deal, or had died. Nick Bertolucci was one of the few left, which made sense because he had to have been one of the youngest men involved. But he had been the one to go on to a major career.

He had become superintendent.

And hidden his secret for twenty-two years?

FORTY-FIVE

GUS'S WIFE HAD made Hungarian goulash, with the lumpy potato noodles he loved. And she'd made French bread in little loaves no longer than six or seven inches. He'd gotten her a bread machine for Christmas a year ago and it had turned

out to be more his present than hers, because she made him special breads all the time. The machine would mix, knead, raise and bake, but Raina didn't like the shape it baked the bread in, sort of a squared column, so she took it out as dough, shaped it and let it rise again, and baked it in the oven instead.

"I guess really I like to play with dough," she had laughed.

And now with all this, plus sweet butter for the bread and salad with his favorite bleu cheese dressing, he couldn't eat.

Raina watched him. It was a second marriage for both of them, and she knew enough to give him space.

"You want some coffee, Gus?" she asked.

"Sure. Yeah. Listen, this was delicious."

"I know." She smiled. "*I* enjoyed it a lot."

When he took the coffee pot from her, she said, "Your hand is trembling again."

"I didn't know you noticed."

"Oh, Gus!"

Soon they'd have to talk about that too, what the doctor had said. But right now he couldn't. Wait until after his appointment, when there was something definite to say. When he was really sure there was something wrong.

Gimball was in no mood for a departmental crisis, even one of normal proportions. He had spent the morning at his doctor's office. Dr. Engleman had given him a full exam, all the ordinary stuff, blood pressure, listening to his heart and lungs, staring into his eyes. He seemed to spend a little more time than usual on the knee tapping and running spiked wheels up and down the bottoms of his feet.

Mainly he asked him questions.

"I notice you stoop forward a little, Mr. Gimball. Is that recent?"

"No, Dr. Engleman. People have told me I looked scholarly since I was twelve."

"Do you ever find yourself making motions like this with your hands? As if you were rolling pills?"

"I don't think so."

"Do you notice more trembling in your hand when you're feeling emotional? Embarrassed, maybe?"

"I don't get embarrassed."

"Well, when does it seem most severe?"

"Oh, maybe when I'm tense or worried. That's probably what it is, just tension."

"Does your wife say your hand trembling disappears when you're asleep?"

"I don't think she's noticed it at all."

Finally Engleman said he wanted Gus to fast from midnight tonight. Come in on the way to work and leave a urine specimen, let the nurse take a blood sample. Come back in a week. He'd have the results, and they'd see if there was any change in the symptoms.

"What do you think's wrong?"

"Let's not rush here. It may be nothing. Let's get these tests done, and meanwhile you try not to worry. Leave it to me."

Very jovial. Gus wanted to scream at him.

Tell Raina when he was really sure something was wrong? Really sure? As opposed to just *plain* sure, which was what he was already? How slyly the mind evaded bad news. All his life Gus had been fascinated with the way his mind worked, had always felt he was standing a bit outside himself, watching. He was considered by the department to be a person of wisdom, not just knowledge, and that was in large part the result of his ability to step back.

Now he felt anything but calm. He felt like demanding,

panicky, of Raina, "Will you take care of me no matter what? Whatever happens?"

He'd been feeling slow-witted lately. Was it illness or worry about the illness? If he were to lose his mental edge, start getting vague, then be unable to walk, maybe unable to talk, what then? If he was dying, paralyzed . . .

And now the trouble with Nick.

Gus's thoughts went back to what he should do about those papers. Wait, maybe. Ask Nick about the Panther raid, or hint to him and see what came out. Also look into the records himself, see what had really happened.

Was this a cowardly approach? Was it, maybe, triggered by his health problems?

No. He owed Nick at the very least the chance to explain. And some careful thought.

He'd pull Heidema's and Withers' files, too. Look at their backgrounds. See if he could tell who was doing this.

Gus had another cup of coffee, which only made his hand shake worse, and now probably he wouldn't sleep, either. Although how was he gonna sleep, anyway?

Shit happens. Well, sure.

But this was more shit than usual. This stuff was dynamite. It would blow open the department if it got out. Nick had deserved the job, but it would look like the old boys, old Nico and his cronies, had set it up, kept the dynasty going, and with old Nico's crummy record on civil rights—shit, it would look terrible. The *superintendent* had killed a black girl during an illegal raid.

It would cause a megaton explosion. This had the potential to make the department look like dirt, like the old days. It could not only bring Nick down, but determine the mayoral election.

There were three or four reporters in the city who would

give both balls to get their hands on this. Their careers would be set for life.

And then it hit him that whoever had sent him the material on Nick probably counted on Gus' specific position in the department. As first dep he was second-in-command. He was the obvious successor to Nick. If Nick stepped down suddenly, ill health, accident, scandal, whatever, it was almost certain that Gus would take over as acting super while everybody started gearing up for a political power struggle for the job. Give them time.

And would Withers or Heidema figure they would eventually win? That the mayor would eventually pick one of them, not Gus?

Well, sure. He had never been political. He had no power base. Didn't want one. He had no taste for politics. He could hold the job a few weeks while the mayoral election was run, then Heidema or Withers could take over. Perfect. Much quicker than getting rid of Bertolucci politically, the way things were going, Bertolucci being as popular as he was.

And they'd counted on him wanting it. God damn! They'd counted on him being so hungry to be superintendent that he'd use this to shoot Nick down and make himself acting super and smooth out the road for one of them!

Raina came in for the coffee pot just then and gasped when she saw his face.

"What's the matter!"

He came out of a half fog. "Department crisis," he said in the tone of voice that always made her decide to let him alone.

When she was gone again, he thought, I don't have to fall for it. If I don't move for a while, it should throw them off. Bury it? There's not much time.

Or could they say I was covering up? I can move forward

quietly, and still leave a paper trail if I need to prove later that I wasn't sitting on my ass. Then there's no way either Heidema or Withers could claim later that I was covering up.

The phone rang. Gus picked up before Raina could get to it.

"First Deputy?" The voice was speaking in a rasping whisper.

"Who is this?" Gimball said.

"You don't need to know that. Did you get my package?"

"What package was that?"

"Oh, come on, First Dep. The one with the Xeroxes and the nice Polaroid of the gun. You'll have to answer me, or we can't talk about how we're going to handle this."

Did the whisper sound like Heidema's voice? Or Withers'? Gus couldn't tell. Do whispers sound like the real voices? He said, "Tell me what you want. Money?"

"If I'd wanted money I'd've gone to Nick."

"Then what?"

"I want Nick Bertolucci fired!"

"Why? Who is this?" Gimball wished he had a recording device on his phone. Voice-print the man.

"Don't play dumb, First Dep! I'm going to give you one week. That's seven days, and I mean it! One week. You can fire him your way, in-house, if you want. If he's not out in seven days, I'm going to the papers. And television."

"What makes you think they'd use it?"

"Don't bullshit. The Panther raid was the biggest scandal the department and the State's Attorney's Office ever had. Basically, we're saying that the superintendent killed a young black woman in cold blood, during a murderous, illegal raid, and covered it up for twenty years! How's the black community going to like having a man like that as superintendent, huh, Gimball?"

"A week is too short. I have to check out—"

"You have to check out nothing! You know this stuff's real! You've got a major scandal here, Gimball. Don't fart around!"

"Why are you doing this?"

"Revenge, Gimball. One week."

The phone went dead.

FORTY-SIX

FIRST THING IN the morning, Gus Gimball had his ADS order a tap on his home phone with a recording device, and a call location identifier to read out the number the call was coming from. At very least, if the man telephoned again, he'd know where he was, plus have a chance to voice-print him. And he was sure he'd call again. He'd call to ask what Gimball was doing, or he'd call to gloat.

The fact that he had phoned Gimball's home was additional proof that it was somebody like Heidema or Withers. Police officers' phone numbers are not in the Chicago telephone directory. And a civilian can't get them just by calling the department. The topcops' numbers were even more carefully guarded. A police officer could probably get the number, particularly if he'd worked in Ad Services someplace, or Communications, but that limited it a lot.

Would Heidema or Withers shoot Nick down at the cost of making the department look like shit? Gimball hoped to hell not. But they might figure they could keep the shit inhouse and out of the papers. A private kind of court-martial. Force Nick out. Blackmail him out.

Mayor Wallace?

By now Mayor Wallace knew Nick opposed his reelection. And of course he could get Gimball's home phone. Would Mayor Wallace blackmail Bertolucci into resigning? Could Chicago politics get as dirty as that? Is Lake Michigan wet?

Still, if Wallace knew Bertolucci was going to back Atkinson, and if Wallace had this material on Bertolucci, it would make more sense to blackmail Nick into supporting him. Christ, with this shit on Bertolucci he'd think he could get the superintendent to give campaign speeches for him all over Chicago! To which, Gus thought, Bertolucci would say screw you, Wallace.

But Wallace wouldn't know that. Politicians usually figured everybody wanted to be a politician but just wasn't smart enough to get elected.

Gimball was working against time. He was also working against dread of the moment when he would have to ask Nick to explain. Which was not yet. He didn't know enough. For now he'd just have to stand the pain alone.

At the morning topcops' meeting he kept quiet and watched Withers and Heidema. He was certain he did it undetectably. Really, he was watching to see whether they were watching *him*. Whoever had talked to him last night would want to see how he reacted and whether he suspected anybody.

He couldn't see anything different.

After the meeting, he sent his secretary, Elaine, to get Heidema's and Withers' personnel jackets. Since he couldn't count on word of this not getting back to them, Gimball asked her for the files on everybody from commander level on up.

He wanted to find out whether Heidema or Withers had been on the department at the time of the Hampton raid. If so, they might have direct knowledge.

Withers turned out to have been on the department

seven years in December 1969. He'd spent a year in the long
course in police science at Northwestern and by 1969 was a
sergeant. But in that specific month, December, he had been
in the Fourteenth District, Shakespeare, as a sergeant on the
first watch.

Heidema was a detective in Area 2, which occupied the
same building as the Fifth District, Pullman. There was no
job-related connection to Shana Boyd.

Then it occurred to Gimball that Withers might have
been related to one of the men killed in the raid. Or one of
the others who was injured. Or even to Shana Boyd. He
knew who could find that out, might know it right off the top
of his head—the pastor of Gimball's brother's Baptist church
on Jeffrey. Hoppy Hopkins knew absolutely everybody.

But it was also a hole without a rabbit. "No, I know the
Withers," Reverend Hopkins said, "but they don't have any
relatives in town. The whole family moved here from Mis-
souri. About 1955."

So much for connections. What about the evidence?
Heidema and Withers had the best chance to get hold of the
data. As deputy superintendent of the Bureau of Technical
Services, Bradley Heidema was boss of the crime lab. Heidema would have free access to any damn thing he wanted.
Who was going to stop him if he wanted to rummage
through bins of old evidence? This stuff—the gun itself and
the ballistics report—may have been buried there for twenty
years. Maybe Heidema stumbled on it through sheer dumb
luck while he was working on something else.

Withers was deputy superintendent of the Bureau of Investigative Services. The Detective Division was under his
command. At the time the Panther raid was investigated—or
whitewashed, whichever—the Detective Division, probably
asked for the autopsy report. Which could have lain around
for decades.

The paper registering the gun to Nick was a little different. It would have been in personnel files at the time of the Panther raid. Now it would be in retired personnel files. Access to these was not casual.

The facts about the Panther raid were key. Gus was going to have to find out what Nick's real complicity was. The investigation into the raid was so screwed up, and so much of the evidence was lost or hidden, that it was possible Nick himself wasn't sure what had happened. Ultimately, he owed it to Nick to ask him for his own version of the facts. But temporarily, he could probe subtly.

Gus called Nick's office, looking for him, and got his ADS, Lester Grimes.

"He's showing somebody Communications," Lester said.

It had to be a heavy somebody, for Nick to be doing it in person. Gus charged out of his office and took the elevator to Communications.

The central core of the entire sixth floor at 1121 South State is the communications room. Around it runs an exterior corridor, which surrounds it on all four sides. The entire communications pool is glassed in, separating it from the corridor that surrounds it. The glass keeps out stray noise and stray people. The definition of stray people does not include the superintendent of police with Alderman Elmer Atkinson in tow.

There are no windows in the communications area. The dispatchers' eyes are on lighted boards, representing the districts they cover. In some areas, there are extra lighted boards, which are aerial maps of parks. These are extremely detailed because of the difficulty of describing park areas clearly to officers chasing fleeing felons. Compared to the rest of the cityscape, with its streets, intersections, house numbers and

apartment numbers, parks are areas where vast and dangerous misunderstandings in communications can occur.

Dispatchers sit at consoles, where they communicate directly with cars and foot patrols. They speak into headsets, use foot-operated mike switches, and receive call sheets from 911 operators. They are juggling which cars are where, which are single-officer cars, where the foot patrols are, who is tied up on a case, who is on lunch, and who is free.

There are a hundred people—dispatchers, message runners, supervisors and assistants—passing back and forth around the central space.

"It looks like a war room," Elmer Atkinson said.

"Which is pretty close to what it is." Nick Bertolucci drew Atkinson to a dispatcher who was handling a ten-one call, officer needs assistance.

The dispatcher was saying calmly, *"Everybody else stay off the air, twenty-one thirty-two has an emergency."*

Meanwhile, cars on the way to help were saying, *"Twenty-one thirty-three, I'm going."*

"Twenty-one twenty-six, I'm there."

And the officer with the problem was shouting, *"I need backup at the end of the alley! Don't let 'em come down Forty-third!"*

Atkinson listened to the incoming messages. He was a man who studied things closely, and he was saying nothing when Gus Gimball came up.

"Gus," Nick said, "do you know Elmer Atkinson? First Deputy Gus Gimball." They walked away from the dispatcher with the emergency.

"I've seen you at City Council meetings, First Deputy," Atkinson said, holding out his hand.

Gimball said, "Welcome to our nerve center."

Gimball remembered seeing the *Trib* poll this morning.

Up to now, Atkinson had been trailing Wallace 44 percent to 27 percent with 29 percent undecided. Today's poll showed him trailing 39 percent to 35 percent, which was interesting. Maybe there was serious dissatisfaction with Wallace out there in Chicagoland. Maybe the name Elmer Atkinson was getting known.

Gimball couldn't talk to Nick or feel him out with Atkinson there. He felt reprieved.

"You wanted me?" Bertolucci said.

"Yeah, boss. But I'll catch you later. Good to meet you, Mr. Atkinson."

As he walked away, he heard Nick say, "Okay. That sounds good to me."

FORTY-SEVEN

THREE FLOORS BELOW, Norm Bennis had come out of the First District locker room in uniform. Suze Figueroa grabbed his arm and pulled him over to where Hiram Quail and Stanley Mileski were leaning casually against the wall. Aldo was late, cutting it close, as usual.

"I gotta tell you guys, I'm passing word to Touhy."

"What, Figueroa?" Mileski said. "You want a better assignment?"

"No. Be serious. I saw Aldo's car in the CPD lot the night Dick-dick was killed."

There was a short silence. Then Mileski said, "This is a big deal?"

Bennis watched the exchange closely.

Suze said, "Stanley, he told everybody he didn't have his

car, it was in the shop, and that's why he walked Dick-dick to the el."

"So?"

"Jeez! Isn't it obvious? He's hiding something."

"You saying he pushed Dick-dick in front of the train?"

"Maybe."

"Why?"

"Money."

Hiram Quail chimed in. "Figueroa, that kind of thing doesn't happen. We *know* Aldo."

"Oh, please! You're like the neighbor of the guy who mows down twenty people in the post office. 'He was such a quiet man, Officer! He'd never hurt a flea.' "

"He's a *cop*, Figueroa," Mileski said.

"You people are impossible! All I'm asking is let's keep an eye on him."

"He's our buddy," Mileski said.

"Really? Tell me something, Stanley. Do you like Aldo?"

"Like? Well, I don't know if I'd call it 'like,' my man."

"What would you call it?"

He considered. "I might say I'm used to him. Although, when you come to ask, maybe tolerate would be closer to it."

Quail said, "You can't know that he actually—um, killed Dick-dick."

"No. But what if he did?"

"Let the detectives take care of it."

"They don't know Aldo like we do. I'm gonna watch him. Plus, I'm going to do a little investigating."

Bennis said, "Nobody—*nobody*—will thank you for it."

"If Aldo killed Dick-dick, Norm, he should pay for it. Plus, in a way, it's all my fault."

"How do you figure that?"

"I knew something was coming down. And I didn't stop it."

"You couldn't have stopped it."

"How do you know? It was brewing up for days. Least I could have done is warn Dick-dick. The person standing outside sometimes sees things insiders don't."

"Wouldn't have believed you."

"I knew Aldo was using Dick-dick—one way or another. So did you three, didn't you? Didn't we all see that?" There was silence. "And we let it happen."

"I liked Dick-dick," Norm said. He paused and after a couple of seconds he added, "A lot."

Stanley said, "I liked him too."

And Quail said, "Yeah."

"Well, if you won't help me, at least don't sabotage me," Suze said. "And don't let on to Aldo."

Norm said, "You got it."

Grudgingly, Quail and Mileski both said, "Yeah."

About that moment, Aldo stomped in. "Plotting to rip off local drug dealers?"

Suze said, "I wish."

FORTY-EIGHT

THERE WAS A new police officer in the squad room when we showed up that afternoon. He had red hair, freckles, and skin the color of vanilla ice cream.

Touhy said, "This is Officer Kim Duk O'Hara."

The young man looked sixteen, but after all, he had to be at least twenty-one to get in the academy. This downy-cheeked sprout had to be twenty-two or more. Aldo

Bertolucci was already saying, "Kim Duk! What kind of a name is that?"

"Um—it's Vietnamese," the rookie said.

Lieutenant Sheehan drawled, "This here's our token Vietnamese, guys."

Sergeant Touhy gave Sheehan a glare, said "Lieu—" in a cautionary tone.

With a sudden flash, Suze took in the red hair, the sweet face, the name Kim Duk O'Hara and knew with a certainty that it was only a matter of time until this innocent kid got nicknamed "Scarlett." Lieutenant Sheehan sauntered off to his desk.

"You'll ride with Officer Bertolucci," Touhy said to Kim Duk.

Suze sent the new kid a little mental burst of sympathy. Meanwhile, three strange men came tramping through the roll call room—a thing that *never* happened. Two were carrying a ladder between them, the third a tool box in one hand, a screwdriver and rechargeable power drill in the other.

The troops watched them pass through. But the one with the tool box stopped and said to Sergeant Touhy, "Can we start in here, now, lady?"

There were snickers and closed-mouth moans. In an altered voice, somebody said, "That was no lady, that was—" and then shut up before Touhy could see his lips move.

"Who said that?" Touhy barked. But there was no way to tell, and nobody would point the finger.

"Start in there, you idiot!" she snapped. She waved at the locker room. "Can't you see we're busy?"

Touhy read a few crimes. They had a lead on the man who was running some of the better-grade streetwalkers in the area. Kept his face off the street most of the time, though.

"Skinny white man. Very skinny," Touhy said. "Approximately five ten, cadaverous. About thirty-five, forty. Usually seen in a midnight blue Caddy. Wears white brocaded vests, blue velvet suits—"

"Yeah, but how do we tell him from anybody else out on the street?" Aldo asked.

"Bertolucci—" Touhy began, and Suze thought, This is where Aldo gets his ass reamed out. But one of the workmen came in fast from the locker room, saying, "Um, lady—"

There was another round of anonymous snickers. Touhy rounded on the workman and yelled, "What do you want?"

"I think you oughta see this."

"Everybody stay put," Touhy said, stomping out.

While she was gone there were calls of "Lady, lady!"

"This man needs glasses," Mileski said.

"Whooo."

"Lady! Those guys better watch their ass—" But the officer talking broke off. Touhy reentered, carrying a bunch of newspaper and looking grimly satisfied. Grimly satisfied was the look on Touhy's face they all dreaded most.

She put the paper down on the desk with a slight thump. Something was inside it.

"Well, group," she said, "look at this."

Touhy folded back the paper and there, in all its fang-baring, half-bald, rotten-eyeball horror, lay a dead and partially desiccated rat. It smelled.

"This was in the air duct," she said softly.

"Whoooey! That's why Come Ag—why the commander's office smelled," Hiram Quail said.

"That's right, Quail," Touhy said.

"I guess we need the exterminators," Bennis said.

"Could be a whole family of them in there," Quail said.

"Yeah," Bennis said. "If more of 'em die in there, we could really start smelling some serious odoriferousness."

"You're absolutely right, Bennis," Touhy said, still softly. "How do you suppose this rat died, though?"

"Beats me," Bennis said. "Boss."

"Seems a little strange to me. These are usually healthy animals, I'm told," Touhy said. "Get along better in the city pollution than most people."

"Yessir," Bennis said.

"Nothing to attack it," Touhy said.

"Mmm. Yes," Bennis said.

"Unless another rat," Quail said.

"Which makes me wonder," Touhy went on, her voice still low volume, but now as sharp as a knife cutting paper, "why this rat has tire treads down his back!"

Coumadin came barreling in from his office. "Okay!" he yelled. "Confess!"

Nobody spoke.

"Aldo, you jerkoff! I know you did it!"

"I did not!"

"You've had a rep as a troublemaker as long as I can re-member."

"Not this time, Commander!" Aldo said, red with out-rage.

Coumadin puffed up dangerously, then let out a long breath that by rights should have been fire. "I've got my eye on you, Bertolucci!" He stomped off to his office.

Touhy said, "Dismissed!"

Just past four o'clock Gus Gimball got a call from Charlie Withers, asking if he could come to Gus's office and talk. Gus thought Aha! but then wondered about it when With-ers added he would bring somebody else if that was okay.

"Okay with me," Gus said.

Four o'clock in Chicago in November is almost sunset. Gus Gimball's office was across the hall from the superin-

tendent's, and it faced east. Mostly he could see the el tracks, and the backs of a couple of decrepit buildings facing the other street, Holden Court, not yet yuppified. Beyond in the distance were the Hilton Towers, the Blackstone, the Sheraton, the Americana Congress and beyond them Grant Park and Lake Michigan. The lower floors of the hotels were in shadow, but the tops gleamed with orange light, reflected from their windows. Even as he watched, the shadows inched farther up the buildings. A golden glow was reflected into his office, on his walls and bookcases, as he turned back to his desk. But the corners were dark. He went over and flicked on the lights.

At 4:20 Withers came in, trailed by a very, very small policeman, one Gus vaguely remembered having seen before, maybe in Area Six.

"This is Detective Ray Moses," Withers said. "First Deputy Gimball."

Moses said, "Sir," but Gus extended his hand and Moses shook it firmly. If he felt any kind of trepidation being in the presence of seriously heavy brass, he didn't show it. Gimball allowed himself a moment of pride in the CPD's selection and training procedures. He liked to find officers who were at home and in control, wherever they were.

"Let's sit down," Gus said, and led the way to three wooden chairs he kept in the far corner of his office. They weren't more than moderately comfortable. They weren't meant to be; they were for business.

He could allow himself to study Withers openly under these circumstances. Naturally, he would be wondering what was going on. He studied Moses as well.

Moses impressed him favorably. He had a sharp nose with flared nostrils that somebody had once told Gus meant a good detective, although Gus knew that was bullshit. Moses was small and thin, but he looked wiry.

"Tell me what this is about," Gus said to Withers.

"Detective Moses here is a detective at Area One—"

"Used to be at Six?" Gimball said.

"Yes, sir," Moses said.

Gus said, "I remember." Moses looked pleased.

Withers went on. "Detective Moses has been working on the case of the police officer who was killed on the el track."

"Richard Dickenson," Gimball said.

"Right. I think Moses should tell you himself."

"Fine. Go ahead, Moses."

Moses nodded, showing no more sign of being flustered or impressed than he had before. Somewhere a window to the east was reflecting the lowering sun. The ceiling was suddenly bathed in orange light.

"Officer Dickenson had been on the department for twenty-seven months. He was just short of twenty-five years old when he died. He's been a good but undistinguished police officer. He seemed to like the work, which was something I particularly looked into because I wanted to know if he was unhappy on the job. If not, that might explain his drinking. Or even suicide.

"He probably could have been distinguished if a distinguished event had happened to him, but he's pretty much drawn routine assignments. There's never been a whiff of anything bent about him.

"Which leads me to the problem. Ordinarily, I would have accepted this as a simple accident—people have accidents when they're drunk, and he certainly was drunk. His blood alcohol was point two five. I would have accepted this as the end of it, except for two things.

"I asked his sergeant for the list of officers he palled around with. He hung out with a gang at the Furlough after work. Nothing wrong with that. Just a drink after the end of

the tour, and most of them were out of there in two hours. As you probably know, the bar is tended and owned by two ex-cops, and I talked to them, too.

"The bartenders both said Dickenson was flush with money the week before he died. In fact, one of them, Mort Gretsky, blamed his death on the fact that he had enough cash to buy whiskey, when he usually stuck to beer. Which, according to the bartender, he was used to and handled better.

"His cronies in the First agreed. He had been chronically broke, but not lately. That's the first thing.

"The second is that his partner"—Moses paused just slightly—"Aldo Bertolucci, was acting a little different, too. According to their sergeant, Officer Bertolucci was usually a pretty—um, rough diamond. Never a cheerful word for anybody."

Moses stopped, glanced at his audience with his face noncommittal, as if allowing them to object if they wanted, then went on. Everybody was well aware Aldo Bertolucci was the superintendent's brother.

"But this last week or two, Officer Bertolucci was particularly friendly to Officer Dickenson. Called him his 'little buddy' according to the sergeant. Which was out of character. He also offered to walk Dickenson to the el the night he was killed. Which also is out of character. I don't like things happening that are unusual, just before somebody is killed."

Moses stopped right there. He was not a person, Gimball thought, who nervously filled silences with extra words.

Gimball glanced at Withers. He could read nothing on the man's face, which looked like copper in the late afternoon light. The orange glow on the ceiling was slowly darkening. The room lights seemed stronger.

"All right. Let's pin this down," Gimball said. "Are you telling me you think Aldo Bertolucci's involved?"

"Knows some background maybe, sir. Involved, I don't know."

"Why so doubtful?"

"I just talked with his commander. Coumadin. Commanders usually have a sense of what their people are like."

"True."

"He says Aldo is just a basic screwup. He was very emphatic about it. Called him a stupid numb-nuts clod. Apparently there was some dumb joke Aldo played just *today*. On the commander. But the commander didn't want to tell me what."

Gimball was thinking about the idiot jokes Aldo had gotten up to in the past. Aldo the fuckup.

Moses said, "I had to agree—psychologically, a guy who plays a practical joke isn't likely to have committed murder just a couple of days before."

"Let me throw some questions at you. You think Dickenson came into some money. Do you think he got it from Aldo?"

"If so, I don't quite see why Bertolucci would be so cheerful."

"Covering up?"

"Always possible."

"You think Dickenson was blackmailing Bertolucci?"

"Also possible, sir. But all reports are that Bertolucci was feeling good too."

"Think he and Dickenson had *both* come into money from some source?"

This time Ray Moses paused longer. Slowly he said, "Yes. That could be it, sir. That's consistent."

"Like a payoff? But if so, is Dickenson's death accident, suicide, or murder?"

"Not suicide, if I'm right. Could be accident; too much celebrating. Could be murder."

"You think it's possible that Dickenson and Bertolucci were both into something dirty, that they both profited from it, and that Aldo Bertolucci then got worried that Dickenson might screw it up somehow, so he shut him up for good?"

"Well, it's possible," Moses said.

"And pushed him in front of the train?"

"Maybe. If the commander is wrong."

"Engineer notice anything?"

"No."

"See anybody with Dickenson?"

"No, but it's a blind curve."

"Anything inconsistent in the autopsy? Bruises?"

"Absolutely nothing. But Dickinson was hamburger."

"Has anybody—any of those drinking buddies—talked about specific hints Aldo or Dickenson dropped?"

"No."

"You need to come down on them harder."

"Yes, sir."

"Have you checked Dickenson's bank?"

"Yes. A recent deposit of $4,600. All in cash."

"Interesting. But by itself it isn't enough."

"No. It isn't. Not nearly."

"Been to Aldo Bertolucci's bank?"

"No. I didn't want to go that far without approval."

Without his ass covered? Gus thought. Well, nothing wrong with that. Nobody wanted to put his foot in shit without being ordered to.

Withers had sat quietly during the questions and answers, not making any move to steer the discussion. Now he said, "Detective Moses wants to know whether to drop the case. Especially because of the—the connection to the superintendent. Somebody needs to make the decision."

Gimball said to Moses, "With such a small amount of

data, guesses really, going for you—and I assume you've tried for everything you can find—why do you feel you should push it?"

"The oddities I've mentioned. If Coumadin is right and Aldo is not directly involved, it could be that somebody was lying in wait for Dickenson. Aldo says he only walked him to the bottom of the el stairs. In any case, I'd like to keep looking."

"I'll buy that, Moses," Gimball said. "Wait outside a minute, will you?"

"Yes, sir."

When he was gone, Gimball studied Withers again. He had never really noticed before how unwrinkled Withers was.

Gimball thought this might be a test. Withers hears about the Dickenson thing, makes a mountain out of the molehill, then comes in and runs the story past good old Gus Gimball and if Gimball says cover up for Nick's brother, then Withers would know Gimball would try to cover up the Panther raid for Nick, too. "All right," Gimball said. "I don't want him to drop it." He continued to watch Withers. There was no particular reaction.

On the other hand, this could be a second string to their bow. A second way to get Bertolucci. Superintendent Bertolucci has a brother who's a murderer—what kind of superintendent can he possibly be? Mud sticks.

Gimball thought he could test Withers.

"I want to follow up on this, Charlie. But I want to do it quietly, until we see if there's anything in it. You know how fast rumors can spread."

Gimball had subtly emphasized the last sentence, watching Withers. But there was no change on the smooth face.

Withers said, "Right."

"We don't want to ruin somebody's career or life with a rumor. What I want to do is to borrow Moses for a few days. See what he can come up with."

"By which you mean—?"

"I want him to report directly to me. Not to the area commander."

Gimball detected no change of expression, no obvious fear that Gimball would keep everything from him, or smother the investigation. So Gimball added slowly, "Of course, you should be in on it at every point."

Charlie Withers' face showed no relief at this, either.

"Okay with me," Withers said. "Personally, I don't think there's anything in it. Some cop drinking too much. Shit, it happens. Happens more than it should."

"Well, get Moses. I'll explain to him what he's going to do."

FORTY-NINE

DURING THE LATE afternoon, an alderman leaving a committee meeting at City Hall was shot from a car that had been parked in front of the building and then sped away. This event was just a bit too late for the four-thirty city news broadcasts. The alderman was rushed to Northwestern Memorial Hospital, where he was in surgery in time for the five-thirty news on all major channels.

He was said to be wounded in the shoulder and abdomen, but likely to survive. The publicity was going to be excellent for his next election campaign. As a colleague remarked, it

was just lucky the alderman wasn't hit in the mouth; that would have ended his career.

It happened that Alderman Elmer Atkinson was leaving the building at the same time. Not having been born the day before, he hung around until the videocams showed up. Naturally, they wanted a live interview. He started out with praise for his fallen comrade. Then he talked about crime, then the money-for-the-police crisis, which he called "our starving police department."

"From 1970 to 1990," he said, "the number of calls to the police for help went up fifteen percent. During the same time period, the amount of city revenue given to the police department has gone down nine percent. The number of police officers has gone down five percent.

"In other words, we're expecting them to do more with less. I don't have to tell you that crime has also gotten more vicious in that period of time. Look at this outrage today! In the last ten years, the number of felony cases that go to the Cook County Circuit Court has gone up *ninety* percent.

"You can't do more with less, no matter how hard you try.

"You do less with less. It's time we stopped financially starving our police department."

The political reporters who battened on City Hall hadn't been born yesterday, either. They could see this was definitely going someplace, what with Atkinson being a candidate for mayor. Maybe Mr. Cool Bertolucci the police superintendent had a deal going with Atkinson.

They tried to get Nick at his office, but he was either out or not answering.

FIFTY

MOSES SAID TO Gus, "Aldo Bertolucci refinanced his mortgage two weeks ago."

"How much?"

"He cashed out ten thousand dollars."

"Put the money in anything else?"

"Not that I can find."

"Did you ask his wife?"

"No," Moses said cautiously. "I didn't think it would be a good idea to start rumors unless we were agreed."

"No. Nooo—" Gus said. "It's better to keep quiet for now. So he got ten thousand. And Dickenson's bank shows a $4,600 deposit. In cash, wasn't it?"

"Right, boss."

"So the sums don't match."

"Course, he could of spent the rest of it. Dickenson. It was cash money after all."

"Fifty-four hundred dollars? That's a lot of spending."

"Maybe he owed a lot of people."

"True. He surely could have. Turned up anything dirty they were into?"

"No. And that really bothers me. I have everybody in the area calling on every snitch they know, and there isn't word one on the street. I don't understand it. When something's going on, people don't always know exactly what, but they usually know there's something out there. There's no whisper of anything."

"Mmm." Gus knew how that worked. There was almost no way to be seriously crooked and not make a ripple. You could do a one-man murder and if you didn't talk about it,

nobody would know. But anything financial had money going from somewhere to somewhere else because of somebody. Moses was entirely right. There ought to be a whisper.

"I've left word around that there's a little money in it if somebody wants to drop a dime on it. I've just used the Dickenson name, though. Not Bertolucci." Moses looked closely for Gus's reaction.

"Good," Gus said.

"I don't understand it. If it was just a personal loan, and there wasn't anything criminal going on—"

"Then we don't have a motive for Aldo to kill Dickenson."

"Right, sir. In which case he probably didn't."

"I know. And Coumadin would agree with that. So. For the moment, we're stuck."

"Yes, sir, we're stuck."

"Keep rummaging around for another source of threat. You've been through Dickenson's apartment?"

"Yes, sir," Moses said, in a tone that was not quite "Of course I did, sir."

"Do it again."

"Yes, sir."

"Check on the street. Somebody may have seen somebody on the platform with Dickenson."

"Yes, sir. It was late, though."

"You never know. And leave me a copy of his personnel jacket. I've reviewed everything but that."

"Yes, sir."

"Now, let me ask you something, Moses."

"Sure thing, boss."

"Did Withers approach you about this case? Or did you approach him?"

Moses was startled. Of all the possible questions, he had

not thought of this one. "No, I approached my commander and he approached Lovici. And Lovici approached Withers."

"You'll forget I asked you that, Moses."

"Yes, sir."

FIFTY-ONE

SUZE LEFT THE Furlough that night after just one beer. She pleaded exhaustion, but nobody but Norm seemed to care what her reason was. He gave her a sharp glance.

In her car, in the CPD lot, she waited for Aldo. Forty minutes later he came out, lurching. He tripped on the curb, but did not fall. He kicked the curb to let it know it had offended him.

Suze half-expected him to drive to an illegal gambling club. Instead he went to hotel row on Michigan Avenue, parked illegally and vanished. Suze waited in her car. He came back in less than five minutes, walking more steadily. From there he went directly home.

She did the same.

When the phone rang that night, Gus knew it would be the blackmailer. The equipment was all set up.

"Hello?"

A hollow voice said, "Five days."

"Who is this?" Gimball asked. The call location identifier had already come up on its digital readout screen with the number of the phone being used.

"Five days," the phone said. The voice's inflection was identical to the first time it had spoken. Gus Gimball began to have a horrible suspicion. This was a taped message. And

if so, it probably wasn't the man's actual voice. He was sure it was taped when it repeated for a third time, identically, "Five days."

"Listen, you bastard! Come see me in my office and we'll discuss it!" He paused. There was a faint humming, but no voice.

"Come out and fight like a man, you chickenshit!" he yelled.

The humming went on. After about three seconds, a voice, speaking in spaced words, as if they had been recorded separately, said, "Four days tomorrow."

If Gus had been able to speak with his caller, he would have detected a change in the voice. Aldo was undergoing an alteration. Feeding his rage had made it grow; he was hungry for more. He wanted more than he thought he had when he began. And he was willing to risk more.

The line went dead. Gus immediately called Rizzo at the department, read him the phone number and had Rizzo identify where the call was coming from out of the reverse directory.

Two minutes later, Gus put down his phone in defeat. The call had come from a pay phone in the lobby of the Palmer House Hotel. There were other equally anonymous, crowded locations in Chicago, but not many.

FIFTY-TWO

"SEE, THIS GUY enters a monastery," Wally Riggs said at the morning topcops' meeting. "It's one of these places where you can't talk, vow of silence—would that be Trappist, Hans?" he said innocently.

"I don't know." Everybody knew Hans Kluger had been a monk of some sort for three years before he came on the department. Everybody knew he didn't talk about it, either. Almost everybody left it alone. If there had been a woman present, Riggs would have been telling a joke on women.

"We'll call it Trappist," Wallpaper said. "They have this rule. You only get to talk once every five years, and even then you can only say two words."

"Wouldn't work at all well for you," Kluger said.

"So he gets his sandals and his hair shirt and his robe and his rope belt and he settles down for his first five years. At the end of the five years, they call him in to the head man's office, the head monk. And the big cheese asks him, 'How are you?'

"The guy points at his sandals and he says, 'Too tight.' So he gets issued bigger sandals and that's his two words.

"Five years go by. He's ushered into the office of the big cheese again. And the head man asks him, 'How are you?' So the guy knows he's got two words and he says, 'Broken belt.' And shows him the rope belt, which is in two pieces.

"They give him a new piece of rope. Five more years go by. The guy gets his regular audience with the big cheese, and the man asks him, 'How are you?'

"He has his two words, so he says, 'I quit.'

"The head man looks at him and says, 'Just as well. With you it's nothing but bitch, bitch, bitch.' "

Nick Bertolucci let the chuckles fade, then he said, "I think maybe *our* vow of poverty is gonna lighten up a little bit. The bill to disgorge money for the new building has just been reported out of committee and introduced in the City Council." Elmer Atkinson had phoned with the word ten minutes before the meeting started. Withers and Heidema smiled. Riggs, News Affairs, TAD and the legal counsel ap-

plauded. Kluger, however, stood up, waved a fist at the ceiling, and shouted, "Hot damn! Way ta go!"

Gimball could hardly focus on the news, although he smiled with the rest of them. He was so tense he had to keep reminding himself not to clench his hands. With four days left of the blackmailer's ultimatum, Gus Gimball knew he had to make some hard choices. He came mentally into the room just long enough to make his own department report, then went back to wrestling with his problems.

Nick caught him in the hall afterward.

"What's wrong, Gus?"

Nick was looking at Gus's hand, which was trembling.

"Oh, hell, I don't know."

Gus made his decision. He would complete his investigation before he confronted Nick with the blackmailer's data.

The lab had the tape of last night's phone call and was trying to figure out whether it was a recording made from a single voice, which might then be the voice of the black-mailer, or whether it was taped from, say, a television program. The blackmailer might have just recorded all kinds of stuff until he got the words he wanted. Gus was well aware that "five, four, days, and tomorrow" were words that had to come up in practically every newscast.

"I don't know, Nick," he repeated, stonewalling.

Nick took a good look at the man and decided to let it drop for now. A problem at home? A health problem?

"Let's talk later today," Nick said.

"Um, sure."

Withers followed Heidema out. Withers' usually smooth face was furrowed.

"You worried about something?' Heidema asked, walking slowly.

"No."

"It's good news."

"By itself, sure it is," Withers said. "Point isn't the new building, point is who's going to get the credit? Last thing Wallace wants is Bertolucci's a hero."

"I know that."

"See, if I were superintendent"—Withers stopped in front of Heidema and stared into his eyes—"you'd be exactly the person I'd want for first deputy."

Back in his office, Gus found more bad news. The voice on the phone was indeed recorded from a television program, the lab thought. It was not live. The words had been patched together. Gus sighed. He knew no more now than he had three days ago.

And he now had four days either to find the man or do what the man demanded.

Gus was almost ready to acknowledge he was stymied when he thought again about the difficulty of getting hold of Nick's gun registration. He called Cole in Personnel. "In confidence," he said to Cole and paused.

Cole said, "Of course."

"Has either Withers or Heidema rummaged around in the personnel files lately?"

"Hey, they never come in, boss. They give me orders to send them stuff."

"Have they asked for any of Bertolucci's records?"

A second, just a beat, of silence. "Never."

Gus turned his mind to the case of Richard Dickenson. And Aldo Bertolucci.

Hell, he thought. The poor little twerp Aldo—he was no more than another of life's losers, had been all his life. But Christ, if he killed Dickenson—you don't kill a cop in my

town and get away with it. And for a cop to kill another cop—that was the ultimate taboo. If he did it—

But it didn't make sense, even now. There didn't appear to be any motivation. No reason at all.

Then Gus remembered he was supposed to get back to Raina.

"Dr. Engleman called," she said. "He wants to see you this afternoon, if you can make it."

"I guess," Gus said, thinking this was the last straw. "Can you call him? I could be there by five."

"Gus? What's happening? What's the matter?"

"Let me get by Engleman, see what he says. When I get home, I'll tell you whatever he tells me."

"I guess that'll have to be good enough," she said. And he knew she was hurt.

By now his hands were shaking even worse. When he got up to get some coffee, his legs refused to respond well, and they felt like he was standing in molasses up to the knee and was trying to walk. He was frightened.

He made it back to his desk, but it had taken him three minutes to get the coffee, which ordinarily would have been a matter of thirty seconds. Whatever was happening to him, it was very bad. Then his phone rang again.

His ADS said, "The superintendent is on line two."

"Gus?" Nick said, "you want to do dinner?"

Gus hesitated. "I have a doctor's appointment at five," he said.

"Oh. Gus, is there something wrong?"

Gus wanted to say no. On the other hand, he wanted to say, "Everything is wrong and it's not just my health." Instead he told Nick what he'd told Raina.

"Let me get to the doctor, and I'll tell you about it to-morrow. Okay?"

"Sure."

"And Nick?"

"Yeah, Gus?"

"I want to send a file over to you. It's on the Dickenson investigation. The guy who was your brother's partner."

"Okay, sure. Why?"

"There's some stuff in it you ought to be aware of."

"Okay."

"I'll get it to you this evening if they can copy it by then."

"Sure. Or otherwise tomorrow morning. I'm giving a talk tonight to one of those damn neighborhood watch groups in the auditorium, after which the little darlings are gonna tour the facility."

"I thought you liked the neighborhood watch groups."

"Oh, I like the concept okay. People ought to be responsible for their own neighborhoods. And the people are good people. What I don't like is the implication that we aren't doin' our jobs and we need help."

"Nick, we *are* doing our jobs and we *do* need help."

Nick laughed. "Okay, I'll try to look at it that way. Come to think of it, maybe I'll use that very line."

"Be my guest."

Hanging up, Gus pushed his call button.

Elaine answered the buzz. Gimball said, "Come in here, please, and get some stuff to copy."

Suze Figueroa stood at Sergeant Touhy's desk.

"Yeah, Figueroa?"

"Sarge—I remembered something."

"That's just swell, Figueroa. Would you like to share it with me?"

"The night Dick-dick died. He and Aldo left the Furlough before me."

"I know Figueroa. You told us."

"Aldo said he didn't have his car. But I saw it. It was in the lot."

FIFTY-THREE

WHEN NICK GOT home, he found Stella on the sofa, reading, a box of pizza on the table. Nick judged from the bill stapled to the box that it had been delivered. For all he knew, she hadn't been out of the house all day.

"Are you okay, Stella?"

"Of course. Why?"

"This is hardly a vacation for you. You're like a hibernating bear."

"I'm not just vegging. I do a whole sequence of exercises every morning and night—"

"Oh, please! I'm not talking cardiovascular fitness. You know that. I worry about you."

"Mmm."

"Have I done something wrong?"

"Dad, be logical! Why would I be here if you'd done anything wrong?"

He sat down heavily in the chair across from her.

"Stella, I won't pester you. You can always come here when you want to, and not be cross-examined. But you *did* come here, and I wonder if that means you actually wanted my—my help, or at least my ability to listen. If not, say so,

and you can just be here and I'll love it, and you won't hear another question from me."

Stella started to giggle.

Nick was delighted to hear that sound and just waited, smiling too, knowing some barrier had been broken.

"Okay, you talked me into it," she said, smiling. "Probably I wanted to ask you all along. Only it's very difficult."

He nodded.

"Good interviewing technique, Dad!" she said.

"Yes, okay. I know you interview suspects in your job, too, Ms. District Attorney."

"Right. Well. Okay. I had a drug case come through. It was my case. Guy was selling big amounts of crack and one of his customers died from it—got nuts, ran in front of a whole armada of cars on the interstate, actually—but we had been keeping an eye on the customer, too, because he sometimes distributed for this other guy. Let's call the guy Herk. Herk has a house where he hangs out and the cops figured that's where he stored the stuff. So they move in, search the house. He arrives, they search him, find a lot of crack. A *lot.* I'm supposed to review the case and prosecute. Unfortunately, his lawyer turns up the fact that the cops didn't have a warrant to search his house. They could have got a warrant, but they were sloppy or rushed, one or the other. The cop, call him Clean Harry, says no problem. They searched the house illegally, but they found the actual drugs not in the house but on him, when he came home while they were in the middle of searching the house. Okay so far?"

"So far."

"Well, that's all right. They had good cause to search him because there were two warrants out on him, so it all seems copacetic. But I said to Harry, 'That seems like a lot of crack to carry. His pockets would bulge.' And Harry says, 'Well, between you and me, it was really in the house, but nobody

will ever know the difference.' With that nudge-nudge 'We're all law enforcement people' kind of sideways grin."

"Uh-oh."

"Yes. Uh-oh. So I worried about it over the weekend and then I went to Gordon, who's been in the office about three years longer than me. He's not my boss, but he's got seniority. And I asked him whether I should go to our boss or what I should do."

"Mmm-hm."

"Gordon said he'd sound out the boss delicately. He comes back to me the next day and says, 'Better go along with it.' The boss is looking for successful prosecutions. There were no witnesses, no jury will believe Herk the Jerk anyhow. I said, 'But it's a lie.' He said it's not a big lie."

"I see."

"So the case should come up in about six weeks depending on Herk's lawyer and what he decides to do. Motions and whatever. So here I am."

Nick was watching her face, her hands, reading as much as he could. He suspected that Stella and Gordon had some sort of relationship, but he was not going to breathe a single question about that. He knew how furious she would be if he did. Still, she must be disappointed in both Harry the cop and Gordon the DA, as well as the system.

"What do you *want* to do, Stella?"

"Oh, both, of course. I want Herk to go to prison, but I want the cops taught that they have to follow the rules, just like everybody else."

"Sure. Which do you want more?"

"I want *not* to get up in court and have one of my witnesses lying. I want to summarize the case honestly. I don't want to lie."

"And what do you want me to say?"

"I don't expect you to tell me what to do. But you've al-

ways made a big argument for teaching and reteaching your cops that they have to follow the rules. I guess I just wanted to hear you say it."

"The police do have to follow rules. There's always going to be crime. Criminals come out of the woodwork, but the cops are always the cops and they build a history. A department history and a history for the criminal justice system. They have to do it right."

Stella put her chin in her hands. "That doesn't make the decision any easier."

"No."

FIFTY-FOUR

"THERE'S ABSOLUTELY NOTHING wrong with your blood chemistry. The urinalysis was normal. I'd like to see your blood pressure a little lower, but 155 over 95 isn't disastrous. I want to start you on some hydrochlorothiazide."

Gimball said, "But?"

Dr. Engleman cocked his head. Gimball hated people who did that. At least he hated this one, right now. "I do a lot of interviews in my own work, Dr. Engleman," he said wryly. "Don't kid a kidder. What is it you're working up to?"

"All right. I'm trying to say I can't find any simple explanation for your tiredness, your trembling—"

"I know what my symptoms are!" Gimball said angrily. "Get to the point."

"I think you have parkinsonism."

Gimball stared. In a softer voice he said, "Is that like Parkinson's disease?"

"That *is* Parkinson's disease."

"I see."

"I'm not sure you do. This isn't a firm diagnosis. There's no *test* for Parkinson's disease yet. There isn't any blood test or genetic marker or definitive pathology we can look for. It's all a matter of assessing the symptoms. I'd like you to see a specialist."

"But you're sure."

"I'm—ah, convinced in my own mind."

"Why? Which symptoms exactly?"

"You report that you sometimes walk slowly when you want to walk normally. You have the characteristic type of hand tremor, and it's the same in both hands. You have no sign of a brain tumor, which you ought to take as good news. You have the characteristic lack of expression in the face—"

"That's my stony-faced cop look, Doc."

"I don't think so. It isn't very marked. You do have facial expression. It's just less than most people's. This is a very early case. You have the characteristic pill-rolling hand motion."

"I told you I didn't do that!"

"Look." Engleman pointed at Gus's right hand. He was slowly rubbing his forefinger and middle finger back and forth against the ball of his thumb.

The el stop was deserted, and besides, this was an hour earlier than Dick-dick had been killed. But Suze had a notion.

Wearing an extra jacket and glove liners to keep from hypothermia, she walked back and forth. In the next half hour she interviewed eleven people who got off el trains and about fifteen waiting to get on el trains. None had seen anything special on the night of the fatality.

She also interviewed two hookers. The first one knew

nothing. But what they say about good police work is true: it's all persistence.

Sabrina was a young-old woman of maybe twenty. Suze had seen her around before. She was the one who had offered Suze a job. She wore a leather jacket with little heart-shaped cutouts in the sleeves.

Suze said, "In this weather? You'll freeze!"

"Naw. I'm used to it."

Her lips were blue under the lip gloss. But she was an adult; Suze couldn't make her put on a coat. She told Sabrina about December 2, the night Dick-dick was killed. "Oh, sure," Sabrina said. "I was right over there." She remembered all the commotion.

She pointed at an alcove, actually a space in a building half a block down where the front door was set in a few feet.

"I was gettin' out of the wind."

"So, did you see Dick-di—did you see anybody go up to the el platform?"

"Unh-unh."

"Oh."

"I sorta backed away from it. I mean, you know. . . ."

"Damn."

"But I know who did."

"What? Who?"

"Starvin'. He was in his car, sittin' there." She pointed directly across the street from where we stood. "Parked his car there. Checkin' up on one of his ladies. They say he's real alert about where they go."

"And he was there—when?"

"All the time. He was there when I got there. I musta been hanging around maybe three minutes, tops, and there was already sirens and cop cars coming. But he was there before. Hadda been sitting there quite a while, car windows all

steamed up like that. He wiped the front one inside. You know, to see?"

"Tell me about him again." Let it be, Suze thought.

"Starvin' Marvin. Skinny guy. Some fancy blue suit. Deep blue Caddy."

"No kidding!"

"No kidding atall."

FIFTY-FIVE

"OH, MY GOD," Raina said. She pulled Gus down on the sofa next to her. Then she took his hands in hers and held them tight enough to stop the trembling.

"Engleman was careful about saying it wasn't a death sentence. People live with this a long time."

"A long time? How long?"

"Years, I guess. I didn't ask exactly." Now they both trembled.

"I'm sorry I thought you were shutting me out," she said.

"I was. Shutting you out. I didn't want to talk about it until I was sure. Probably I was hoping it would be less—less likely to be true if I didn't say it out loud."

"What happens now?"

"He wants a specialist to confirm it."

"Yes, but what then?"

"He says it's an early case. He seemed rather proud of that, as a matter of fact. He says there are several drugs that weren't available before. We'll start with something called amantadine."

And as it got worse, they'd switch to stronger drugs, like
L-dopa. And stronger drugs, and double up on them. And
someday none of them would have any effect any longer. But
he didn't say it to Raina. He had asked Engleman, "Will this
affect my mind?"

"No. Sometimes patients get depressed—"

"I can imagine. What about the drugs? Will they affect
my ability to do my job?"

"They have some side effects. We'll try different ones if
one of them gives you a problem."

Which was not exactly an answer. Gus said to schedule
the specialist, but no drugs this week. He had to be entirely
himself until the crisis at the department was over.

"We're going to beat this thing into submission," Raina
said.

"You're darn tootin', mama."

Trouble was, all her sympathy and all her love and all his ac-
ceptance of her love and sympathy were in one way just another lie. Because what he was really thinking of was how to
save Nick. He was being frank with Dr. Engleman when he
said he couldn't do anything about his disease this week, not
if it meant distracting him. Everything else was on hold. He
didn't even want to be bothered with the Dickenson matter,
really, except that he knew he had to.

Gimball had brought home his own copy of the Dickenson file. The best thing would be to go through the whole
thing again. At the very least, he'd come back fresher to the
problem of how to save Nick's ass. Yeah, all right. Take his
mind off his health, which he couldn't do anything about,
and Nick, which he didn't know what to do about.

He opened the folder.

Gus reread the description of the crime scene first. He

knew those el stops. There were a few on curves, and depending which way the train was coming they could be blind stops to the engineer.

He read the report of the first uniform on the scene, Fiddleman. It was laconic, but it was clear and thorough.

Lab reports. They'd gone so far as to fingerprint the railings going up to the elevated station. That was good. Vacuumed and swept the platform. They'd found hundreds of fingerprints, but most of them were smudged. Well, naturally, it was a busy el stop in winter, when most people wore gloves. They'd found any amount of gunk when they swept and vacuumed. Cigarette butts, mud, spit, hairs, pieces of fingernails, candy wrappers, filter tips, a couple of rubber heels, one from a woman's shoe, one from a man's. A carnation, stepped flat. Part of a hot dog bun. Fritos. Cheetos. Potato chips. Doritos. An unused tea bag—what had anybody been carrying *that* for? A used condom. A feather which was probably from a man's hat. Pieces of newspaper. Tickets. Lots of coins, in which pennies greatly predominated. No paper money. A lipstick, Chanel Light Coral No. 2. A wet, frozen scarf. Paper cups. Styrofoam cups, all of them ripped or flattened. Pieces of cups. Beverage cans. Dust. Lint. More hair. And a dead chickadee.

If there was anything that identified a killer, he couldn't see it. A junk food addict with a heel missing from one shoe, known to wear a scarf and a carnation in his lapel, who was caught by Richard Dickenson while illegally shooting a chickadee and who popped Dickenson to cover the crime?

Sure. Except it wasn't funny. Dickenson was twenty-four years old and dead.

Interviews with the other cops in the First on the third watch. Not much. Interview with the bartender, Mort Gretsky. Not much. Interview with Officers Norm Bennis and

Susanna Maria Figueroa, not much. Moses made full notes about Dickenson's bank account. And Aldo's, and Aldo's mortgage. Nothing new there.

Here was Aldo's personnel jacket. It made sorry reading. Nick had given Aldo one great opportunity after another and the damn idiot always fucked it up. Most cops would give their left nut for even one boost like that. What a fool the man was!

But he was a screwup, not a killer.

Well, if there was nothing to it, so much the better. If they'd done a sincere job of investigating, which they had, and were not covering up for the superintendent's brother, which they weren't, then maybe it was a simple accident after all.

Gus turned to Dickenson's record. It wasn't very thick. He hadn't been a cop very long, the poor doomed kid.

It was all there. His high school grades, athletic background, his All-Iowa gymnastics championship. His near miss in the Olympic. Almost at the top, poor guy, but not quite. Missed by a hair. College courses, apparently while waiting to get into the academy. Seems he didn't want to be a high school gymnastics coach. A lot like him would have. Really liked the CPD, it seemed. His entrance scores. Psychological testing. Average-plus sort of guy. No problem. His academy scores, also good. Qualifying scores with his sidearm, repeated at proper intervals. And that was about it. No sign of anything funny. No hint of dishonesty, although admit it, some cops hid it real well until a scam got out of hand. But really—nothing.

Nothing at all.

Then—Gus could feel it coming. It was like just before you knew you were coming down with the flu, or maybe approaching thunder you didn't hear but felt. Something—

Something. Pow!

Gymnastics!

Oh my god, the blackmailer!

The voice on the phone! Somebody who wanted to get Nick Bertolucci! Somebody who'd hated him for decades!

Where would that gun registration have been all these years? The personnel files! How could anybody have got it recently? Unless you were one of a very few topcops, you couldn't. And they hadn't. Cole would have said so.

Why hadn't he seen some sort of guilty knowledge in Heidema's and Withers' faces? Because they didn't have guilty knowledge.

Who hated Nick Bertolucci? Aldo Bertolucci.

Who might have found some of those papers, or the gun at least? Aldo.

Yes, yes! After old Nico died. Someplace at home. Of course! What would he need to add to old Nico's papers? The gun registration!

But Aldo could never have gotten into the personnel files for the final proof. Never! They'd surely never let him go through the files.

And Aldo, overweight, clumsy Aldo could hardly climb up the wall and break in. But a gymnast could.

Easy. *Easy!* HOLY SHIT!

Two hours later, Gus Gimball had managed to fall asleep. He hadn't resolved anything, but at least he had his next steps firmly in mind.

The phone rang.

He rolled over, away from Raina. The phone was on his side of the bed, because the late night calls were always for him.

"Hello?" he said.

The taped voice said, "Three days." It paused. "Three days."

Gently, Gus replaced the receiver. He looked at the clock. Past one A.M. Yes, three days was right.

Wait until tomorrow, Aldo, he thought. Aldo Bertolucci was going to get a little surprise. That little cocksucker was gonna get the surprise of his life. For the first time in several days, Gus fell asleep with a smile on his lips. And his hand wasn't trembling, either.

FIFTY-SIX

GUS BLEW INTO his office like a one-man tactical unit. "Get Ray Moses for me! Try Area One!" he told Elaine. She went back to her phone, fast.

A minute later she was in his office. "Moses isn't due there until noon. Do you want me to try his home?"

"Yeah, and don't just try. I want him down here as soon as he can move."

"Yes, sir," Elaine said, leaving.

"Wait a minute. Call and see if the super and I can meet any time today. *Any* time."

"Yes, sir," she said, turning to leave.

"Wait! Call Commander Cole in Personnel and ask if there's a convenient time for me to go *there* and see him today. This morning if possible."

"Yes, sir," she said, turning back to the door.

"Wait! Once you get the meet set up with the super, call Hans Kluger and set up a meet with him for sometime today."

"Yes, sir," she said. This time she stepped into the door-

way, but stood there waiting for any further orders. Gus had to smile at this, and she smiled wryly back.

He said, "And call the First and leave a message for Sergeant Patricia Touhy to call me here the minute she gets in."

"Should I try her home, sir?"

"No. Enough is enough."

A couple of minutes later she was back.

"Detective Moses isn't at home. I called the Area again and they said he sometimes has breakfast at a place called the Fat Cat on Diversey. I thought of phoning, but would you rather I sent somebody to try to get him and bring him in?"

"You'll go far," Gus said.

"Does that mean yes, sir?"

"It means yes."

Three days left, Gus thought, sorry he'd wasted time up to now. He'd scare the living crap out of Aldo Bertolucci. Aldo was always five pounds of shit in a two-pound bag, anyhow.

Gus hiked out of his office for the morning briefing, leaving Elaine tracking down everybody he wanted to see. He ran into Wallpaper Riggs at the door of the conference room.

"Hey, Gus!" Wally said brightly.

Gus thought, Oh hell, here it comes.

"Did you hear the one about the ad for the Mercedes in *Ebony?*"

Gus sighed, too quietly for Wally to hear. "No, Wally. What was it?"

"It says, 'You've got the radio, now get the car.' "

"That's swell, Wally," Gimball said, forcing a smile. He was thinking, I am surrounded by idiots.

The meeting went well, though. Nick was in good form,

and yesterday's news that the City Council looked like it would approve the money for the new building had everybody in high spirits. In fact, Gus could see them already circling the new building like sharks, each one trying to gobble up as much space for his own division as he could. No problem—it was the job of the top man to keep the sharks in line.

Nick caught him in the hall afterward. "You wanted to talk with me?"

"Yeah," Gus said, his heart sinking. "Yeah, I did."

"You've been trying to catch me for a coupla days. It must be serious."

"Important, anyhow."

"How about dinner?"

"Good. That'd be just fine." Gus would have preferred three days guard duty at Comiskey Park during a winning streak, rousting barfing drunk and disorderlies.

Nick started to walk away.

"And boss," Gus said.

"Yeah, Gus?"

"I sent over a file about the officer who was killed. Dickenson?"

"Got to me this morning. I haven't had a chance to read it."

"If you wanted to take a look at it—"

"Before we talk?" Nick smiled. "Sure. Catch you then."

Gus was accelerating. He'd get the facts that nailed Aldo. Then he'd just back the man down. Scare the living shit out of that slimeball. Threaten him with prosecution for murder, which should shut the little fuck up, then tell him to turn over the gun and the ballistics evidence.

Offer him manslaughter in exchange for silence?

But wasn't it Murder One, no matter how you looked at

it? It surely was premeditated. Walking Dickenson to the el, intending to kill him? Also, burgling the Personnel office was a felony. Killing Dickenson was murder to cover a felony. The problem would be the apparent lack of motive if people weren't told about Nick.

Could they claim that Aldo just lost his head and killed on impulse, thinking Dickenson was going to blow the thing open? Not if they didn't know what "thing" it was. What a mess.

Almost everything in the world had been plea-bargained someplace, sometime. Maybe they could offer to fruitcake him—plead him NGI, not guilty by reason of insanity.

But he'd know that almost never worked in the courts.

All of this wasn't important. What was important was scaring Aldo pissless. And for that, he needed ammunition. First let's nail the little fucker. Then we'll decide how much of him gets chopped off.

Gus pushed his intercom. "Why isn't Ray Moses here yet?" he demanded.

"I found him, sir. He's on his way."

"What about Larry Cole?"

"Gonna be in all morning. He awaits your pleasure."

"Don't get cute."

But she was right. Keep a sense of humor. Let's take this slowly. Gus knew he'd be better off staying calm. There was no point in telegraphing to everybody that there was serious shit coming down.

Gus charged out the door, took the stairs up to the eighth floor. On the way, he noticed he was really feeling much better today. That leaden feeling in his legs just wasn't there. Maybe he didn't need drugs. Maybe he wasn't sick after all.

Oh, how the mind can deceive.

He had a quick five minutes with Cole in private, and was down in his office before Moses arrived.

* * *

"Got a biggie, boss," Moses said. "One of the cops remembered seeing Aldo's car in the CPD lot. Aldo said he didn't have it that night."

"Excellent! Fits with what I have. Now, Moses, I have to warn you, you're going to get only half an explanation."

"Yes, sir."

"And even that you're going to have to keep to yourself."

"Certainly, sir." Moses's bright black eyes were sparkling now. Gus saw the enthusiasm of the born detective for the hunt. Moses knew from Gus's manner they were on a warm trail.

"All right. All you really need to know is that Aldo Bertolucci got Richard Dickenson to break into the Personnel Division offices."

"The *Personnel Division!* The office in *here*, sir? This building?"

"That's right, Moses. You are to go on the assumption that Dickenson climbed up from the annex roof to the Personnel Division windows and entered. Looking for a file. Now stop being so amazed and let's get down to work."

"Yes, boss."

"I've alerted the commander—have you ever met Commander Cole, Moses?"

"Yes, sir. Nice guy."

"Yes. And discreet. Now, mind you, he doesn't know the full story, either. But he knows he may have been burgled and he's hopping mad. You are to go up there now. Get a camera issued to you first. You will check the outsides of the windows in the Personnel offices—only the ones over the annex. You can forget about the ones facing State Street. You will look for any sign that they've been pried up from outside. Then you will check the sills, all the sills facing over the annex, insides and out, for fingerprints. Lift all the prints. There'll be

plenty inside. There are a lot of people working in that office. Then you will do the same on the file cabinets and some boxes they have stored there, and a certain file."

"A certain file, sir?"

"Cole will show you which file."

"Yes, sir."

"It's now nearly eleven. You have to finish by one."

Moses's eye widened, but he didn't object.

Gus went on. "Then I need those prints run through AFIS and I need the results by two-thirty. Specifically, have them compared to Dickenson's, of course."

"Two-thirty! Sir, it takes them—there's always a whole lot ahead of you when you go in—"

"This time, Moses," Gus said grimly, "there will be *no* one ahead of you."

"Uh—yes, sir. Sir, will I have an evidence technician with me?"

"Can you do it yourself?"

"I think so."

"Do you *know* so?"

"Yes, sir."

"Then do it by yourself."

"Yes, sir."

"Do you have any questions? See any problems?"

"One question."

"Go ahead."

"Shouldn't I try to print the outside of the building? The drainpipe, maybe? And try to find the window he went out of to get to the annex. Print that?"

"Sure, that's fine! Sew him up!"

"And one problem."

"Go ahead."

"Won't the other people in the Personnel Division wonder what I'm doing?"

"No. Cole's going to send them all to lunch at the same time. Which he doesn't usually do. He's telling them there's an extremely sensitive conference going on there at noon and any of them who come back before one-thirty will be shot dead on sight."

"That's great, sir!"

"Get moving, Moses. The camera is waiting for you downstairs. And the other equipment."

Moses nodded and got moving. After he was out the door, Gus rang Commander Cole.

"He should be up there inside of twenty minutes. Clear the decks for him."

He walked over to his coffee pot, and while he was pouring himself a cup, the intercom buzzed.

"First Deputy Gimball," he said to the instrument.

"Sir, Deputy Superintendent Kluger can see you any time in the next hour. After one o'clock, he's got a conference with some union attorneys that he says he can't cancel."

"Tell him I'll be in his office in half an hour."

He had thought of calling Kluger back and asking him to come to his own office. Then he decided his first instinct had been right. People were always more comfortable on their own turf. Plus the gesture of going there would be good—both a courtesy and unusual enough to emphasize how serious it was.

Let's see. Kluger at eleven-thirty or thereabouts, then Moses at two-thirty to make sure they had Aldo nailed down. Aldo would be coming on for third watch by three o'clock, probably get in at quarter of.

Before he left for Kluger's office, he said to Elaine, "When Sergeant Touhy calls, if I'm not back from Kluger's office, put the call through to me there."

FIFTY-SEVEN

GUS SLAMMED THE folder down on Kluger's desk. Kluger opened the file. He looked at the picture of the revolver, slipped that aside, studied the autopsy sheet, the ballistics photos. While he read, his face got redder and redder and he started to chew on his upper lip.

He turned over the last sheet, the copy of the registration of the revolver.

"Shit! Shitshitshit!" he said, standing up so quickly his chair slammed back against the wall. "God damn it! Just when things were startin' to go well!"

He paced rapidly back and forth along the wall for half a minute, then apparently getting control of himself or wearing off the worst of his fury, he sat back down.

"Okay," he said to Gus, "what're you gonna do about this?"

"No. What are *we* gonna do?"

"Do we know who sent this?" he said suddenly.

"Yes."

"Wanna tell me?"

Gus hesitated. Then he said, "Aldo Bertolucci."

"*Christ!* You sure?"

"Yes. But I'll confirm it in about—in a little while."

"Well, as I see it, we can do any one of several things."

"Go ahead."

"Number one. Kill Aldo and snatch the originals." Kluger grinned.

Gus smiled back. "Won't work. We don't know where he keeps them."

"So scratch that. Number two. Blackmail Aldo back."

"That may be possible. I'll explain in a minute. Go on."

"Number three. Have a quiet in-house investigation and clear Nick."

"Aldo goes to the media."

"I'm assuming Nick didn't know about the girl—"

"I assume so, too. I'm going to try to confirm that tonight."

"Number four. Have a quiet in-house investigation and not clear him. He resigns."

"What's number five?"

"Go public. Have a public hearing. The press crucifies him. His name is shit in Chicago. Just like his father, they'll all say. Screaming and yelling in the media. Maybe specials on PBS. *People* magazine does a thing on it with pictures. Nick looks like Hitler. Really nasty. The department looks like shit, too. The City Council turns down the budget. Everybody loses. Everybody bleeds."

"You got any other numbers?"

"Not really. Maybe six. Nick quits now, today, quietly, and moves to Sarasota to play shuffleboard for the rest of his life. No hearing. Nobody cares anymore, nobody follows up. Nobody suffers."

"Except Nick."

"No matter what you do, Gus, Nick loses."

"Not with number one or two."

"So tell me about two, we blackmail Aldo back."

Gus told him about Aldo and the murder of Richard Dickenson, the telephone ultimatum. "Can't pay him off with money. He wants Nick out. Period."

"He killed a cop!" Kluger said. "That cocksucker killed a cop!"

"And he *is* a cop. And we had just better keep calm and play this right." Gus looked at Kluger while he spoke. Kluger's face was purple with fury.

Kluger said, "Aldo doesn't know you know he's doin' this?"

"Nope." Gus added, "I'm gonna meet with Aldo in an hour. But he doesn't know that yet, either."

"Good! Gus, about that dead girl. Don't you really need to know the truth? What'd Nick really do during that raid?"

"I think he never knew."

"Suppose he knew all about it, killed the investigation through his Pa, and then *he* kept the evidence all these years."

"Oh, come on, Hans! Keep the evidence! Keep evidence that could hang him? In his mother's house? That'd be crazy!"

"Did Nixon keep the Watergate tapes?"

Gus couldn't speak. Finally he said, "The main thing is to shut Aldo up."

"You're gonna have to scare the livin' crap outta him. Get him to plead to a lesser offense in exchange for giving up the evidence."

"I know it."

"Capital punishment. Tell him you got the goods and you're gonna watch them slip in the lethal injection needle and stop his heart."

Sergeant Touhy returned Gus's call at two-fifteen. Moses had just come into Gus's office, but hadn't had a chance to report yet.

"You have an interview room down there someplace?" Gus asked Touhy, knowing that they did.

"Yes, several, sir."

"Hold Aldo Bertolucci when he gets in. Don't send him out anyplace. Put him in a room. Make him wait. Don't tell him why. Just say somebody wants to see him about some-

thing. And then *close the door.* I don't want him to see me when I walk past. Then set aside another room for me to interview him in."

"Yes, sir."

"I mean this. It's essential he doesn't see who's coming to talk to him. If he does, Sergeant, it's your ass."

"Yes, sir!"

Gus hung up. "Okay, Moses. What do you have?"

Ray Moses smiled. "A partial from one of the windowsills. It has four points of similarity with Officer Dickenson's. Not enough to take downtown by itself. But—"

"It's confirmation."

"Yes, but there's more. From the file on Sup—the file in question, plus the outside of one file drawer, we got four good prints. They're Dickenson's."

"Got him!"

"You bet, sir."

"Got him breaking in and got him in the files."

"Nothing from the drainpipe outside, though. Either he wore gloves, and he might've, or the snow or rain washed it off. Or I wasn't good enough to find them," he added soberly.

"You did good, Moses."

"Thank you, sir. There are a couple of partials on the metal file cabinet and a couple of usable prints on the box where the retired papers are kept."

"Then we've got him."

"Who, sir? Dickenson or Bertolucci?"

"Aldo Bertolucci killed Dickenson. He had means. He had opportunity. He was at the el with Dickenson. Just to put the icing on the cake, keep trying to find somebody who saw him up on the el platform."

"Means and opportunity. Did he have motive?"

"I can't answer that, Moses."

*   *   *

"Bertolucci is waiting in the locker room, First Deputy," Sergeant Touhy said. "He'll stay there until I call him."

"Okay. Have you got a small room around here? Very plain?"

"Yes, sir."

"Show me."

They walked down a short, drab hall painted cream and brown. The room she showed him into was painted pea green. There was a table and two chairs. That was it.

"I'll wait," Gimball said. "Send him in here."

"Do you want me to say anything specific, First Deputy?"

"No."

Gus knew she would do precisely what he told her. She was a cautious one, this female sergeant. Probably had to be.

It was seven minutes to three. He waited patiently. Like most cops, he had learned to wait. Would this technique work on Aldo? Aldo still thought nobody knew what he was up to.

After a couple of minutes he heard heavy footsteps in the corridor. Before the door opened, he was sure it was Aldo. Just for a second Gus thought about Nick and his light, quick step. Two brothers, completely different.

The door opened.

Aldo walked in like a cop, no hesitation, assertive, a man who always knows where he's going. Then he saw Gimball.

The first deputy sat, unmoving, unspeaking. Aldo Bertolucci froze. His eyes widened, he stopped breathing briefly, and when he started moving again, he was very, very cautious.

"Good afternoon, First Deputy," he said, the tone just short of irony.

"Sit down, Officer Bertolucci."

Aldo sat and waited. After a while, Gimball said, "What do you want?"

"What do I want? You called this meeting, First Deputy."

"Bertolucci, you know what I'm talking about. What do you really want? Money? A better job?"

"I don't know what you mean, First Deputy," Aldo said. This time his tone was sarcastic.

Gus stared at him. A minute went by, then two. Aldo simply waited, placid and calm now. Gus thought Aldo looked a lot like a wild boar, full of some bloody dinner.

"You won't say anything. All right, Aldo, but we're going to talk. You figure I'm wired, right?"

"Could be, First Deputy."

Gus walked over to him. "Pat me down."

Aldo stood up. He ran his hands over Gus's chest and back, down his pants, then up inside his pants legs. Then he pulled off Gus's jacket and felt down his arms. Gus stolidly let him work. Finally, Aldo felt Gus's hair, which was too short to conceal anything anyhow. Gus let him finish.

"I guess you're not wired, First Deputy."

"Let's talk."

"I don't think so, First Deputy."

"Why not?"

Aldo gestured at the room.

"Search it," Gus said.

"Oh, no, First Deputy. I don't have the expertise."

"All right! Get your coat and follow me."

They went out the front door of the building, Gus leading the way, bulling along, Aldo with his heavy shoulders and heavy gut following and breathing hard. They turned left, rounded the corner of the building to the parking lot.

It was cold. The orange sun was already low in the sky, hidden behind the jumble of buildings that lay west of the department. It would set in another hour in its winter posi-

tion to the southwest. The south windows of the Chicago
Police Department were sheets of brass in its light.

"Okay. Let's talk," Gimball said.

"Not here." Aldo kept walking, through the parking lot
where the squad cars clustered. One took off with its Mars
lights flashing, and the brightness of the stroboscopic blue
light emphasized the overcast afternoon.

The el tracks ran behind the building about two stories
above ground level, set on arched metal legs, a long iron cen-
tipede meandering past the building and disappearing up
State Street.

"Over here," Aldo said, standing directly under the
tracks.

Aldo looked up at the CPD building. He moved farther
forward, under the tracks, to where the metal intervened between him and any windows in the building. It was very dim
back here, in the shadow of the big building and with the el
tracks between them and the sky.

"You can't seriously think we'd set up a—"

"Seriously, First Dep? I seriously think anybody would do
almost anything. If you were the Red Squad, now, you'd have
me taken out, wouldn't you?"

"I'm not the Red Squad. And those guys are long gone.
Those days are over."

"And human nature has changed, huh?"

Gimball balled his hands. Then he relaxed them.

"What do you want, Bertolucci?"

Aldo was listening to something. Far off, to the north, the
tracks were humming. The southbound train was coming
closer.

"I told you what I wanted."

"What do you *really* want?"

The sound built in strength. The tracks rumbled. A
girder groaned. A clatter like rocks tumbling in a cement

mixer grew louder, and Aldo smiled, "You know what I really want. I want Nick fired!"

"Why?"

"It's not your fucking business," he said louder and the tracks screamed and the clatter grew. "I want him out of there or the stuff goes to the press. And the TV channels. And the muckraker papers!"

Soot and pieces of rust rained down on them. The noise was deafening.

"I know you killed Dickenson!" Gus shouted.

Then the train was past and the noise diminished. A few flakes of rust sifted down on them. They paid no attention.

Aldo had his head cocked back, arrogant, slit-eyed. He took a punch, finding out Gus knew.

"And I can prove it," Gus said quietly.

Aldo simply stood there leering, fists propped on the sides of his big belly. Gus figured he wouldn't say anything until the next train came past. So Gus did the talking.

"You got that poor chump to break into the Personnel Division. He left his fingerprints everyplace. He got a paper or two for you."

Still Aldo just stared. Gus went on.

"Then you discovered he couldn't hold his tongue because he couldn't hold his liquor. Don't you think you should have thought of that beforehand?"

Still nothing.

"So you walked him to the el, saying you didn't have your car that night, and you pushed him in front of the train."

Aldo's little pig eyes stared back. On the el above them, Gus heard a train coming northbound.

"You said your car was in the shop. Didn't you realize it would have been seen in the lot here?"

Aldo blinked. "Maybe I forgot I drove to work."

"We have more than that. And we'll use it. You'll lose

your job and your pension and your freedom. And eventually your life. You are going to death row, and wait there, and you'll be thinking about how that lethal injection really feels."

The northbound train was approaching. Over the din, Aldo said, "You don't have shit. You can't connect me to Dick-dick. But you're making one basic mistake in all this, First Dep."

"What's that?"

Aldo snarled, over the train racket, "You will *never* back me down by threats. And you know *why*, First Dep?" He pushed Gimball in the chest with two fingers.

"No."

"Because *I don't care.* I used to think I could get out of this without anybody else the wiser. Okay, maybe I didn't think it through. Nick always said I was too impulsive. I don't care. If I get Nick, I don't care what other shit happens. If I bring him down, big First Deputy, the risk is worth the reward."

"Why? Why do you hate him so much?"

"Drop it. Don't outpsych me; you can't do it." Aldo smiled. "The beauty of it is, it doesn't matter. I'm still good here. I'd rather bring Nick down than *anything*. Your job is to bring him down *for* me. You won't talk me out of it, and you can't threaten me"—he lowered his voice as the north-bound train pulled away—"and you will never find where the documents are hidden, either. You can't steal them and you can't scare me off. If I died tomorrow, they'd be sent to the press. There's *absolutely nothing you can do!* You got that now?"

Gus wanted to slug him. Aldo saw it in his eyes.

"Can't hit me, either, huh, big guy? Wouldn't look a bit good. Huh? You'd have to explain why. Or I would explain why, see? So you're stuck. The sun's setting, big guy. And as of tomorrow you've got two days left. You can't stop me. You bring Nick down for me. Hang him. Figuratively speaking,

of course. Don't look so grim, big guy. Hey, you know the old saying—if you can't stop it, why not relax and enjoy it? If you play your cards right, maybe you can get to be superintendent!"

FIFTY-EIGHT

"I READ THE file, Gus," Nick said gently. "The Dickenson file." The waiter laid the egg rolls on the table and padded quietly away, as if he knew they didn't want interruption.

"Good," Gus said. He felt sick. His hands were shaking worse than ever.

"Gus, you look like you lost your best friend."

Christ. "Sorry, Nick."

"Will you cheer up, please? Aldo didn't kill his partner. He knows cop taboos. There wouldn't've been anything worse he could do on the job. Aldo is your basic fuckup, but he's not a killer. He's exactly the kind of person who could get himself into a mess, though. He's made a career of getting himself into messes. Totally unnecessary messes."

"That's true."

"So he's exactly the kind of guy who stupidly can *look* guilty. I've read Moses' notes on the bank balances and so on. I don't know why Aldo refinanced his mortgage. I don't know—but I'm afraid I can guess. He has a gambling problem. He can't stop himself from betting on games and horses. The poor stupid putz probably thought he had a sure thing. And I'll bet he's holding out on Regina."

"Dickenson made a deposit—"

"The deposit Dickenson made and the mortgage money

Aldo got were two widely different amounts of money. That by itself should prove there isn't any connection."

"His buddies said Dickenson was talking about Aldo hanging him out to dry."

"I read those statements. Dickenson never said clearly what he meant. It could just as well be that he was complaining about Aldo making him do the paperwork on the job, for instance. Aldo would do anything to get out of paperwork."

"That's true. But there's more—"

"And anyway, Gus, you know what the main thing is?"

"What?"

"There isn't any motive. There's no evidence of the two of them being involved in anything at all, any—any chicanery. Not even a whiff. Aldo simply didn't have any *reason* to kill Dickenson."

Gus sighed and looked down at his egg roll. He wouldn't be able to eat.

"Nothing ever goes right for Aldo," Nick said. "When Aldo and Regina first settled down, they wanted to buy a house. It made more economic sense than renting, which they were doing up to then."

"Right. S'what I figured too, when I bought."

"Aldo couldn't afford it, though, and Regina was pregnant and sick; she couldn't work. So Pa offered to loan Aldo the money for the down payment, and then he could get a smaller mortgage and he had enough income to start paying on the mortgage."

"That was nice of him," Gus said, vaguely surprised, since he had heard old Nico was a bastard at home, just as much as he had been on the job.

"Seemed so. For a while. Then Aldo did something Pa didn't like—I don't remember what, wanted to take a vacation, whatever. Pa said no. And Aldo said he was gonna do it

anyway. Well, Pa had had a complete, legal loan agreement drawn up when he gave Aldo the loan, and it had a clause he could call at any time."

"Uh-oh."

"Uh-oh is right. Either Aldo did what he said, or he'd call it. See, Pa really just wanted to have something to hold over Aldo's head. Basically he wanted to control everybody all the time. Whatever he didn't like—I think it was the vacation, because I remember thinking that Regina really needed it. Hadda be after the baby was born. Well, they canceled the vacation, naturally. Regina through the years kept telling Aldo to stand up to Pa, but what was Aldo gonna do? Finally he got enough money together to pay the old man back, but by then it was kind of too late."

"In what way?"

"Oh, Aldo and Regina had fallen out of—of understanding with each other. I guess they might have anyway, but who knows? I always thought Pa jinxed their marriage. Who knows? Who knows?"

Gus dipped an egg roll in hot mustard. "Hey, this is pretty good."

"You haven't eaten any yet."

"Oh. No, I guess not. I don't feel very hungry." When Nick looked disappointed, he took a bite and added, "But this is good, though."

Going back to the CPD they walked south down Michigan Avenue, past the hotels. The lighted bank sign said it was seventeen degrees Fahrenheit at 8:27 P.M. To their left was Grant Park, thirteen city blocks long, lying against some of the city's most expensive real estate on the west and Lake Michigan on the east. At Congress Parkway, Nick gestured east over the Plaza at Buckingham Fountain, closed down now for the winter and barely visible over the long sweep of

grass. The fountain was a city block in size. "That thing was modeled after a fountain at Versailles," Nick said.

"I heard that. But bigger."

"Naturally. It's the American way."

They strolled past the Americana Congress. Gus was tense and miserable. What was he gonna do? Just flat out *ask* about the Hampton raid? He said, "I heard the lake shoreline used to come up to Michigan Avenue. Grant Park was supposed to have been built when they shoved all the refuse from the great Chicago fire over here and then dumped dirt over it."

Nick grinned. "That's very symbolic."

"Right about here, in 1968, we were setting up riot equipment," Gus said. He was leading up to something, but Nick wouldn't know.

Nick stopped to look briefly, then went on walking. "You're right. You're right. We had barricades along here during the convention."

"And tear gas launchers."

"And machine guns."

"On tripods!"

Nick said, "God, I remember blood in these streets. Literally." He stared at the well-dressed people heading to the Auditorium Theater. "Right here. Twenty-nine years. A generation ago."

Finally Gus said, "Nick, what do you remember about the Hampton raid?"

"What brought that on? Grant Park? The riots?"

"Yeah. I guess."

"What do I remember? I was on that raid, you know."

"Yeah. I know."

"They didn't tell us anything ahead of time. Me and a couple of other young guys. The older ones knew. I'm not sure exactly what they were planning to do, even now. But

you've heard all the evidence that came out later about Fred Hampton being drugged, probably by the FBI informer. He put secobarbital in some Kool-Aid?"

"I've heard."

"And then the informer left the apartment and the raiders swooped down on it. So the question was, did they intend to go in there and murder Hampton in cold blood? Or did they just kill him after they got there because they were enraged because they thought they'd been shot at?"

"Which was it?"

"Who knows? The people who know aren't telling."

"Probably never will."

"Probably. He was lying on the floor when the two shots were fired into his head. He hadn't moved, all the time all that shooting was going on. That sounds like murder to me. I asked Pa once, pretty soon after the raid, how he would have expected people to react? They're sound asleep. It's four A.M. Suddenly a bunch of armed men, none of 'em in uniform, burst in shooting. How would you react? How would anybody react? It's kind of amazing that they only fired one shot."

"What did Nico say?"

"I could've saved my breath. With him, I always would have been better off saving my breath. But me—I'll tell you, for me those three or four weeks after that raid were just like being stepped on by a giant over and over again. First it comes out that the two guys leading it didn't know where the fuck they were half the time. Then it turns out there wasn't any running gun battle at all. The guys who came in the front door and the guys who came in the back door were basically shooting at each other. *We* were shooting at each other. Then it turns out these idiots at the front door came *in* shooting! And I was along with them! I felt like I feel sometimes when—"

"When what?"

"When—oh, I don't know. Maybe it's better not to talk about it." They turned off Michigan on Ninth to go west to State Street.

Gus didn't often see uncertainty on Nick's face. He was surprised at the intensity of it. "What, Nick?"

"When you were a kid were you ever in this position— like, you're out with some other kids and go into a Wool-worth's or something. And then one of the other boys starts snickering and sneaking around, and then he takes some-thing? Shoplifts some candy or a squirtgun or something? And you're standing there, horrified. And you're thinking, I'm not one of these people. I look like them and I'm sort of here with them, people will think I'm one of them, but I'm not one of them. Count me *out*."

Gus smiled. "Yeah. I know what you mean."

"It was like that. I got dragged in there, on that raid, and I wanted to say, count me out. It's a lot like when"—he sighed and hesitated for a couple of seconds, but went on— "when I hear these white bigots carrying on. I know I look like them, I'm white too, and I feel like yelling, 'Leave me out. I'm not one of these people.' But there isn't anywhere to get left out to. I'm trapped by the way I *look*."

"Join the club."

"Well, I know. I understand. It's worse if you're black, and for that reason most white people who feel this way won't even talk about it. They don't feel they have a right to complain. About feeling trapped this way, and not having any real way of saying so—after all, what am I going to do, wear a sign reading 'I am not one of *them*. I haven't caused this situation. I'm a prisoner of history just like you are. I am not a bigot!'? So you just go on hoping your actions at least say something. But I hate it.

"I hate it! I really resent walking down the street and some black guys pass me and I know they hate me on sight.

And I can't even be angry at them for it, because I know perfectly well what kind of nastiness they've been through all their lives. But I don't want this! I don't wanna be in this loop! I want to be seen as just myself. I know, I know, so do you and so do black people out there and so do most people, but *so do I*, is all. I want to have my friends and not worry about whether they're white or black. I hate being a prisoner of history this way. Once in a while I get a fantasy—like maybe we can all blink, and then open our eyes and start over fresh. Which, of course, is total lunacy. But I wish it just the same. The way we are, it's like walking around on glue paper. You never get free of it. It slows everything down and gums everything up. I can't stand it and I *can't fix it*, and that makes me mad!"

"Oh lord, Nick," Gus said. "Why haven't we ever talked about this? In all these years."

"Beats me." They hung a left and were coming up on the CPD from the rear, passing under the el tracks. There were squad cars turning into the alley under the el, and some officers on foot nodded as they went by. Gus knew now that Nick had never realized he'd shot the girl. Old Nico'd never told him.

"Maybe we never needed to," Gus said.

They were just outside the front glass doors now. Instead of going inside, Nick stopped. He said, "About Aldo and that officer—Dickenson . . ."

"Yes?"

"That isn't all, is it?"

"All?"

"You're worried about something else, too."

Gus took in half a breath. This was what he feared. Nick was too astute to be easily fooled. He waited a minute while his heart stopped pounding. Nick let him wait. Finally Gus said, "Well, yes."

"What is it?"

"I can't—"

"Hey, Gus. This is old Nick here, remember?"

"I remember."

"Tell me."

For just a second Gus was going to tell him. Then he thought, No, I have to hold it. One day. I have to follow procedures. I promised Kluger. I have to do what I said I would.

"Tell me, Gus. Trust me. I don't like to see you looking so sad."

Knowing he was deceiving his old friend, Gus said, "Nick. I have Parkinson's disease."

Nick's head came up and the corners of his mouth drew in. He stared at Gus a few seconds, then started shaking his head. "No, no."

"I'm supposed to see a specialist, but I'm afraid it's true," Gus said.

"What does it mean?"

"It's progressive. But slowly."

"What happens?"

"Muscle weakness. Shaking hands." He saw Nick register that; he had noticed. "Slows your walk. Your face gets expressionless, I'm told."

"Oh my god. What do they do about it?"

"Something called amantadine for a while. Then as it gets worse, I guess you go over to another thing called L-dopa."

"Progressive over what sort of period of time? Months?"

"Years."

Nick put both arms around Gus and held on, never mind the officers coming out the door staring. "Thank God for that much, anyway." Then he let go and Gus put one arm over Nick's shoulder.

"I should report it, shouldn't I?" Gus said. You were sup-

posed to report to the department anything that might in-
terfere with your performance. In fact, there was a rule that
every officer, even the topcops, should be able to go out on
the street and perform full street duties, if necessary.

"You should," Nick said.

"Yeah. Okay."

"But don't."

"What do you mean?"

Nick gave him a grin. "I'm the boss. You've just told me.
That's good enough."

Gus felt like Judas.

FIFTY-NINE

"LISTEN, LARRY," GUS said, "I'm hoping—"

On the other end of the phone Commander Larry Cole
in the Personnel Division said sure, go on.

"Remember the file on that person Ray Moses was print-
ing couple of days ago?"

Cole said yes.

"Remember you said it was odd that the registration of
his—the subject's—" Gimball paused for a second. He didn't
think anybody would dare bug his phone, and he had it swept
every other week, but how could you be sure of anything?

Fortunately, Cole caught on immediately and said yes.

"—the registration of his earlier sidearms wasn't there,
either in the old file or the current file. And you said you supposed it could have been lost over the years, but not likely?"

Cole agreed.

"Well, Larry, is there any way to be sure? If it was there

up to a certain time? Is there anybody who might have gone through the files any time in the recent past and *noticed?*" Gus was reaching now, and he knew it. But years in the Detective Division had taught him that—assuming you had both the time and the money, which, of course, you never did—you could never ask too many questions.

Cole said let him think a couple of minutes. Something at the back of his mind. He'd call back.

A night's sleep had not helped Gus. It had not been refreshing. It was shredded by dreams of death, disease, dishonor. He had wakened once with the conviction that he was liquefying, putrefying, running away in a broth of blood, pus and decay in his own bed. He woke up screaming and found that he was screaming silently.

And in an hour he had to go see Nick. And explain. The deputies had decided. They would hold a hearing on the Shana Boyd shooting this afternoon. Nick would have to appear before a board of his own deputies. Nick would have only two hours to review the evidence before the hearing.

Gus needed one thing—Nick's acknowledgment that he knew nothing of those papers, had never in his life seen them, and didn't even know that he had shot Shana Boyd. It had to be presented to the deputies unequivocally.

Then Gus had to nail Aldo for the break-in and the murder of Dickenson.

He thought he could force Aldo to plea-bargain. Your silence for your life. Down deep, Gus did not believe Aldo's boast that he would chance death just to get Nick. He was vicious, but he wasn't suicidal. He wouldn't take a Murder One rap. Not capital murder.

While Gus waited, he drummed his fingers on the desk. Once in a while he'd stop and hold his fingers out and see whether they were still trembling, hoping he'd find he was cured. They trembled. He wasn't.

Less than two minutes later, Larry Cole was on the phone. He'd thought he remembered something, and he had. His office had photocopied all their material on the person in question, old file and current file both, in mid-October for News Affairs. News Affairs wanted to make up a new bio of the—um, person. Would that help?

Would it? Gus did everything but blow a kiss to Cole over the phone. He punched the intercom button for his secretary.

Elaine came in.

Gus said, "I'm calling News Affairs. They've got a copy of a personnel jacket down there. You head down to get it. You personally, yourself. Now. They should have it ready for you."

They had it! It was in there! The gun registration, pretty as a picture, just like the one in the package Aldo had sent. Which meant it had been in the Personnel Division offices up to the middle of October and wasn't there by the middle of November, after which it was in Aldo's hands. Beautiful!

"Now I've *got* him!"

SIXTY

TWO HUNDRED YEARS ago, the place where the center of Chicago now stands was a swamp. Some people think not much has changed.

It was a northern sort of swamp, with hummocks of beach grass, bullrushes, muskrat domes, blue herons and seagulls. The sand dunes were partly dry in the summer and

flooded when the fall winds blew down over 350 miles of Lake Michigan and piled up the water at the southern end of the lake. In the winter the sand froze as hard as cement and the muskrats hid in their dens.

When Chicago was a young frontier town, the swampy areas were mostly left as they were, filled with water and mud and garbage, and as the town grew, they were filled with the poor, living in tents and shacks. After the great Chicago fire, things were different.

There was big money in Chicago—lumber money, meat-packing money, money from making harvesters and combines, money from the burgeoning railhead. Chicago was the transportation center of the nation. Almost all the trains in the northern half of the country passed through Chicago.

Big money went into improving the city. The downtown streets were raised above the swamp or flood level. Whole areas of the Loop were built on iron stilts, the pavements were raised, and gradually the sidewalks were filled in and the vacant land between stuffed with buildings until you could walk from one end of downtown to another and not realize it was underlain by swamp.

The only remnant of all this raising of the city was a series of secondary streets below the level where the sun shines. Some, like Lower Wacker, which runs under Wacker Drive, are regularly used and are favorites of taxi drivers and city cognoscenti for getting places in a hurry.

Others are used primarily by loading trucks and delivery vans, picking up and delivering to the subbasement levels of hotels and restaurants. Even more carry heat conduits, sewer mains or parts of the underground transportation system.

Occasionally, one of the daylight-level streets will collapse without warning, leaving a hole at street level, a few cars in the muck at the bottom, pedestrians standing around on top gaping and the rats underneath scurrying away. The

last time this happened a passerby took one look at the hole, which was fifteen feet deep and forty across, and threw himself into it, hoping to collect big damages from the city. Several bystanders saw him do it, however, and the ploy failed.

But many of the tunnels and leftovers under the city are unexplored and forgotten. People say there are homeless living there. Down in these tunnels it is always dark. There are no pedestrians. These are perfect places for people or deals that don't want to see the light of day.

Norm Bennis and Suze Figueroa were rolling along Lower Wacker, patrolling the underground, Norm driving. Suze had told him she'd found another lead in Dick-dick's murder.

"I suppose you gotta call the detective."

"I will when we take our break."

"This kills me though, my man, if he did it."

"I know."

"Mileski's beginning to believe you. Quail thinks you're nuts." Just then Suze caught a glimpse of the man driving a midnight blue Caddy next to them in the right lane. He was a thin white man wearing a blue suit.

"Hey, Norm!" she screamed. Bennis jumped a foot.

"Jeez, don't scare me like that."

"It's—it's—uh-oh, my! It's Starvin' Marvin and he's wearing a shoulder holster."

"How can you see a shoulder holster from here?"

"It's for a left-hand draw. Keep parallel and look. Don't let him see you're looking."

They were in a marked car. Marvin maybe didn't see them, but probably studiously ignored them.

"Yeah, you're right," Norm said.

"Drop back a little. Pretend to be looking at those parked trucks. I'm gonna run the plate."

Suze got on the air and read the plate to the dispatcher. It came back clean.

The radio said, *"One twenty-seven."* The dispatcher was calling Aldo and Kim Duk, who were in the south part of the district.

"One twenty-seven," came Kim Duk's excited voice.

"We got this number-one parker, twenty-seven. Somebody parked a Rolls-Royce in front of a fire station driveway. Can you believe?"

"Sure. What's the address, squad?" Kim Duk said, sounding like he knew what he was doing.

"Scared of Aldo, I suppose," Suze said to Norm.

Norm, who was paralleling the Caddy, said, "Mmm."

Aldo's voice came on. *"One twenty-seven."*

"Go ahead, twenty-seven."

"Listen, we could take that fire station, but we got some young gentlemen here on the corner lookin' good and actin' bad. How about we get to the parker in a few minutes?"

"Sure, twenty-seven. Put it on your clipboard. Corner of Superior and Michigan."

"All right, my man," Norm said to Suze. "Whaddya want to do?"

"I wanta pull him over."

"We got probable cause?"

"Hey! He's the one Coumadin wants. I want him too. Plus, that's an unlicensed gun."

"Like you know."

"He won't look at us. Anyway, if we don't brace him now we don't know where he'll go. Michigan Avenue, probably. You wanta think for another five minutes and then stop him up on Michigan Avenue, a hundred high-priced lawyers on the hoof goin' by?"

"No. No."

"Pull up next to him and hit the lights. Don't use the siren down here; I don't wanta go deaf."

It didn't work. Norm hit the lights. Starvin' Marvin hit the gas, scooted around a white panel truck and tried to make it to an up-ramp. But the cars ahead were in both lanes solid. The Caddy cornered squealing into the underground cross street.

Bennis snaked around the traffic and screamed into the cross street. Suze was on the air, saying, "One thirty-one. That Caddy took off and we're in pursuit someplace just off Lower Wacker—"

But the cross street turned out to be no cross street or any street at all. It was a tunnel running off at an angle from Lower Wacker. For the first block it was lined with loading docks. There were delivery trucks and one or two semis unloading. Sheets of newspaper blew around behind the wheels of the Caddy. Some rotten oranges lay in a small drift against a wall.

Beyond this first block, the lighting dropped off quickly. The loading docks were illuminated with a dim yellow bulb or two over each metal door. The next block vanished into gloom, with one bulb a hundred yards down, and another a hundred yards beyond that. The pavement ahead was stained and greasy. There were slicks of mud and oil, as if it were hardly ever driven on. The roof of the tunnel was laced with heat pipes and electrical conduit and telephone cables.

The Caddy knew it had made a mistake.

It spun toward the right-hand wall and stopped there. Then it reversed, screaming rear-end down the tunnel, stopped, rocking, and started forward.

Norm had already sent the squad car into a turn. He stopped, dead across the tunnel. But there was room for the Caddy to pass on either side, if it chanced running into some pipes and cables on one side or scraping by the wall on the

other. Norm jumped out instantly and Suze jumped out two seconds later, because she remembered to shut down the car and take out the keys. Otherwise next thing they'd see Starvin' Marvin in their squad car speeding away.

Then a shot whanged into their windshield.

Norm Bennis dove right and Suze dove left. Norm opened fire, and Starvin', now revealed as an exceedingly skinny man, dove behind his own car. He miscalculated, hit a pylon with his shoulder, and the gun spun out of his hand and clattered across the pavement into a streak of slime that ran along the lower part of the ancient roadway.

Norm jumped up and started running toward the man. But Starvin' had the back door of the Caddy open, and as Norm sprang toward him, he pivoted, displaying a 9mm automatic.

Norm screamed, "Drop, Suze!"

The man fired in the same instant.

Norm was blown off his feet and backward, where he collapsed into the slime and grease near the man's other gun.

"Shit!" Suze screamed. She loosened a round, then took an airborne dive behind the squad car. Firing another round, she grabbed the mike and yelled, "Ten one! Ten one! One thirty-one off Lower Wacker! About two blocks north of Jackson."

She fired another two rounds. What did that make? Four?

Don't forget to reload! She fired again—four?—five?— and was grimly satisfied to see that Marvin was staying behind his car. Now she had a little space to be more specific to the dispatcher.

"I've got an officer down. We need an ambulance here immediately! I have a man with a firearm holed up here! Use caution! Use caution!" She felt like she was screaming. She didn't wait for a response; she was too worried about Norm.

Now she risked sticking her head out to look at him, lying some twenty yards away. He didn't move.

Suddenly she realized that Marvin could back away from the Caddy into the tunnel. He could get quite a distance beyond his car and still be protected by it. Then he could turn and run into the dark tunnel and God only knew where he might come out. The fucker could get away clean!

Up on Michigan, Hiram Quail and Mileski were well into an uneventful tour, rolling south on Michigan, a block south and twenty feet above Suze and Norm. They had heard the exchange. Part of it. Being under Wacker and surrounded by power cables had fouled up Suze's transmission. Quail and Mileski heard something like *"En one. Bazzt! Urmmmmmmmmmmmmm.—orth of Jackszznnnnnnn. Zeet!"*

But they hit their lights and sirens and started moving.

Then quite clearly they heard *"—ambulance."* It cut off in static, then *"—up here. Use caution. Uzzzzz—zmmmurt!"*

Hiram swung around in traffic, freezing two buses in their tracks. Mileski yelled, "Take Monroe! They were somewhere near there when they first asked them to run the plate!"

The dispatcher was saying, *"Talk to me, thirty-one."*

Down under the street, Suze had backed away, desperately searching for access to Marvin, terrified that Norm was bleeding to death. Or dead. She needed more cops; she couldn't hold him down with firepower and creep up on him at the same time.

Suddenly the dispatcher's voice was crystal clear. *"We have a ten one on Lower Wacker—off Lower Wacker in a cross street someplace north of Jackson. Units to respond?"*

"One thirty-three. We're almost there," Quail said.

Then the air was full of units all over the First, plus the Twenty-first and Eighteenth, responding or asking to respond. The dispatcher okayed the nearest, then said, *"Every-*

body else stay off the air, one thirty-one has an emergency. Thirty-three?"

"Thirty-three," Quail said.

"Ambulance is responding."

"Ten four."

Quail and Mileski were under Wacker themselves now.

Suze saw the flash of their Mars lights on the roof of Wacker up ahead. Mileski pulled to a stop diagonally, blocking part of the Caddy's escape route. They crept up behind her car.

The Caddy was twenty yards away. Suze crouched near it. The perp, Marvin, was well blockaded between a pylon and a dumpster. She couldn't get any closer without exposing herself to the man's fire. Quail and Mileski couldn't get to Norm, either, without being shot at. After a few seconds of looking around wildly, Suze backed away toward Quail and Mileski. Norm lay still on the pavement. He did not move, didn't even groan. What he did was bleed. As they assessed the situation, they heard the radio inside Mileski's car. The transmission was totally garbled. Nobody up top could be told exactly where they were.

"What we got here, Suze," Mileski said, "is your basic clusterfuck."

"Hey, Norm!" she called. "We're back here and everybody else is on the way."

No answer.

"But that's not gonna help," Quail said, just barely keeping the desperation out of his voice.

Suze said, "I know it. We got to get to him and stop the bleeding at least."

"Sure, Supergirl. What do you suggest?"

"That's Superperson, you clod."

"Right."

"What I suggest is you wait right here and distract the

perp with random shots. I'm going to get on that pipe. The one that runs over the slimeball. I'm gonna climb over and get the drop on him. And destroy him."

"What! He'll see you."

"No, he won't. The pipe's too fat and the other pipe runs next to it."

"He'll see you get up onto it."

"I'm gonna go back around the corner."

"I'll do it."

"You can't, Quail, you're too fat and ugly."

"Hey!"

"Come on! The pipe's too close to the ceiling. You wouldn't fit. Now quit this. We're wasting time. If I make any noise, you distract him."

"I'll distract him whether you make any noise or not."

Suze ran back to the intersection of the tunnel with Lower Wacker. Even the running seemed to take too long. For all she knew, Bennis might have one minute's worth of blood left.

She jumped onto a dumpster, which tipped wildly, forcing her to stand spraddled with her arms out for balance. Then it righted itself. There were some cables within reach. The heat pipes or whatever they were ran near the roof, farther up and beyond her reach even from here. The roof was a good fifteen feet above the pavement.

Her only choice was to grab the cables or conduit or whatever they were and swing up. But these could be electric wires—probably were—and for all she knew they were live and uninsulated. She knew nothing about electricity and it was too late to learn. For a second she hesitated, frightened. But she was far more terrified that Norm was dying. She reached up, grabbed the cables and swung up onto them.

Still alive, she thought. Excellent. She stood on the cables. They stretched, swung a little, but from there she

grabbed the big pipe, threw her leg over it and crawled on.

There was a smaller pipe running next to it, the one that should help hide her from Starvin' Marvin. Creeping on hands and knees like a crawling baby, she reached the tunnel mouth. Both pipes split here, one section continuing along Lower Wacker, the other turning into the tunnel. She kept moving, fast.

From up here she could see the situation well—and it was bad. Norm didn't seem to be moving. The gunman was well barricaded from Mileski and Quail, and Quail couldn't get nearer to Bennis without exposing his body to the gunman. If Mileski and Quail didn't keep the man pinned down, he could be off, rabbiting down the dark tunnel and God only knew where he would come out.

There was also no way to explain to Bennis that she was up there without also explaining it to the gunman.

What Suze needed was to get a good line of sight for a shot. She could climb right over the gunman. As long as he didn't look up. Because it was now pretty obvious that both pipes, the large one and the small one, still weren't really big enough to hide her.

If he looked. Mileski saw her coming along above him, saw the problem, and immediately yelled at the gunman.

"Hey, dog burger!"

The man didn't answer. But Suze could see he was listening to Mileski. She inched closer. She was maybe twenty feet away from him now, halfway between Bennis and the perp.

"You fucking slimehead, there's a hundred and fifty squad cars on their way!" Suze inched closer. She was increasingly aware that she didn't have a good shot yet, but the gunman could blow her off the pipe by shooting through it.

Shit, at that range, he'd hardly have to aim.

Mileski screamed, "Give it up! They're gonna come in

here blasting. You're gonna be a Swiss cheese! You're gonna be training material for all the little medical students, that's what you're gonna be!"

Suze was within seven feet of the man. A little closer, she could jump him.

"You're dog meat, cocksucker!" Mileski screamed, sounding terrified.

Mileski stopped long enough to take a breath. Suze crept forward, almost over the man now. The pipe groaned. She tensed, started to reach for her sidearm.

The gunman flinched. Right then Bennis raised his head an inch and said, "Help me." It was a thin, weak sound, nowhere near as strong as a scream. But it was too much for Mileski. With a roar of fury, he leaped from behind the squad car and charged the gunman. The man spun, gun barrel pointing at Mileski, who suddenly realized his danger, turned and dove away from the man.

The gunman fired. Mileski, who was already dropping to the pavement, screamed, rolled and lay still.

Suze didn't have time to get out her gun. She dropped out of the air onto Starvin' Marvin's back. Her weight was only a hundred and ten pounds, but it carried the man down. As he fell, she fended off the barrel of his gun with her left hand. With her right, as the man hit the cement, she cracked the back of his head with her palm, smashing his forehead into the pavement.

Then Quail was there. He piled on the gunman, yelling "Now you're mine, pal!"

Suze rolled off the man, while Quail planted a knee in the small of his back, and Suze handcuffed his wrists, backs together and palms facing out, in less than two seconds.

"Give him his rights," she said. She got up to run to Bennis, and she heard behind her, "You have the right to remain silent . . ."

Bennis lay still as death, breathing, but breathing in short shallow gasps as if taking in a full breath of air was too painful to do. His whole upper body was slick with blood.

His face was bluish. She tore open the front of his shirt. In the right chest was a ragged hole. Blood and air were bubbling out together. She knew a sucking lung wound when she saw one. She knew she was supposed to patch something over the wound, something impervious to air, but she couldn't think of anything until she remembered the chocolate bar in her pocket. Quickly, she stripped the wrapper. Then, watching for a moment when he exhaled, she gently flattened it over the wound, holding it in place with her hand.

Now that the right lung was not uselessly sucking air and blood, the left breathed better. But he was still losing blood fast, internally.

His eyes popped open. "Hey, Suze, my man," he said, ragged and faint, but just as if they were in the middle of a conversation.

"Hey, Norm."

And then he started to swear. At that instant Suze knew that he wasn't dying. She could tell because of the constant flow of rich, ripe curses, delivered with great conviction, even though spoken in a very faint voice.

He closed his eyes. He was breathing stertorously, stopping between breaths. Where were the damn paramedics? She kept her hand on the flap of plasticized paper over the open lung. She closed her eyes and prayed. When she opened them she saw flashing lights shining on the tunnel wall.

There was a hand on her shoulder. She turned around. Johnny on the spot. Two EMTs.

Suze stood back. One of the paramedics got next to Norm, lifting his eyelid, listening to his heart, getting a blood pressure cuff in place. "You did right," he told her. The other

EMT, on Norm's other side, slid a needle in the vein on the inside of his elbow.

Mileski had taken a fragment of a ricochet somewhere in his thigh. He had torn most of the shoulder out of his uniform blouse. He got up, limping.

Suze and Mileski strode over to Starvin' Marvin, who was now leaning over the hood of the squad car, guarded by Quail.

"Marvin," Suze said, "look at me."

He looked.

"Why?" Suze asked. "Why did you run?"

He shrugged. She grabbed his elbows and spun him around.

"Unlicensed handguns?"

"Yeah."

"Pretty stupid. Now you got a real beef. Attempted murder of a police officer."

"Shit."

"You want any help from me on this, Marvin, you gotta help me first."

Some light dawned in the sullen eyes. "What? How'm I gonna help you?"

With Mileski and Quail both listening, she said, "Tell me everything you know about the night of December second."

SIXTY-ONE

"YOU UNDERSTAND THAT you have the right to have an attorney present?" Gimball, his face impassive, said to his best friend.

"I understand that," Nick Bertolucci responded. "I waive any attorney."

"You understand this is not a trial."

"Yes."

"This is a hearing. You are under oath. You understand that there is no specific precedent for these proceedings. That we could hold a trial board, but that all parties have agreed to this hearing first, because of the attendant danger of publicity with a full trial board."

"I understand."

"That except for me and Deputy Superintendent Kluger, none of the people present knew anything about this until today. Including yourself. Is it true that neither I nor anyone else spoke to you about this before today?"

"Yes."

"The intent of this hearing is to determine whether there is cause to go to a trial board. This hearing is being held without a stenographer, although we are tape-recording it for your protection, and if it is decided that there are no grounds for a trial board the tape recording may be destroyed."

"I understand."

The room was too warm, but to Nick Bertolucci, Gus looked cold and drawn. And very sick. Nick thought of this morning when Gimball came to him with the papers and the photograph of the gun. A frozen Gimball, who said only, "These were sent to me."

Nick had shuffled through them quickly, not understanding what they meant, then again, very slowly. He was too stunned to ask questions. The world buzzed around him; he had *killed* a young woman—almost a child?

Gus had said, "I have to hold a hearing. This afternoon. The person who has this material is threatening to go to the papers and television."

"Who is it?"

"Aldo."

"Aldo? *Aldo?*"

On top of the other horror, he almost laughed, the way the pain of breaking a bone can cause a laugh of physical outrage.

The name hung for a minute. Finally Nick said, "Does he want money?"

"If he'd wanted money he'd have gone to you."

"What does he want?"

"He wants you fired."

Nick held his breath. "Do the others know it's Aldo?"

"No. Yes, Kluger does. The others don't know anything."

"Good."

"I guess," Gimball said.

"How long have you had these papers?" Nick asked.

"Six days." Gus didn't lie. And then Nick knew Gus had held them and not told him.

"I'll come up with something," Gus said, very quietly.

Nick wanted to scream, "Bury it! Don't let Stella know!" but he didn't. And of course Gus couldn't hide this. Even if he wanted to, he didn't have the originals of the documents. Nick held himself firmly in check. Courteously, calmly, he made himself say, "Thank you, Gus. I hope you will."

"I had to call the deputies together. This is too serious to do anything else."

"That's true."

"Basically, we'll see whether we can face it down, or—"

"Yes. Or."

"Today at two-thirty," Gus said politely. "Just the deputies." Nick and Gus were courteous with each other. They had never before, in twenty-six years, been courteous. Never had to be.

Nick had spent the intervening hours sitting, not planning, not preparing, just sitting. Once he got up and put on

a sweater. A little later, finding he was still cold, he put on his
outdoor coat.

Now Nick stared around the hearing room. He was finding it difficult to know what to do with his face. He was the
boss still, but his own deputies were sitting in judgment on
him. Stony and rigid, that's how he looked, he thought. And
inside an aching and roaring . . .

Gus was still talking.

"You understand that we will first take your statement as
to what precisely happened to Shana Boyd. How she met
her death. Second, we will determine how the data was originally suppressed and whether that was done in a criminal
fashion. Third, we will assess your part, if any, in the ongo-
ing suppression up to this moment. We have to know exactly where we are."

"I understand."

"And then this hearing board will decide whether it can
support you against any revelation or criticism that might
arise in the future out of this incident."

"I understand," Nick said.

The silence sang. Unspoken were the words, "If we can't
support you . . ."

It was snowing outside, heavy pellets falling fast, just visible through the small window far down at the end of the
room. And Nick was at this end sitting on an oak chair apart
from the other five. Trial boards were sometimes held here.
It was an ugly room, painted a yellowish cream color, nothing to look at but a flag. Between him and the window were
Charlie Withers, Hans Kluger, Wally Riggs, Bradley Heidema, and Gus Gimball. Kluger was belligerent, angry, his
face all frowned down on itself. Withers looked sleek. Heidema was ramrod straight, as usual. Wally Riggs' face was
very solemn. For once, instead of talking stupidly, he waited
and watched.

Nick thought, Wally Riggs to be sitting in judgment on me!

He studied Gus. Gus, who was his friend. His hands were shaking faintly, visible if you looked for it. His eyes were red.

Gus had been sitting, but now he stood up—out of formality, taking on the role of prosecutor, or just because his tension needed an outlet.

Gus said, "Deputy Superintendent Withers?"

So Withers was going to lead off. Nick turned to focus on him and turned his side to Gus Gimball.

Withers got up, too. This way, he loomed over Nick. He looked puffed up, inflated with the interior pressure of a pleasure he couldn't show openly.

"Superintendent," he said to Nick, "why did you go on the Hampton raid?"

"I was ordered to."

"Why were you detailed to the state's attorney's special police at all?"

"My father, who was then first deputy, assigned me to it."

"Weren't all the SPU men volunteers?"

"No."

"No?"

"I wasn't a volunteer. I don't know about any of the other men. I heard some were volunteers."

"When were you told you were going to take part in the raid?"

"Late in the afternoon of December third, 1969. That is, about eleven hours before it happened."

"What were you told?"

"To study the floor plan. And to expect seven to ten people in the house. And to expect armed resistance."

"Now, let's move ahead to the raid itself. What was your part supposed to be?"

"Backup. I was to go in with three men behind the front door team and keep the scene secure."

"Into the apartment?"

"I don't understand the question."

"You were to go into the apartment?"

"Yes. We were told to follow inside as far as the living room."

"Did you see the initial entry into the house?"

"Not clearly. We were too far back."

"When you did enter the living room, what was happening?"

"The front door team was firing. One officer was spraying the living room wall with machine gun fire. Another man in the living room yelled something like 'There's more of them back here!' and they all started firing again toward the back rooms."

"When did you discharge your weapon?"

"Just after that. I saw motion, which I took to be a threat to the forward officers, and I fired."

"Had you been ordered to fire?"

"Not specifically."

"Did you see who you were firing at?"

"Not well."

"Did you see who you were firing at *at all?*"

"Only motion."

"So you fired blind?"

It hadn't been blind, not exactly, not through a wall, like the man with the machine gun. But he had not stopped to make sure who or what he had shot at. Withers waited, staring at him.

"I fired blind."

Withers sat down. Gus said, "Does anybody have additional questions on this point?"

Heidema said, "Were you under the impression that you were supposed to protect your superior officers?"

"I was told to."

"Were they firing blind?"

"Yes. Into the dark rooms and through the wall."

"Through the wall without any inspection of the back rooms, or any way of knowing whether the police officers from the back door could be behind that wall? Is that possible, Superintendent?"

"That's what happened. It came out later that one of the officers who thought he had been shot by the Panthers had been shot by one of our men."

Heidema nodded, signifying he was finished. Nick was surprised. Heidema's questions had been almost friendly. Kluger said to Nick, "How many rounds did you fire?"

"One."

"During the whole incident?"

"One during the whole incident."

"How old were you at the time, Superintendent?"

"Twenty-three."

Nick waited. Nobody asked anything more, and after a few seconds Gus walked closer to the table. "I suggest we go on to the second issue," he said. "Since we're engaging in an informal hearing, I want to say if you think of any other questions about the raid itself you can come back to them later." Nick watched Gus work, wondering to what extent he and Kluger had orchestrated their part so far.

"Very well," Gus said. "I want to take up the matter of how this was originally suppressed." Withers raised a finger and Gus nodded.

Withers said, "When Shana Boyd was found to be dead, did you know that you had killed her?"

"No."

"Why not?"

"Well, actually, I don't think anybody knew who had shot anybody, except for whoever shot Hampton himself—point-blank—and he or they weren't telling."

Withers frowned. "Are you saying nobody knew what they'd done?"

"That's exactly what I'm saying." Nick was annoyed at Withers' pretense. Half the world seemed to know that the raid was totally fucked up; Withers knew as well as anybody. "Nobody knew what they were doing, or what they'd done, spraying the walls with firepower, and nobody tried to figure it out later, either."

"Then exactly how was the data from the raid, like the ballistics evidence and so on, suppressed?"

"It hardly was suppressed at all. Most of it was never collected in the first place. What was collected wasn't analyzed."

"But, Superintendent," Withers said smoothly, "we know the bullet from your gun was analyzed and so were many of the others. The FBI did their own analysis, isn't that true?"

"The FBI hid documents for years until they were ordered by a court to produce them. And then they tried to send the court just a small portion of them. Most of the spent pellets disappeared. Where are the ones that killed Hampton, for example? They went through him into the floor. Easiest thing in the world to collect."

"But shots were traced to some of the raiders' guns."

"In most cases shotgun pellets were traced to police shotguns by the type of shot and wadding and so on, not ballistics striations. And the police Thompson submachine gun rounds were obvious. Almost everything else disappeared."

Withers folded his arms over his chest. "Then you took part in a—a—" He couldn't think of a word.

Nick said quietly, "Whatever name you want to call it, I've called it over the years myself."

At that point they all stopped. Nick saw Heidema throw

back his head, a gesture he often made when he was deciding to do something he knew was unpopular. Riggs just listened.

"Anybody else?" Gus asked.

Kluger sat forward on his chair. "Did you at that time ask anybody to hide the fact that you had shot Shana Boyd?"

"No."

"Why not?"

"I didn't know I had shot her."

"Were you given any reason whatsoever to think you might have killed anybody during the raid?"

"Nobody said anything to suggest it. I turned in my Colt thirty-eight and never heard that any ballistics test had ever implicated it in any way."

"And then the incident faded into the past?"

"It did. And I was relieved that I hadn't—I thought—done anything irremediable."

Heidema held up his hand. "If you had learned then that you shot her, would you have tried to get the evidence suppressed?"

"I hope not. How can I say, now?"

"A very honest answer, Superintendent."

Gimball strode around to the front end of the table again. "All right. I want to go on to the third aspect. The suppression of these materials in the years following the raid."

Nick was watching the other men, but they made no sign that they wanted to ask a question. Gus almost seemed to expect that. He straightened his slight stoop. "Superintendent, were you aware that these materials existed?"

Gus gestured at the papers and the photograph of the gun and spent pellet that lay on the table.

"No. Not until very recently."

"How recently?"

"You showed them to me this morning."

"Yes. And can you make any guess as to where they were up to now?"

"I think so."

"Tell us, please." Gus would be aware that this was distasteful. Nick always avoided talking about his father unless it was forced on him.

"I believe my father kept them."

"All right. Do you have any idea why?"

Nick paused. There was something a little bit wrong here. It was something about Gus, and Nick couldn't quite get what it was. He watched him. Gus was his friend, wasn't he? Still his friend, despite this? He was trying to help him, wasn't he? But looking at Gus now, Nick sensed an avidity, an eagerness that he wouldn't have expected. Gus's regret earlier had surely been genuine. But now he looked more vigorous. He stooped less. His face had more life. But that wasn't all. It was as if he were a detective on the trail, on a scent. And yet there was nothing in these questions to explain that. Surely Gus wasn't trying to pin Nick, was he? Back him into a corner, pin him, get him to admit he'd known about that evidence? Could Gus possibly be trying to force Nick out and take over the department?

"Um . . ." Nick hesitated.

Gus pushed harder. "What do you think your father kept them for?"

"To put pressure on me if he had to. I mean, if he wanted to."

"And he never showed them to you?"

"No."

"Never tried to use them to force you to do anything?"

"No."

"Never alluded to them?"

"No."

"So you've never seen them in all these years?"

"Not . . ." Nick stopped again.

"Not *any* of them?"

Suddenly Nick knew what was teasing him. Gus's hands were not trembling! It made no sense. His hands trembled worse when he was tense, and he should be very tense now. What was going on here? To look at Gus, Nick would have thought the answer to this question was that Gus expected a victory of some kind. Gus was confident.

Nick knew better than to go ahead when he didn't understand what was happening. He said, "I'm going to ask for a short break."

Gus backed up, surprised. "All right," he said cautiously. "That's your prerogative."

As soon as Nick was out of the room, Wally Riggs said, "What're we gonna do if he's gone someplace to eat his gun?"

Gus said, "He wouldn't do that."

"How do you know?"

"I know him."

Kluger said, "He's on the verge of losing everything he loves most in life."

"I'm not so sure," Heidema said. "He can see this last hour hasn't gone entirely against him."

Gus looked at Heidema for a second. Gus was surprised and maybe not so surprised. Heidema didn't like Bertolucci, but he could perfectly well vote against his own preference. It was that uprightness of Heidema's, the self-righteousness, really. He was perfectly capable of saying never mind if it's difficult or the mayor criticizes us if this comes out. What's right is right. If Bertolucci didn't instigate the raid and if he was following orders, and if he could not have known that he did anything wrong, then morally we are not justified in blaming him.

This would leave Riggs and Withers voting to pop Bertolucci and Gus, Heidema, and Kluger voting to support him.

Gus threw himself into a chair.

SIXTY-TWO

NICK PACED THE hall outside. He had to get the sequence right. Something dangerous was happening here and he didn't know all the facts.

Some of the sequence was obvious.

Pa had got hold of the gun and the autopsy report, of course. Nick realized he had never really been in doubt of that, however much it hurt to admit it. Sounded right, first time he saw them. Pa figured he'd hold the documents over my head, he thought, and if he ever wanted to really come down hard on me, he had me skewered.

Collected them from the Detective Division, probably. The gun from Tech. He remembered they were all asked to turn in their weapons. The pellet in the girl's brain would go from the coroner to Ballistics. Sure.

So Pa gets to be superintendent and he takes the stuff. And then what did he do? Takes them home and keeps them safe, like a nice supply of strychnine or a pet cottonmouth. Keep the poison. That's Pa, all right.

So when did Aldo come into the picture? That's easy. When he cleaned out the attic for Ma, naturally. And hugged it to himself for a while, too, just like Pa.

Except Aldo wasn't like Pa. He could never wait when he wanted something. Pa died two weeks ago, so why not send

them to Gus sooner? The whole thing was not right. Not right. Not Aldo.

Why wait? What was he doing those two weeks after he found the papers? Maybe he was upset that his partner, Dickenson, was killed. Except that his partner hadn't been killed until later—

Dickenson! The gymnast!

What did it mean? In his mind's eye he saw a picture of Dickenson climbing the outside of the building before his thinking brain understood what it meant.

The other papers and the gun could all have come out of the Detective Division at some point, or out of Tech, but the gun registration would have been in the Personnel Division all the time—from long before.

But what did that mean?

That it wasn't with the rest. Old Nico had been moved to superintendent right after the raid, and he'd whitewashed it as fast as he could. Then the whitewash started to come off and it hit the papers and in a few months he was out as superintendent, down in General Support, largely disgraced. So maybe he had part of the stuff, but never got the rest. Thought he had plenty of time and didn't. Or didn't even think of the gun registration. Or for his purposes didn't need it.

The gun registration?

Nico might not need it. But Aldo had to have it. He needed proof of the sort that newspapers and television reporters would buy. And of course, Aldo couldn't walk in and ask for it.

Dickenson, the gymnast!

Aldo had worked on Dickenson, and got him to go in the Personnel Division windows. Probably late some night. It wouldn't have been all that difficult.

And that's where the money went. To pay Dickenson.

And that meant—didn't it?—when he, Nick, had said it was ridiculous to think Aldo had killed his partner, that Aldo didn't have any motive, it meant that Aldo had the greatest motive in the world.

Dickenson may have been about to talk.

It all fell into place.

Gus knew.

And Gus was going to nail Aldo.

Gus was trying to save him, Nick, and pop Aldo at the same time. All he had needed from Nick was the word that he had never seen the documents before, so that there was no evidence that any copy of the gun registration was with them before this month. Gus would argue that Nick was not morally guilty in the death of Shana Boyd. At most he was guilty of too closely following the orders of his superiors.

And judging by Heidema, he might succeed.

Then Gus would go after Aldo and hunt him down.

Nick allowed his mind to dwell on Aldo just briefly. It was too painful to think about him for long. To know he had harbored that much hatred all these years felt like hitting a brick wall at eighty miles an hour. Nick had been aware that Aldo envied and resented him; he'd shown it openly. But not this black hatred. Enough hatred to be willing to risk his life to destroy Nick!

And to kill his partner! It was the ultimate evil, the thing no cop did, to kill another cop. And it was evil piled on evil to kill the partner who trusted you. You relied on each other on the street. You built an automatic reliance on the man at your back.

How could Aldo be so steeped in poison?

Nick straightened his shoulders to go back to the hearing room. It was up to him alone now. To take care of everything.

SIXTY-THREE

"**I WAS ASKING** about the documents, and you were saying you had not seen them before," Gus said.

"Yes, that's what I said."

"None of them. The ballistics photos, the autopsy report, the gun registration?"

Gus said "gun registration" casually, almost the way he spoke the other words, but Nick *knew*. He was right. Right.

"That's not exactly what I said."

"But you—"

Nick interrupted. "If I gave that impression, I want to change that testimony."

"*What?*"

"I was trying to protect my father. I've thought it over and I now see I was wrong."

"What are you saying?" Gus pushed his glasses up on his nose. He was struggling to keep his cool. His hand started to tremble.

"I'm saying that my father showed me the papers once."

"*What? Why?*"

"To tell me that if he ever wanted me to do anything for him, I'd better be ready to do it."

Gus stared. He swallowed. "Including the gun registration?" he finally said.

"Yes. Including the gun registration."

Nobody looked at Nick.

"In view of the fact that the superintendent suppressed this evidence, I don't feel we can successfully support the superintendent against any political attack," Heidema said.

Withers glowed, his smooth face stretched in what was

not quite a smile. Riggs watched Withers to see what it all meant.

"Or against the publicity that would follow," Heidema added.

Withers said, "That's right."

Kluger slouched in his chair. He was seething.

Gus's hands were trembling again.

"Given the plans of the anonymous person to publish unless you step down," said Heidema, who still did not know who the person was, "I imagine some announcement should be made soon." The five men waited.

Nick stood up. "I'll clean out my desk this evening. Gus can tell News Affairs in the morning that I have stepped down because of ill health." He turned directly to Gimball.

Gus would not meet his eye, either.

Withers had three or four suggestions about how Gus could inform the press in the most politic way. Nick let them talk.

Finally he said, *"All right!* All right. Listen up!"

"What?" Withers said.

"Now it's my turn."

"Turn what?"

"To speak."

"Well," Withers drawled, "I guess we can grant you that."

"Thank you so much," Nick said ironically. "Now I'll tell you exactly what we're going to do next. Pay attention, because this is my last order."

"You shouldn't be giving orders—" Withers began, but Kluger and Gus both told him to be quiet and then Heidema, who hadn't said much for the last few minutes, said, "Let him talk."

Nick said, "My last order is this. We will all unanimously appoint Gus Gimball acting superintendent."

"But the mayor appoints—"

"The mayor appoints superintendents. Which he can do when he gets around to it. We can delay sending him names. Meanwhile, we put Gus in as acting superintendent. Mayor Wallace is locked in a close primary race with Atkinson. He's not gonna risk a fight with the CPD on top of everything else right now."

"Wait!" Withers barked. "By then—"

"By the time you send him names, Wallace may be a lame duck and he'll realize that to throw out the acting super would only make enemies. And if Atkinson is elected—"

Kluger interrupted. "Maybe the Republican will win."

"And maybe the earth will turn on its axis and we will find ourselves in the tropics. If Atkinson is elected, he is likely to keep Gimball."

"But Nick," Withers drawled, "you don't really get to dictate, do you? You haven't any power now."

"No. No power, exactly."

"So we don't need to do what you tell us."

"I think you will, Charlie."

"I think you're wrong."

"Go on," Kluger said, seeing Nick's calmness.

He was bluffing; he could not let Stella find out. Never. But they wouldn't know that. He said, "I have no power but blackmail. I can let the stuff about me come out."

"And make the department look like shit?" Heidema said.

"Sure. And maybe turn over the whole anthill from the top. Including all of you."

Withers said, unbelieving, "You'd screw yourself?"

"I'm screwed now, Charlie," Nick said. "I don't have anything to lose."

SIXTY-FOUR

"GOD *DAMN* YOU!" Gus said. He shoved open the door of Bertolucci's office so hard it blasted into the wall and the handle made a round dent in the plaster.

"Hey! Hiya, Gus." Nick gestured at the packing material, cardboard boxes and newspaper. "You want to pass me that small box? Figured I'd put the photos with glass on them in it. Our unit in 1983, you and me in our graduation photo, all that kind of stuff."

"Don't bullshit me!" Gus pushed the cardboard box onto the floor. Half a dozen papers wafted out to settle near the window.

"Bullshit you? I'm the one moving out," Nick said.

"Yeah?"

"And you're the one moving up."

"And fuck you, you goddamn turncoat. I tell you, I never figured you for a traitor, Bertolucci."

"Oh?"

"You never saw that gun registration."

Nick swept his arm across his desk. The clock, the pen holder, the blotter which never was used to blot anything anyway, the papers, and three folders all went flying.

"Fuck!" Nick yelled.

"Fuck yourself!"

Nick stared at Gus's eyes. Held them.

Gus repeated, "You never saw that gun registration."

"I never saw that gun registration," Nick said.

"Or any of those papers."

"You know it, babe."

Gus strode around the end of the desk, up to Nick's toe caps, punched his index finger, sticking out of a tightly

clenched fist, into Nick's face and snarled, "You've betrayed everything we ever stood for!"

Nick grabbed Gus's fist.

They stood there frozen in anger, fist inside fist, eyes locked, toes touching, both furious. Both hurt.

Nick dropped his hand first. "Christ," he said.

Gus put his arms around Nick. Nick hugged Gus back, and when they stepped apart both were crying. "Oh, shit. Oh, I don't know anything anymore," Nick said. They sat down in Nick's green chairs. Drained.

"I'm still mad, though," Gus said.

"I know you are."

"Aldo is guilty."

"I would never have believed it."

"Would you have believed he wanted to destroy you?"

"Not that he'd want it this badly."

"Well, I talked to him, and it's all he wants in life. He's guilty of killing a cop, Nick. And you let him off, just because he's your brother."

"Just because he's my brother? No. Not at all. Gus, you don't know about me and Aldo. When he was a little kid, he was kind of pudgy. Soft. And trying to cope with a very large, very tough, Italian street cop."

"Nico."

"Nico, sure." Nick told Gus about the time Nico had told Aldo to go to the dark cellar and he wouldn't. And Nico took him to the cellar and handcuffed him there. "And left him all night."

"So Nico was a bastard. Not your fault, Nick," Gus said.

"I'm not so sure. See, I was smarter than Aldo and I was on to my father. I knew he could smell fear. Lot of cops learn to smell fear, but he had an instinct for it. Smart bastard, too. When he told Aldo to go to the cellar to get whatever it was, I knew at any second he could turn around and ask me,

and I knew that I would *die* sooner than let him see I was scared to go down there. But I was totally terrified of the cellar, too. I was smaller than Aldo, and younger. So he was still on Aldo, yelling at him, this big guy, cuffing a little kid, couldn't have been three feet tall. So you know what I did?"

"What?"

"While he was still cuffing Aldo, I said, 'I'll go, Pa.' "

"You did?"

"Not to help Aldo. I was showing Pa I wasn't scared of it. I knew, I *knew* that he wouldn't let Aldo off that easy, see. I knew by saying that, I was making sure he wouldn't make *me* do it. He just slapped me up against the wall, got me out of the way, and went on yelling at Aldo. And finally he grabbed Aldo up and carried him down in the dark basement, carried him by the back of his shirt and pants, and handcuffed him to a pole down there. And Aldo screamed and screamed all during dinner, but we were made to eat everything on our plates.

"I let Aldo take the heat, all my childhood. So you see it makes some sense Aldo hates me."

"You were younger. It wasn't your fault."

"I'm not so sure."

Gus stood up again. He was angry, didn't want to be angry, felt the pressure of sympathy for Nick but he was utterly outraged—

"You think poor little Aldo never had a chance!" he said.

"In a way he didn't—"

"He had more chance than a hell of a lot of people who manage to be honest and kind. He grew up in a house with a roof and heat and food and he had clothes and two parents. And even if he hadn't, it's not up to us to decide who gets excused for murder. *Murder*, Nick! How many times over the years have you and I said it isn't up to the police to decide what's extenuating circumstances and what isn't? Judges do

that. Or juries. Legislatures. One of the characteristics of cops is that they don't want to look too close into the background of people they arrest, because if you look hard enough you can excuse anything. You know that statistic that ninety percent of the people in prison for violent crimes were abused as kids? I believe it. And it doesn't make one damn bit of difference to what we do. We aren't asked as cops to decide what background somebody has. All we need to do is ask *whether he did it!* And leave the punishment to the judge."

Nick watched Gus. He was afraid maybe Gus was going to start staggering and shuffling again. The trembling in his hands was worse.

Finally, Nick said, "In this case, I'm not a cop."

"Oh." Gus turned to look out the window, but it was very dark. "Yes, you are."

"I don't want to talk about it. Hey! You want to help me pack these pictures? Here's one with you—1973."

"Nick, *please!*"

"Well, what do you expect me to do? Get drunk? Shall I throw something through the window? Knock you unconscious? Pitch *myself* out the window? What?"

"How about be honest?"

"What do you mean?"

"It's not Aldo. You'll settle with Aldo your own way."

"No. Aldo is gonna settle Aldo. Have you seen the way he looks lately?"

"Let me finish. Aldo isn't why you did this. He's not why you gave up. You turned over and gave them your belly to stab, Nick, feet sticking up, kill me, just when I had it all greased for you."

"They hadn't voted yet."

"Heidema was leaning my way. And you noticed it, too. Don't play dumb with me."

"It doesn't matter."

"Yes, it does. I know why you gave up. It's because you shot that girl. Because you shouldn't have fired at all."

The silence drew out. Nick just stood still, not angry, not much of anything, as far as he himself could tell. Numb. Drained. Everything was over. It was all very simple.

"The rule is you don't fire blind," Gus said. "You don't fire into a darkened room where you can't see where your shot is gonna go. It's the rule now; it was the rule then; and the fact that three superior officers, at least three, were firing right through walls isn't an excuse for you, you think. You should have known better. Youngest one in the group, but *you* should have been better than best."

"I should have."

"You were just a kid."

"Well, Shana Boyd was eighteen and she'll never grow up."

"You're too hard on yourself. What did you know?"

"It's what I know now. I'm guilty." He stood, looked at the room, looked at the door, then dropped his arms to his sides. "And I will be punished."

SIXTY-FIVE

GUS HAD BEEN at the window for four hours now. His back had hurt so much about nine P.M. he thought he'd take some aspirin he had in his pocket, but he didn't dare leave the window and go to the bathroom for water. Finally things got so bad he chewed them dry, retching a little.

Down in the CPD parking lot it was dim, but not dark. The sodium vapor lights bathed it in a uniform Venusian

glow. The guard's shack squatted on the side near Gus. In his car, parked in the spot of honor, the superintendent's slot, sat Nick Bertolucci. The snow had stopped hours ago.

If Gus's own office window had faced the parking lot, he would have been more comfortable. But his window faced east and the lot was on the south side of the building. Gus sat in the anteroom to a courtroom, on a bench at the back which was built into the window arch. He had amused himself for a while by imagining all the deals that had gone down on this bench over the years. The ripoffs, the scams, the bribes. This had been the courtroom of a judge now in federal prison for extortion. The guy used to ask for personal loans from attorneys who had cases before him. Didn't ever get around to paying back the loans.

Gus couldn't quite see Nick. The car roof was in the way. But he saw his hand once in a while, knew he was there, and he knew why. The First District officers would be coming off their tour at eleven.

SIXTY-SIX

SUZE, HIRAM AND Stanley got to the Furlough nearly an hour before Aldo was scheduled to arrive. They had all been early cars. And Suze, having followed Norm to the hospital, then reported to Touhy, then dealt with the paperwork, hadn't been back on the street all evening. Aldo was late car as usual.

Mileski's ricochet had turned out to be not precisely a thigh wound. A tiny piece of a pellet had lodged in his scrotum.

"No real damage," Suze said.

Quail said, "Hmm."

"Hmm what?"

"Guess that makes him Lead Balls Mileski, don't it?"

But nobody laughed. The three sat waiting in an atmosphere as thick as clotted blood. They sat at tables instead of the bar—tables which in their entire memories they had never used. At one point Mileski said, "Aldo was one of *us.*"

Unbelievably, Hiram Quail began to cry. Nobody joked about it.

Twenty-five after eleven. Several other First District officers had crossed State Street heading for the Furlough. Nick still sat in his car watching. He felt suspended. One life was over and he had no idea where the next life lay. He watched.

The street was deserted.

And finally, there was Aldo, with a smaller, younger man who must be his partner. They came out of the department, onto the sidewalk. Nick's car door opened. They stepped onto the street. Nick stepped out of his car.

From his window, Gus saw them and he started down the stairs, fast. His feet weren't equal to the urgency in his head. He dashed down the first flight, not even thinking about his illness. On the second flight, five steps from the bottom, he tripped and went down hard.

Aldo stood in the middle of State Street just across from the Furlough. Nick was in front of the CPD parking lot, maybe fifty yards from Aldo, also in the middle of the street. Behind Aldo stood the younger officer, frozen and confused.

A cold wind was blowing from the north down State Street, tumbling discarded paper along the pavement. The street lights cast an orange glow with no warmth to it. Aldo

and Nick were connected by the dashed white line that ran
down the center of the street, made pinkish by the light.

Nick strode toward Aldo, one foot before the other, methodically, along the white line. Aldo's hands hung at his sides
as if he were going to wait; then he walked toward Nick.
Kim Duk followed. Kim Duk's face was pale and his eyes
widened when he saw the superintendent.

The two men met. Neither man unholstered a gun. Nick
feinted with his right hand, then plowed his left into Aldo's
gut. Aldo whoofed. But he came up with both fists into
Nick's face. Nick rolled his head, taking only part of the
blow, and standing his ground, punched Aldo in one side of
his head and as his head spun around, smashed his other fist
into his ear.

Kim Duk said, "Come on, Aldo! No—now stop!"

Aldo backhanded him, like swatting a bug, knocking him
out of the way.

Aldo punched at Nick's gut but got him higher, in the
chest, as Nick leaned forward to backhand Aldo's neck. Aldo
drove a second punch hard and got Nick over the eyebrow,
splitting the skin. Aldo's ear was bleeding and Nick hit it
again; then when Aldo tipped his head back, looking punchy,
Nick threw an uppercut to his chin.

Aldo's tongue must have been between his teeth. He
screamed and spat blood. Blood cascaded down his chin into
his collar. Now Gimball came limping out of the CPD main
entrance.

Kim Duk O'Hara hopped around the bleeding, grunting
men to Gus Gimball.

"Uh, sir?" O'Hara said.

"Yes?"

"You're a boss, aren't you, sir? I mean"—he hurried on
over what he knew was surely a big verbal mistake—"I mean,
I think I ought to stop this, but I don't know who you are,

and you're just standing here—not that there's anything wrong with that. Probably there isn't. I mean, I just don't know what I ought to do. And isn't that the superintendent?"

Gus gave him a look. The kid was bouncing from foot to foot, totally nervous, but his heart was in the right place.

"I'm Deputy Superintendent Gimball," he said.

"Oh, gee. I mean, yes, sir."

"Look, kid"—as he said it, Nick's fist collided with Aldo's jaw in a sickening thump—"your assignment is to stand behind Aldo there and make sure his hand never goes to his gun. Me, over here, I'll be doing the same thing."

There was a car coming down State Street. Its headlights caught the fighting men and the blood. Kim Duk whipped around and gestured to the car to pass. It slowed. Kim Duk vehemently waved it on. A few people were trickling out of the CPD building now, stopping to stare.

Nick took a punch on his cut eyebrow. Blood was trickling down his face. He punched out again at Aldo's mouth.

"Don't you know who you were trying to get even with, Aldo?" he gasped out. "You've always been such a stupid fucker."

Aldo didn't say anything, just drew back his fist. It was so obvious, Nick ducked before the blow landed and punched Aldo's nose. "Don't you even realize why you suddenly went hog wild on me after he died?" Nick coughed blood.

Aldo moaned and struck out at Nick's eyebrow. He missed.

"Every time he made us fight?" Nick hit Aldo twice and twice again, left hand, right hand, left hand, right hand, in the gut. "Don't you know who you hate? Don't you know who you really hate?"

Aldo threw another punch at Nick's chin. Nick dodged. He said, "You couldn't get back at him anymore. And when he was alive you were too scared."

Aldo leaned slowly backward, then folded, plopping down on his ass like a baby, feet stuck forward. His eyes were flooded with tears. His belly flopped over his belt. The middle of his shirt had sprung its buttons and his belly stuck through, flabby, white, covered with black hairs. His face looked like lard, sweaty and bloody and fat, and the folds of his neck hung slackly over his collar.

Sitting, he sobbed like a child.

Nick sank down to sit on the curb. Gus walked to him and put a hand on his shoulder. How slippery blood was, Gus thought. Like oil. Not at all sticky, like they say it is.

Nick leaned against Gus. A minute more and he'd break down, too. Gus beckoned Kim Duk O'Hara. "Hey, kid, go over to the Furlough and get half a cup of brandy, okay?"

"What? Um, sir?"

"Hurry up!"

"But sir, boss? It's illegal for a bar to let the patrons take drinks out on the street!"

Gus stared at him. "Listen, you raisin-brain! Look around here! What do you see? Who exactly do you think is gonna arrest you?"

"Oh." Light dawned. "Yes, sir. Right away, sir!"

Suze, Hiram, and Stanley heard screaming in the street. They blew through the door into the street at the instant Kim Duk came in yelling for brandy, and gasping, "Aldo and the brass! Aldo—"

They didn't wait for Kim Duk.

Nick was just getting to his feet, helped by Gus. Suze and Hiram didn't give them a second look. They pulled Aldo to his feet.

"You shit!" Suze screamed. "Dick-dick had his whole life ahead of him!"

"Leave me alone!" he blubbered.

"I have you dead on it, Aldo."

He punched Suze. He got her on the ear, and she reeled but came back at him.

"I have a guy saw you come down the el stairs *after* the train pulled in. You are history!"

The two older men staggered closer, but Suze shrieked at Aldo. "I've got you and I'm gonna make you pay for this!"

Aldo yelled, bubbling blood, "I'm gonna publish it *anyway!*"

Suze saw Kim Duk step into the road with the brandy. For just a second they all took their eyes off Aldo. In that second he turned and started to run, blundering, heavy-bellied, maybe not seeing through his tears and the blood in his eyes. Gus yelled, "Look out!"

The bus coming from the Loop saw him, too, but not soon enough. They heard a dead thump like bread dough dropped on a floor, and Aldo fell and passed under the wheels of the bus.

SIXTY-SEVEN

ALDO WAS DEAD. At the Furlough Bar the next night, nobody wanted to be the first to mention his name, until Kim Duk broke the logjam.

"How tough was Aldo, really?" he asked.

Suze thought it over, and decided to cheer the kid up. "So tough—" she began.

"So tough," Mileski repeated. "There was this time when he was a detective, before he was dumped back, he's called to a scene. Some civilian sees some fingers sticking up out of a

garbage can, gets suspicious, can't blame him, so the uniforms go screamin' over there, and it's a body part. They call the techs, the detectives, you know the drill.

"Well, this is late at night. They're in an alley. Techs take some pictures, get some samples, by then the neighbors start tricklin' out. Two or three big apartment buildings around, lotta people.

"What the techs find is there are half a dozen body parts in the garbage cans in the alley. I mean, all of the guy is there but he doesn't all hang together, see what I mean?"

"Yeah," said Kim Duk.

"So more and more people are comin', and the crowds are gettin' in the way. Finally the detectives get exasperated. Aldo says, 'I know how to clear 'em out.' And he lifts up the guy's leg. That backs the crowd away, I can tell you!"

Kim Duk laughed.

"So the other detective, Dugan or Deegan it was, holds up the guy's head, holdin' it by the hair. Aldo says, 'Hey, he looks familiar.' Then he says, 'That looks like Skag Ruddles.' Looks again. 'Except ol' Skag was a taller guy.' So Deegan lifts the head way up. Aldo says, *That's Ruddles!'* "

"Jeez!" said Kim Duk.

Early in the morning, on the third day after he left the department and one day after Aldo's funeral, Nick piled Stella's two suitcases in his car and drove her to O'Hare. They parked in the garage and threaded their way along the elevator maze, the skyway over the road, through the various terminals to her gate.

"I'm sorry about your visit, Stella," Nick said. "Coming home and having two funerals had to be the least—"

She didn't answer for a couple of seconds, then said, "I guess I've been pretty much of a pest."

"No! I told you I'd love having you here, and I did. And I always will."

"I mean, I wasn't in a very pleasant mood."

"You're entitled."

"Still, I was pretty horrible."

"Stella, I'm very proud that you came to me and I'm even prouder you wanted to talk with me."

"You helped. Come see me sometime?"

"Maybe sooner than you think."

"What do you mean?"

"I'm going to retire, Stella."

"I don't believe it."

"I'm burned out." For just a split second he thought of confiding in her, even-steven, as she had in him. But he decided it wouldn't work. There was too much baggage attached. "It's time to let Gus take over. He'll be good."

Stella stared at him, trying to understand. Her flight was called, and she shook her head. She held still a few seconds, with her hand on his arm, weighing the reasons, weighing him in her mind.

"Okay," she said finally. "I guess I have to treat you like a grownup, too."

From there Nick drove down to the old neighborhood.

He parked in the alley, went into the tiny backyard. Snow was starting to pile up in half moons around the post footings of the chain link fence. He walked slowly through the snow, up the back walk. He glanced into the DiNicolas' yard next door. For a moment he thought there was a gravestone at the rear end of their yard, leaning sideways, as if shy, away from the house.

But it was their shrine. He hadn't thought of it in years. The shrine made from a half-buried bathtub. Looking closer,

he could see the statue of the Virgin, but she was all gray. Her blue paint and gilding were almost gone, peeled and chipped off. Snow was beginning to pile up behind her in the tub.

Bertolucci went to his mother's back door and knocked. After several minutes he heard a bumping as she came down the hall, peered out, and started unlocking the three or four bolts and the deadbolt into the floor that secured the back door.

He entered without a word. She knew something was wrong but she didn't ask, and instead preceded him into the living room.

Knickknacks lined the shelves and windowsills, and littered the tables. The walls crowded into the room with their load of framed aphorisms and pictures of saints.

Neither Nick nor his mother sat, just studied each other's faces.

"When Pa was hurting us," he said evenly, without heat, without inflection, "why didn't you stop him?"

She didn't answer.

"You were our mother," he said, not noticing that he'd used the past tense. "Why didn't you stop him?"

She stared at him, black Italian eyes alive in their nest of tiny wrinkles. Finally she shook her head. "You don't know what my life has been like," she said.

He didn't know whether it meant that she couldn't stop him, that she didn't want to stop him, that Nick shouldn't have asked the question, or that she simply refused to answer.

He waited a couple of minutes, with the small, hard pellets of snow streaming past the window the only motion visible. Then he turned and walked out.

Aldo had left his papers and the gun in a big manila envelope marked "Open in the event of my death." The envelope was on the table in the mud room. Regina found it a couple of

days after his funeral. She opened it, but saw that there was nothing of value inside, and threw it onto the top shelf of the closet. It is there still.

from *Chicago Today:*

BERTOLUCCI RESIGNS

FROM POLICE DEPARTMENT

Superintendent Nicholas Bertolucci has resigned from the Chicago Police Department, effective immediately, according to a department spokesperson. "Superintendent Bertolucci resigned today on grounds of ill health," said Ted Ropac, of the department's News Affairs Division. Former First Deputy Gus Gimball has been named Acting Superintendent. Reached at his home for comment, Bertolucci said, "I've been a Chicago police officer for 33 years and it's time to take a vacation. I'm planning a trip to do some deep-sea fishing."

Good cop, bad cop /
FIC DAMAT   745543

D'Amato, Barbara.
WEST GEORGIA REGIONAL LIBRARY

Chicago
December 4, 1969
4:15 A.M.